THE *lies* WE TELL OURSELVES

THE *lies* WE TELL OURSELVES

a novel

Maura Pierlot

First published in 2025 by BIG IDEAS PRESS
An independent press based in Canberra

bigideaspress.com

ISBN: 978-0-6450998-3-6
Cover design and typesetting: Nicola Matthews, Nikki Jane Design

A catalogue record for this
book is available from the
National Library of Australia

Important note: This novel explores mental health themes including
body dysmorphia, distorted eating and eating disorders. If you find
these topics triggering or distressing, please take care of yourself
while reading. Your wellbeing is important, and it's okay to step
back if you need to. If you, or someone you know, is struggling,
consider reaching out to a qualified health or mental health
professional for support. Remember, you are not alone.

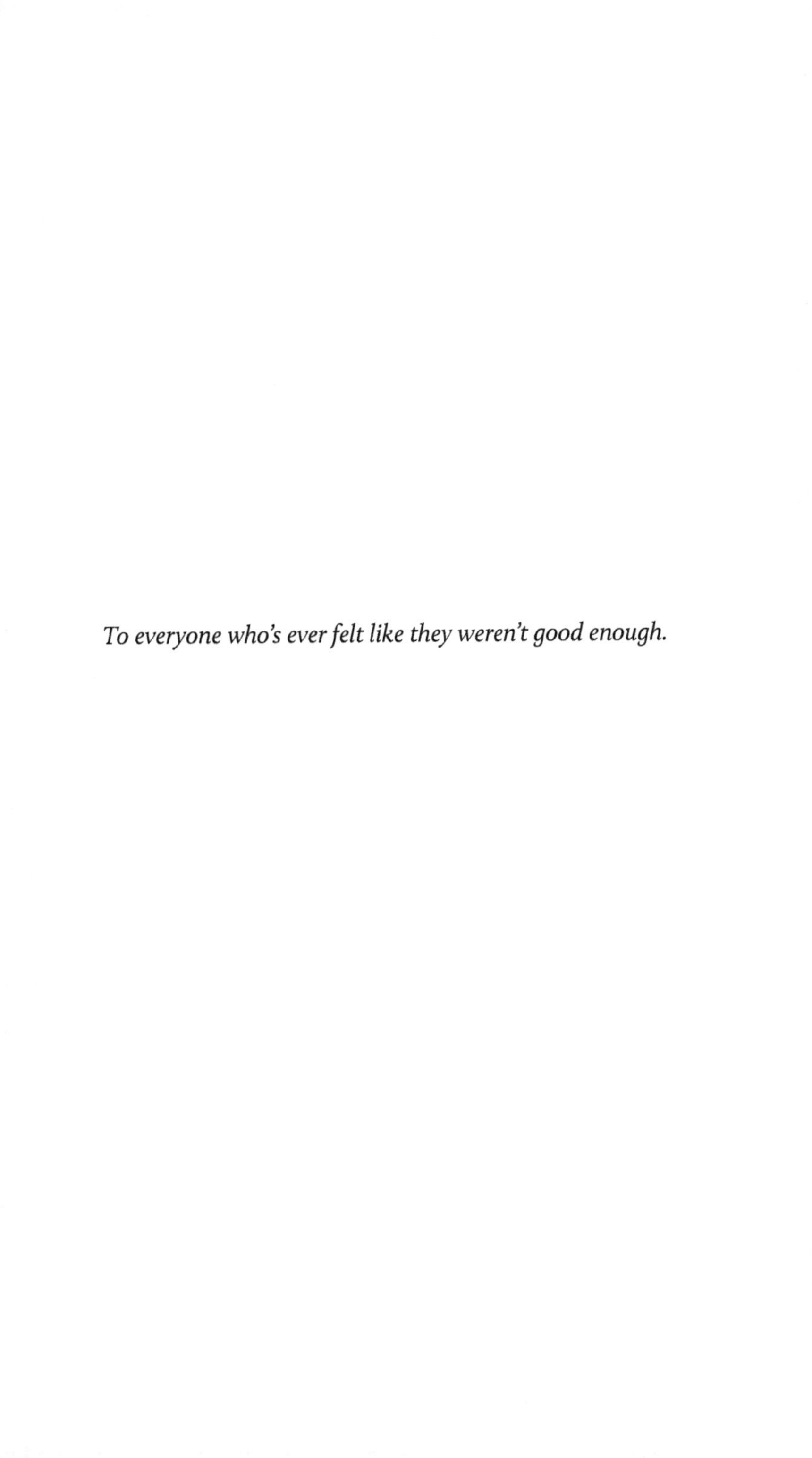

To everyone who's ever felt like they weren't good enough.

Prologue

Perception is cunning.
It plants a seed in your vulnerabilities, where it burrows
like a parasite, feeding on nameless fears. It's everywhere
but reveals itself only in glimpses: the shadow that follows
you mercilessly; the emptiness that can never be filled;
the voice that taunts you from the mirror.

SUMMER

CHAPTER 1

The Year of Harley

One cannot step twice in the same river.
(Heraclitus)

I'm standing face to face with my biggest enemy. It's the first day of school and I've only been awake half an hour, but here we are. I step back until my head touches the wall, but the girl in the mirror doesn't look any smaller.

Nan's voice sings in my head, telling me I'm beautiful and school uniforms are always unflattering, but I'm not buying it. Nothing would make these thighs look thinner.

Talia's name pops on my screen: *8.05 bus?*

Yep, I reply, suddenly nervous. She's been overseas all summer and never even messaged me when Nan died. It's not like I expected her to fly back for the funeral. But she's my best friend. I thought she'd at least make sure I was okay.

One last mirror check. I scrunch my hair for a beachy wave then touch up my lips with peach-tinted balm. May as well make the most of my two best features.

There's no time for breakfast so I pack last night's beef rendang for lunch. No matter how hard I try, I can't unsee the apple slice on the top shelf and snatch that from the fridge too. One voice in my head tells me I can share it with

Griff. It's his favourite, after all. Then the other voice kicks in right on cue: *You're disgusting!*

Mum pokes her head out from the laundry room. 'Try to take it easy today, Harley, okay?' Her words come out happy and light but her eyes say, *I'm worried about you.*

Falco is barking. Maybe he's worried about me too. I toss him his squeaky toy.

'I will,' I call out to Mum from the front door. I wonder if she believes me.

I cover two blocks in no time, praying Talia will wait for me if I miss the bus. The faster I go, the more the stiff fabric rubs between my thighs, making a weird squeaking noise. I'm a walking accordion.

'Behind you!' I burst through the cluster of Year 7s with a half-hop, half-run because I haven't exercised in ... forever. Sweat's pouring off me like I just finished a marathon. This is so *not* how I pictured the first day of Year 10.

When I turn the corner, I hardly recognise Talia. I swear, she's two centimetres taller and at least three kilos lighter. I have a good eye for detail, so I can tell these things, even from a distance. She's waiting at our bus stop, doing mini bicep curls with her backpack. The second she spots me, she breaks into a funk routine, throwing in a hip roll to make it her own. I hug her longer than usual to make up for a summer apart, nearly overdosing on her grapefruit body spray.

'First day of Year 10,' Talia squeals, drawing me in tighter for a selfie.

I was hoping she'd tell me her phone had been lost or smashed. Something to explain why she only messaged me twice all summer. Instead, she sends the pic to a contact list way longer than last year's. I'm too distracted by her boobs to comment. They're much bigger than I remember.

'Tal, don't take this the wrong way but you've ... grown.' I try to make eye contact but her cleavage is distracting me.

She grins. 'Yeah, Mum says she was the same. Suddenly, it was goodbye baby fat, hello C-cup.'

I want to smile but it's hard, considering my boobs haven't announced themselves properly yet. 'How was Italy?'

'*Molto bene!* Milan was to die for. Florence too.' She steps onto the road, looking for our bus. 'What'd you do all summer anyway?'

'Nothing much. I landed a modelling contract and starred in a few music videos. Oh, and I have a new boyfriend called Phoenix.'

Talia laughs. A big back-of-the-throat guffaw that morphs into giggly hiccups and, right on cue, her unmistakable snort. It's more full-on than I remember.

'Griff and I didn't do much,' I explain. 'We just hung out at the pool and went up The Mount most days. He's been taking some nature photos for ... *stop it, Tal!*' She's pretending to hold a notepad, like she's a journalist recording my fascinating story, nodding between hiccups. 'Anyway, same old, really. Except for Nan dying, of course.'

Talia drops her bag, her eyes and mouth wide open. 'Oh my God. How? When?'

'Blood clot on the brain,' I tell her, figuring she wouldn't understand *cerebral aneurysm*. That's what the doctor called it. She looks genuinely shocked. Maybe she really didn't know.

'Mum and her stupid social media ban,' she says, jogging my memory.

And I thought *my* mother was hormonal. But surely, she could've tapped into wi-fi somehow, somewhere.

A tear falls down her cheek, then others follow in an unbroken stream. It's official: everyone's crying over Nan except me. Dad says showing your emotions is healthy, which is strange, because he never seems to be around to show his. Mum keeps telling me to let it all out – no surprise from the Queen of Venting. But if I start, I don't think I'll be able to stop.

Nan was my superhero, always saving the day with a few simple words or a smile. And I never bothered to ask, 'How did you always make everything better? Did it take years of practice? Did you make lots of mistakes?' I didn't even get to say goodbye, but doubt I could have found the words anyway. How do you say goodbye to someone you've known forever?

'Did I miss the funeral?' Talia's words are full of melodrama, like her Lady Macbeth in English last year.

I nod, thinking, *Words fail at times like these*. That's what everyone kept telling me at the service last week. And they're right.

'How's Gi-Gina?' she splutters.

Mum's always telling my friends, 'Call me Gina,' but it sounds weird when Talia says it. Even Griff calls her Mrs Hastings and he's known her forever. I shrug because I don't want to waste valuable catch-up time on my mother. Talia accepts my offer of a crumpled tissue, releasing a trumpet-like honk that nearly knocks me off the kerb. We surrender to a tsunami of pent-up laughter after a summer apart. I'm so glad she's home.

Our bus pulls up and the doors heave open with a loud belch. Larrikin Lou, as he was always known at Mount Pleasant High, is behind the wheel, rocking some serious dreads. Strange that the guy who dropped out of school is driving us there. He offers a half-hearted salute. My motto is 'never diss the driver' so I return the greeting. Not that it matters. Lou's eyes are locked onto Talia 2.0 behind me.

I head down the aisle, sizing up the boyfriend potential that's loading the seats. From what I can see, it's next to nil.

'He's not here,' Talia sighs, pushing past me for a better view.

'Who?'

'The new guy.'

'New guy?' Funny how she seems to have caught up on all the news except mine.

'Yeah, from the States.'

'The States, like America?'

'No, the states, like Victoria and Queensland.' Then she performs an eye roll so spectacular it seems choreographed. 'Of course, America.'

WTF? Did Talia do a *How to Be Sassy* workshop in Italy? 'And he's meant to be on our bus?'

'No idea. Just wanted to be prepared, you know, check him out before everyone else does.' She flashes me a pouty look to drive the point home.

At the back of the bus, Eden is holding court. Chief wannabe, Paris, seems mesmerised by Eden's new hairstyle, white-blonde and cropped short, showcasing her sculpted cheekbones. Wannabe-in-waiting, Sydney, is running her hand over the cut, like it's so spectacular she has to touch it immediately.

Any guy would think Eden is the total package. Beautiful face, super fit, dazzling smile, flawless nails. She's perfect. Well, close to perfect. The only thing I've got over her is personality, but boys don't give a shit about that. I scan the faces on the bus. No matter where I look, one thing's brutally clear: all the girls have *blossomed*, as Nan would say, while I spoiled – like mayonnaise left out of the fridge for too long.

Gloppy, spludgy, fatty mayonnaise.

Talia lets out a little '*Eep!*' when Eden's name flashes on her phone, flying to the back of the bus where the queen and her fake-tanned entourage ooh and aah over her summer transformation. They've been sworn enemies since forever so I figure Talia will soak up the love and head back, but she squeezes in between Eden and Paris instead.

What the hell? My best friend has ditched me on the first day of school, for girls she doesn't even like.

I keep walking, hoping I don't look as desperate as I feel.

'*Hairley!*'

There's only one person who calls me that.

Another shriek from Eden, the human megaphone. 'You're just *bursting* at the seams to get to school, aren't you?'

Then an explosive cackle – her I'm-so-hot-I-don't-care-what-I-sound-like laugh. Eden's group howls in support, throwing their heads back and thrusting their chins to the ceiling, like they're doing Mum's neck exercises. Talia's smile is frozen.

Out of the corner of my eye I see Stu staring at me. He runs a hand through his hair. It's so thin I can nearly see his scalp. The colour's off too, like he tried to go light over the summer and ended up with beige.

'We don't need to see that,' he grimaces. Ty, his partner in ignorance, nods to my right hip.

I reach down and confirm my worst fear. The side seam on my dress has split open, treating the back of the bus to a glimpse of my undies. The phones start clicking, no doubt for Snaps that will be all over school before we even get there. I try to look on the bright side: at least I'm wearing my cute new pineapple and cherry briefs, not my usual grotty ones. All it takes is one loud exhale for my hip flab to sneak through the seam, like sausage meat popping out of its casing.

I blame all the sympathy eating. Since Nan died everyone's been bringing us so much food that we could cater for a small wedding. Mum's been telling people, 'Oh, thank you so much, you really didn't need to do that,' but she loves the meals because they give her a break from cooking. And I love that they give me a break from eating her cooking.

A few rows back I spy a familiar grin. Griff. I can't help but smile back. He's patting the seat next to him with the energy of a morning person. He looks cute. Not *cute* cute, but cute in a quirky rock-star-just-got-out-of-bed-at-noon kind of way. His unruly dark curls clearly haven't seen a comb in a while, but the messy look works for him.

'What's up?' I ask, tossing my bag near his feet then flopping onto the seat. It's too early for meaningful conversation.

'Not much.' There's a slight gap between his two front teeth when he smiles, like they shifted overnight. 'Year 10's gonna be *sublime*.'

With Griffin Tobias Laettner, conversation is always a journey, destination optional. His idea of fun is to master ten new words each week, in alphabetical order. A good spinoff: I've picked up heaps by *osmosis* – that one came in handy for a science test last year. Sometimes I think Griff comes up with all his wacky ideas – his word games, his cartoons about alternate dimensions, his obsession with photographing leaves – because he's bored. It must be lonely being an only child, but with an idiot brother like

Luke roasting me all the time, I'd be happy to give it a go. Most of the boys at Mount Pleasant High are like Luke, but Griff's a bit different. He's smart and interesting and not a jerk, which helps. Dad says Griff's better with details than the big picture. He should know – he's a scientist.

I turn to Griff, gathering my split seam. 'Got any safety pins?' Worth a try.

His eyes drift to the fresh wads of chewing gum overhead, the start of the annual ceiling mural. He fumbles in his pocket and presents his haul: a key, seven dollars thirty in coins and – yes! – a small chain of safety pins. I snatch one, worried that my wobbly bits aren't going to stay put much longer. Three pins later, I'm left with a lump of fabric nearly as big as the rip.

I feel everyone's eyes on me but when I turn around, no one's looking. They're too busy having fun. Especially Talia, who's ditched her awkwardness to gush over something on Eden's phone.

All summer I kept telling myself 2019 is going to be The Year of Harley, when everything I do finally turns to gold. But I can already tell this is going to be The Year of Same Old.

When I get tired of counting flags still up from Australia Day (seven) and trash bins lined up on the kerb (twenty-three), I remember my list and dig it out of my backpack.

'You've got yours, right?' I pass Griff the words I laboured over all week, suddenly feeling nervous.

Each year, on the first day of school, Griff and I trade our wish lists – a delayed version of our New Year's resolutions. And each year, mine sounds more and more pathetic. I watch his lips move as he silently reads my words:

Harley's Year 10 Wish List

Get a job.

Get a boyfriend.

Get a life.

'Short and sweet,' he says, reaching into his pocket. 'I like it.'

Seconds later, a bright orange origami bird lands on my lap. I carefully unfold the corners, marvelling at Griff's intricate design. His words, printed neatly in blue ink, leap off the paper.

Take risks.

Make memories.

Help someone.

'Man, you're deep,' I tell him.

The bus pulls up in front of school, announcing our arrival with a gasp and a shudder.

The Year of Harley starts now.

CHAPTER 2

Good Skinny

There is always some madness in love.
But there is also always
some reason in madness.
(Friedrich Nietzsche)

I leave Griff at the canteen and head off to find my locker, which couldn't be further from my classes. Mrs Stevens, the Year 10 coordinator, allocated them and I wonder if she's trying to tell me I need the exercise.

The thought's still in my head when I see her marching across the quadrangle. Her long, flowy skirt can't disguise a serious case of cankles. The top half's not much better: a peasant-style blouse so uncomfortably tight, it's a wardrobe malfunction waiting to happen.

Before I know it, she's standing right in front of me, her fingers doing a mad drum solo on her arms. 'Emergency, Harley!' she hisses. 'Hairspray!'

'I don't have any,' I tell her, wondering why she can't just pack her own.

'The Year 10 production.' She sighs with an eye roll even I wouldn't attempt. 'Auditions are next week and there's not a single name on the list.'

'But it's only the first day back,' I try to explain, 'and I bet—'

'I emailed everyone over the summer,' she cuts me off. 'Twice.' Her eyes narrow and I can practically hear the wheels in her head turning. 'You did get my messages, didn't you?'

The door creaks open to a conversation I don't want to have. If this is really going to be The Year of Harley, I know I need to put myself out there. I love to sing and everyone's always telling me I have a beautiful voice, but I'd rather break both my legs than work with Mrs Stevens for two terms. But I panic and the words spill out of my mouth. 'Should I try out for Penny Pingleton or Amber von Tussle?'

'Harley,' she insists, 'I want you to audition for the lead.'

'Tracy Turnblad?' The biggest person in the whole musical.

She looks at me like it's a no-brainer. 'Do you know anyone else who can sing and dance like you?'

Like me? Why doesn't she just spit it out: *Do you know any other fat* girls *who can sing and dance?* There's absolutely, positively no way I'm going to play Tracy ... especially if some tool like Stu or Ty is playing Link.

Why did Mr Gonzalez, the best drama teacher ever, have to leave? He headed off to St Anthony's just when I'd signed up for music theatre lessons with him. Now we're stuck with Mrs Stevens who's never even been in a play before. And my dog Falco is a better singer.

'Here's the thing, Mrs Stevens,' I start off, hoping the right words come out this time, 'I really don't think I can ...'

When she purses her lips, new lines appear at the edges of her mouth, like millimetres on a ruler.

'Learn it, live it, love it,' she sings out, pointing to a

highlighted scene on the script she's holding before shoving it into my hands. Not that I need it. I've seen the movie at least thirty times and know every line, song and dance by heart.

My brain's telling my body to move but my feet aren't listening. I stare at the words until they go blurry.

'Harley, is everything alright?' Her grip on my shoulder is firm but her tone is soft.

When I press my fingers to my eyes, a determined tear escapes. It lands at the top of the page, blurring 'Good Morning Baltimore'.

'Something's in my eye, that's all.'

<center>~~~~~~~~~~~~~~~~</center>

I slip into class on the second bell, notebook covering my split seam. Philosophy was a breeze last year, so I opted for the stepped-up version: Ethics, Existence and the Good Life. I can be deep when I want to be.

Talia and Eden are sitting near the front and Talia hasn't even saved me a seat. *What the hell?* First, she dumped me for Eden on the bus, and now they're so caught up in whatever they're talking about that I might as well not exist. I grab a seat towards the back of the room, leaving my notebook on the chair beside me for Griff. Before I can even take out my laptop, Stu has parked his ugly butt there.

My death stare works. Stu leans forward to retrieve the notebook from under him, sniffing it like a rare flower before tossing it to me. *Gross.*

'Morning, all,' calls out Dr Kanter.

I'm five-foot nine and she's easily got a few centimetres on me. And she looks old – maybe late thirties. Her simple, classic style – navy pencil skirt just above the knee and tapered floral blouse – says feminine, but her olive-green lace-up boots give her an edge, like Army Reserve meets sass & bide. She smiles as she tells us about herself. She's been teaching for five years, has a kelpie-labrador cross named Zoe, and she plays the saxophone.

Maybe I should take up sax? Dad used to play so how can Mum say no? On second thought, it's bad timing. She's still pissed off that he never made it to Nan's funeral last week. Mum nearly chucked the phone across the room when Dad told her he had to stay in Switzerland a while longer, something to do with a big study he's presenting there.

'Oh, and my nickname is Ick,' Dr Kanter adds.

Ty laughs. 'And you're admitting that, why?'

'To show all of you there's no reason to be embarrassed in this class. No question is wrong. No idea is dumb.'

Griff breezes past Dr Kanter without a note, just a smile that she quickly returns. His hair looks messier than usual, like he battled a windstorm. He frowns, thinking I didn't save him a spot, then claims the nearest seat.

'Oh, Iris Chastity Kanter, in case you're all wondering,' Dr Kanter adds. 'My initials.'

Ty snickers. 'Chastity! That's even worse.'

'Yeah, I copped a fair bit of ribbing in high school from the boys,' she laughs. 'From a few girls too.'

Note to self: high school humiliation is amusing with the passage of time.

'Now it's your turn to share some snippets from your wonderfully exciting lives,' Dr Kanter says, 'so go ahead, dazzle me.'

An uncomfortable silence follows, interrupted by random fidgeting and the annoying screech of a few nervous chairshufflers.

'Are we meant to call you Ick?' Paris calls out. 'Dr Kanter sounds so ... formal.'

She smiles. 'I have a better idea. How about you call me Doc?'

I can't work out whether that's lame or cool, but I start off anyway, eager to redeem my crap day with a good first impression. 'Hi, Doc. I'm Harley. My best subject is English, and I love to sing and cook.'

'And eat,' Stu mutters.

Dickhead.

He runs his hand through his hair, probably making sure there's still some there. I tear a scrap of paper from my notebook and quickly scrawl a few words.

'Sounds great, Harley. Anything else?'

'Well, my brother Luke's in Year 12,' I add, flinging the note in Stu's direction when Dr Kanter's not looking. I feel strangely satisfied when it hits him in the head.

'And is school captain,' someone calls out in a sing-song voice from across the room.

I want to kick myself for even mentioning Luke's name. I'm so sick of hearing about The Golden Boy. All the girls love him because he has the face of an angel and an eight-pack. And the guys love him because he brought Brolympics to school last year, *A Day of Testosterone-Fuelled Insanity* according to the marketing hype. Luke insisted it was a fundraiser for new cricket nets and everyone believed him. Everyone *always* believes him.

'And I have a jack shit named Falco,' I add, eager to flick Luke out of my head.

'Pardon? A what?' asks Dr Kanter.

'A jack shit. You know, a jack russell shih tzu.

Out of the corner of my eye, I see Stu reading my *You will be bald by 21* note before crumpling it and whipping it back at me, just missing my right eye. I should have written *bald and blind.*

'Thanks, Harley. Anyone else?' She flashes Stu a stern look before scanning the room for her next victim.

Addy's waving her hand frantically, like she's lost at sea.

'Hey, Doc, my name's Adelaide but everyone calls me Addy. I play netball and hockey in winter and do swimming and tennis over summer.'

She's putting herself out there as a future Olympian, but it's not natural to do that much sport. And what's with her name, anyway? Did someone pass a law fifteen years ago, saying everyone had to name their child after a city? In our school they're taking over. Along with Adelaide, there's Paris and Sydney. Worse, they hang together at recess and lunch, as if forced to by some weird geographic bond. And they're just like their names suggest: Adelaide is pretty but slightly distant, Paris is the resident style queen, and Sydney ... well, she's warm and sunny but overrated.

Now that the ice has been broken, half the class is itching to volunteer, thrusting their hands in the air, calling out to Dr Kanter. I urge Griff to have a go, but he shakes his head robotically like he's in a trance. Then he opens his notebook and starts sketching – mutant superheroes, I think.

***

At recess, I spot Luke leaning over the Pit Stop counter, probably trying to sweet-talk the canteen ladies into a free meal. All my friends say he's so good-looking – *yuck!* The seniors swarm around him like his popularity is contagious.

And Luke's loving it. Now that he's school captain, he's on even more of a power trip than before. He was sure to get the job, thanks to his friendly vibe and natural aptitude for bullshit. But I doubt he'll be any good – he has the leadership skills of a toddler.

I plant myself on a nearby bench and try to get comfortable. The safety pins are stabbing me in the hip, which makes the rip even bigger. If that's not bad enough, I look like an overgrown shrub thanks to the colourblind school committee that chose seaweed green for our uniform. Sweat is trickling down my back, sticking the itchy fabric to my skin. Why does school have to start in summer when nearly every day's a scorcher?

I sink my teeth into the apple slice, instantly losing two chunks near my collar. A quick peek on my phone confirms 1) the stain's not too bad, and 2) I look terrible anyway. Random videos even more boring than my life distract me on TikTok for a few minutes till I remember the slice and take another bite.

Luke's latest girlfriend, skinny little Meika, is prancing around the café tables like a demented fairy. She's wearing the boys' uniform – pleated maroon shorts and a green-and-white-striped cotton shirt that only she could pull off. She looks fresh, immune to Warmageddon.

When I'm halfway through the slice, Luke shoots me a disgusted look, like I'm stuffing my face.

'Here, you can have it,' I tell Griff when he plops down next to me. 'I can't eat with Luke staring at me.'

'Why do you even care what he thinks?'

The real answer? I don't know. But I say the only thing that makes sense right now. 'Because it's too hard not to.'

'I wouldn't worry,' he says, nodding to Meika. 'I think he

has his eye on other things.'

Meika's still flitting about, and I wonder how she always has so much energy. She's tiny – about a hundred-and-sixty centimetres tall and maybe forty-eight kilos, if that. She looks like she's been shrink-wrapped. But in a good way. There's bad skinny, when you look sick, and good skinny. Meika's definitely good skinny.

Griff polishes off the slice. 'Got anything else?'

His eyes light up when I pass him the beef rendang.

'Save some for me,' I joke after his third mouthful. Then I realise all this food's better off in his stomach than mine.

I've begged Mum to lay off on the takeaway and desserts, telling her they're no good for us. I say 'us' to make it a shared struggle, figuring maybe we can bond over better eating habits, but she just thinks I'm being paranoid about my weight. She's always saying things like, 'You're just tall, like your father'. I'm fifteen, not stupid.

It's like there's an unspoken rule: you can tell people they've lost weight; you can even tell them they're too skinny. But tell them they need to lose weight? No way.

But I don't need anyone to tell me. I already know.

CHAPTER 3

What's in a Name?

*Love is a canvas furnished by nature
and embroidered by imagination.*
(Voltaire)

The next week the new guy finally arrives, bursting into Food Tech on Valentine's Day like an avatar for gorgeousness. Call it bliss, nirvana, whatever. It's like that *Doctor Who* episode where Rose looks into the heart of the TARDIS, straight into the vortex, and experiences everything in the universe in a single moment. I try to catch Talia's eye, but she's already locked her gaze on him, smiling dreamily.

'Well, hello! Colt, is it?' Miss Zhang's voice is higher than I remember, chirpy even. She takes a step back, as if to admire the living, breathing work of art before her.

'Say hello to Colt Carter,' she sings out. 'He's just moved to Mount Pleasant from sunny San Diego in the USA.'

'Hey, everyone,' Colt calls out. His Hollywood smile sends bright sparks throughout the room, like a mirror reflecting sunlight.

His California vibe is clearly unnerving some of the jacked guys, whose appeal is fading faster than Eden's fake tan. Addy is clutching a stack of recipes rather than passing them, eyes glued to the star attraction. A few girls break into spontaneous applause as if they've won a lucky door prize.

Miss Zhang's eyebrows shoot up as she ticks his name off the roll. 'I see your name's listed here as Coltrane.'

'Well, my dad was a huge jazz fan,' he starts to explain.

He holds out a handful of Sweetheart lollies, and she hesitates before taking one. I wonder if someone gave them to him for Valentine's Day. And who. But my ears are too busy processing his smooth, hypnotic voice to care.

'So he named me after one of the greats, John Coltrane.'

'Of course.' Miss Zhang pops a pink lolly in her mouth without even reading the message. 'I love the trombone.'

'So do I.' A smile takes over his face in slow motion. 'But he played sax.'

'Oh, yes, silly me.' Miss Zhang's cheeks turn at least five shades of red, settling somewhere between crimson and magenta. 'That's what I meant.'

Colt walks down the aisle, nodding to everyone. There's too much to take in – peacock-blue eyes, full lips and a strong jaw in perfect proportion, broad shoulders, tall, lanky frame, and tousled, sun-streaked locks that make me want to go blonde and take up surfing. My pulse is racing and my chest feels tight. Colt's eyes meet mine and he smiles, revealing killer dimples. Could this guy be any cuter? Eyeing the empty seat next to me, he approaches, swinging his long leg over the back of the chair before claiming the spot.

'Hey.' He tosses his notebook onto the space between us. *Our* space. I can hear my blood pumping – a deafening, pulsating rhythm, like when Griff and I mucked around with the stethoscopes in Health class. I wonder whether he hears it too.

'Hey,' I reply, trying to sound nonchalant. I shoot Talia a

look across the classroom that practically screams, 'OMG, best day ever!'

She nods vigorously. I want to kick myself for my uninspiring reply, but there'll be plenty of time to make an impression. Bumping into Colt at our lockers, hanging out in the quad at lunch, chatting on the bus, maybe catching a movie. I sit back and smile, thinking Food Tech has just become my all-time favourite subject.

'Everyone calls me Carter,' he explains with another wink.

Either he's flirting with me or he's just super friendly. Or maybe he has something in his eye. I'm trying to work out how his eyes can be so blue and green at the same time and whether they're aqua, turquoise, teal or azure that I almost forget to reply. 'I'm Harley.'

'Don't you mean Tracy?' Ty scoffs.

'Tracy?' Carter's confusion is adorable. *Everything* about him is adorable.

'It's some drama thing,' I tell him, wondering who blabbed to Ty and whether he's auditioning. I don't want to be Tracy Turnblad. I *can't* be Tracy Turnblad. I just need to figure out how to break the news to Mrs Stevens.

'Listen up, everyone.' Miss Zhang claps loudly for attention. 'Turn to the person next to you and say hello to your new cooking partner.'

Carter spins towards me, holding up his man-sized hands for a double high-five, laughing when I jump up and barely make contact.

Addy's looking around desperately for a cooking partner.

'I'll put you down with Griff,' Miss Zhang tells her, and Addy slumps in her seat.

I message Griff. *Where are you?*

Across the room, Talia and Eden are giving each other

little air kisses in a mutual love fest. Ever since Talia sat next to Eden on the bus it seems like they're best friends.

'And for our budding chefs,' Miss Zhang announces, hands on hips like she means business, 'Teenline's hosting a fundraising brunch at the end of next term, and we've been asked to contribute a dish.'

'What kind of dish?' Paris calls out, no doubt gearing up for the challenge.

'Good question,' she replies with a smile. 'One that will soon be answered with a bake-off.'

Yes! I have to stop myself from doing an air punch. I'm a great cook, and I'll gladly take the express route to Carter's stomach ... and heart. I just hope this bake-off doesn't require a lot of taste-testing. I need to look my best to grab his attention. Then I need to quickly figure out a way to keep it.

'Just to *sweeten* the deal,' Miss Zhang adds, looking too pleased by her pun. 'The bake-off will be your major assessment item and the winner, of course, will receive top honours.'

The class buzzes with excitement, I'm guessing more about the grade than the cooking.

'So it's never too early to start planning,' she adds.

'Can we use our own recipes?' Addy asks. 'My mum's zucchini fritters are the best.'

'Sounds great, I was just getting to that,' Miss Zhang says. 'Easy recipes, please. No more than five ingredients. Something you can eat with your hands.'

'I eat everything with my hands,' Ty says, which doesn't surprise me, coming from the poster boy for Neanderthals.

'Savoury or sweet?' Sydney calls out.

'Your choice, but remember, something simple like a

quiche or a cake. Maybe a slice, or even biscuits.'

'Biscuits?' Carter asks. 'Like the kind you eat with gravy?'

Cue raucous laughter.

'In Australia, biscuits are what you call cookies,' I lean over to whisper, eager to grab any opportunity for close contact.

'Aah,' he exhales, his toothpaste-ad smile revealing no hint of embarrassment. 'What other lingo do I need to know?'

'Well, where do I start?' I blurt out, suddenly energised. 'There's *beaut*, which means great, *arvo* is afternoon, *bludger* is a lazy shit, *ranga* means redhead.'

He laughs. 'Are you serious?'

Now that I think of it, no one under sixty uses these words. But I can't backtrack so I simply say, 'Would I joke about my native tongue?'

Those killer dimples appear again at the corners of his mouth.

'*Dinky di* and *true blue* are the same thing, *wanker*'s an idiot.'

I'm on a roll for old people sayings but I'm liking our banter, so I keep going.

'Oh, and there's *Bob's your uncle.*'

He laughs again. 'Who?'

'It just means *it's all good*,' I tell him.

His eyes meet mine. Then he smiles and my body stops working. I sit there frozen, like a garden statue.

'Man, I'm gonna need a translator,' he finally says. 'You up for the job?'

My pulse skyrockets as my future flashes before my eyes. Carter and me, high school sweethearts. Our gap year travelling the world, picking up odd jobs, living week to week off bread, cheese and wine. Then uni – Melbourne, probably. Carter studying medicine, me pursuing my acting or singing career, maybe teaching if I'm broke. Our wedding in the Blue Mountains, then a ...'

'Earth to Harley,' he leans in to whisper.

'Sorry,' I mumble. 'Yeah sure, translator it is. A girl's gotta start somewhere.'

'Hope you're up for a challenge. I can't even make toast without burning it.'

I fiddle with my pen, trying to look carefree. 'And you're taking Food Tech, why?'

'Dude,' he laughs, 'to learn, of course.'

Dude? Am I being friend-zoned? When my brain's done body-slamming my heart, I catch him looking at me. His eyes are saying, *I like what I see.*

'How am I going to manage a cake?' he adds. 'Or, um ...'

'Biscuits!' I call out, overwhelmed by a sudden desire to help him – anytime, anywhere. 'Or bikkies.' Now we've graduated to Nan-speak.

'Bikkies. Cute.'

I smile, even though there's no reason to. I mean, it's not like he's calling me cute. Or is he? I realise I've been doing a lot of smiling since he sat down, so I stop; I don't want him to think I'm simple. 'I can write them down for you,' I offer.

'Write what down?'

'All the Aussie lingo.'

He laughs again and reaches for his phone.

'Say cheese!' He takes my photo before I can even process what's happening, then passes me his phone.

I'm surprised to see how good I look on his screen. My messy bun hits the mark, and I'm not sure if it's the lighting, but my hazel eyes really pop. I start to add my details to his contact list then wonder how many other girls are on his phone. I wish there was some way I could check.

Carter leans in, his shoulder touching mine, sending lightning bolts through my body. 'You do know your number, don't you?'

'Yeah, it's coming back to me,' I joke, punching it in. He drapes his arm around the back of my chair, my pulse instantly doubles.

The bell rings, sending half the class to Carter, drawn to his force field. I grab my notebook and a pink Sweetheart spills out from the pages.

It says, MARRY ME!

CHAPTER 4

The Climb

Courage is knowing what not to fear.
(Plato)

By the end of the week, nothing has changed. First, Griff's still not at school. It's like five days of Mount Pleasant High was too much for him and he needed a break. Second, I'm still avoiding Mrs Stevens – at least until after today's auditions. And third, Carter is still gorgeous. Correction: even more gorgeous.

My phone buzzes with a message just as the final bell rings. Griff. I thumb a quick *kk* and am out of school in two minutes flat, at The Mount in under ten and rethinking my decision to meet him in fifteen. I didn't factor in climbing over 700 metres in this heat. I stop every twenty or so steps to catch my breath, sitting on the rock wall just past the halfway mark to take in the view. In the distance, the hills mark the edge of town, framing the six-block-long town centre.

The good news about Mount Pleasant – population 11,583 according to the welcome sign on the main road – is it's so small that everything's an easy twenty minutes on foot – the shops, movies, school, the swimming pool. The bad news: it's boring. Except for The Mount (more of a big hill, really) that gives the town its name. Griff loves the solitude and the fresh air, always insisting the smell of green could be bottled there. I love the space and serenity, and the fact that we've been going to The Mount forever. Mum says my first glimpse was from a baby sling although I can't picture her ever using one of those things. I'm still waiting for her maternal instinct to kick in.

When I finally get to the clearing, Griff's orange runners are easy to spot halfway up his favourite tree, *Ficus carica*, as he's always calling it, instead of fig tree like everyone else. It's the only fruit tree amidst a sea of gums and the perfect climbing tree, with a wide split near the base and gnarled roots doubling as toe-holds. When we were little, we'd squeeze into the forked V-seat then shimmy along the tree's sturdy branches, eager to survey the world. Before long, we were heading skywards to nestle in its upper limbs, like hugs from heaven.

'You coming up?' Griff calls out.

'Nah, wardrobe issues.' I fan out the edges of my sweaty uniform as proof, wishing I had ducked home to change.

He slithers down effortlessly, dumping a shirt-load of figs on the ground. Then he cuts one open with his pocketknife, passing me the sun-warmed fruit. 'Soon the tree will go into shutdown mode, dropping its leaves to conserve energy ...'

'To make fruit that will bud in spring,' I finish for him, having heard this growth cycle talk way too many times. 'Hey, where've you been all week?'

'Home.' Griff always takes the express route when answering questions. He slices another fig.

'Yeah, I figured that,' I tell him, popping the fig in my mouth. 'But why?'

He shrugs without making eye contact. 'Dunno. Just felt a bit off.'

Why couldn't he just answer my messages? It would've taken less than five seconds. Knowing Griff, he didn't even bother to check his phone all week. I banish the thought, relaxing into a makeshift seat of dried grass, and immerse myself in the sounds and rhythms of the bush. The screech of cockatoos, updating each other on the day's news. The whistle of a breeze through the tall gums. The curtain of light streaming through the trees, casting shadows at our feet.

A text from Mum quickly destroys my nature vibe.

Dinner at 6, don't be late x

'Mum's doing her drill sergeant routine,' I tell Griff. 'Ever since she lost her job, she's got too much time on her hands. Either that or she has PFSD.'

He sits down next to me, polishing off another fig in two bites. 'PFSD?'

'Yeah, Post-Funeral Stress Disorder.'

Griff spots a stripped-back gum and begins neatly stacking sheets of bark near the base. 'By the way, I thought you held it together pretty well.' His voice is calm, reassuring.

'Really? What funeral were you at?'

The moment the priest had said, 'Let us commend Maeve O'Connell to the mercy of God,' it hit me. Nan was dead. One day she was here, the next day she was just a name like all the other Dearly Departeds read out each week at Mass. My eyes had teared up at the graveside but I didn't cry. All that slobbering, it's so ... *unbecoming*, as Nan would say. Then the violinist played the saddest music ever and I nearly lost it. Mum tossed irises, Nan's favourites, into the ground as the casket was being lowered.

Strange thoughts popped into my head.

How's Nan going to breathe under all that dirt?

Does she have everything she needs?

I remember gulping big pockets of air, trying to swallow my emotions. Then I lunged forward. Mum's arm yanked me so hard that I stumbled, nearly falling into the grave. A few oldies gasped.

Mum shouted, 'Luke, help your sister!'

He did … after snapping a photo.

When we got home that night, I told Mum I didn't want to go to Mass for a while. All my life I've believed God exists but suddenly I wasn't so sure. Her mouth twisted and I thought, uh-oh, verbal missiles ready to launch, but she said not to worry, I'd know when I was ready.

A gum leaf as sharp as a steak knife jabs me in the thigh, abruptly ending my daydream. 'I wish Nan was here.'

Griff is staring at me, his brown eyes intense and questioning. 'It gets easier, Harls. Promise.'

I guess he'd know. Losing your mum trumps losing your grandmother any day of the week. He was in Year 7 when his mother died in a car accident. I still don't know how he and his father got through that time.

'Feels like forever that Mum's been gone,' he tells me, gathering a few stray gum leaves. 'And like yesterday, too.'

He rubs his hands together and takes a whiff of the leafy eucalypts.

'Sometimes, when I close my eyes at night, I panic because I can't see her face,' he continues. 'You know, like those old photos that are so faded you can make out the shape of the person, but there's not enough detail to be sure.'

I don't really know what to say about his mother, about Nan. About anything. I place my hand on his arm and he meets my gaze. His eyes look lighter in the sun, caramel swirls, rather than their usual chocolate brown. I wonder what they're searching for and whether that's why he seems far away at times. When the corner of his mouth turns up ever so slightly, so does mine, and for a brief moment, I feel better. Until my stomach demands: *Feed me now!*

An army of bull ants marches past a pile of dead leaves, straight into a massive nest. The ants seem full of energy and purpose. Direction. Everything I don't have lately. Griff grabs his Nikon from his backpack, tossing the fluoro strap around his neck before snapping on the zoom lens. He takes a few shots of the leaves, manoeuvring for the best angle. Then he aims the camera skyward, working it with ease, like a musical instrument mastered long ago.

A wedge-tailed eagle circles overhead before settling on a twisted branch. Griff clicks furiously.

The bird takes flight, and for a split second, I'm convinced my relentless stomach rumbling has scared it off. Since Nan died, it's like there's an animal gnawing at my insides. I'm always hungry but the more I eat, the emptier I feel.

'I don't suppose you've got anything to munch on?' I ask Griff. 'Besides figs,' I add with a smile.

He drags over his backpack and takes out a couple of ham and cheese salad rolls, a bag of potato chips, and two slices of carrot cake. His hair has fallen over his right eye and I almost reach over and brush it away. He offers me the slice with the iced carrot on it. He knows me too well.

'Thanks but, um, I'm trying to be healthy,' I tell him, hoping I sound grateful. 'I feel so gross and spongy lately, like I'm inflatable.'

Griff pulls a face. I'm sure he's sick of hearing me complain all the time. My weight, my brother, my boring life.

'You look totally normal,' he offers, and I'm tempted to say thanks, but somehow I doubt he'd know what normal is. I sweated out a few kilos in the heatwave at the start of the summer – thank you, global warming. Then the funeral meals-on-wheels started and I gained them back ... and more. Now, every time I see food, my brain says, *Don't touch that!* But my hands are disconnected, like someone cut the wiring.

My phone buzzes with a text and I figure it's Mum again, since nagging's her part-time job.

Oooh, much better. Carter!

You didn't audition!

My pulse races then my brain catches up. Carter auditioned? I didn't even know he could sing. Why didn't he tell me? Why didn't I ask?

I have no idea what to say so I just tell him the truth.

Nah. Chickened out ;)

More rumbling but this time it's not hunger. It's disappointment. Maybe I should have auditioned. I don't think I'd mind being cast as the fat girl if Carter was Link Larkin. I'm sure that's what he went for. I can't imagine someone like him in any other role.

My phone buzzes again, this time with an unknown number. Acid's brewing, working its way to my throat.

'You okay?' Griff asks. 'You look like you've seen a ghost.'

My eyes are glued to the image on the screen, a moment captured for eternity. It's me at recess on the first day of school. I don't know what's worse. The apple slice shoved in my mouth or the chunks of filling strewn across my uniform. I look like a well-fed zombie.

Griff leans over my shoulder to see what I'm staring at. 'Okay, so it's not the most flattering shot.' He takes my phone, peering at the image from every angle, like he's trying to find some hidden code.

'Don't waste your time searching for a reason,' I tell him. 'Luke is evil, pure and simple.'

'Luke?'

'Who else would do something like this?'

Griff shrugs.

I take a deep breath. 'He's convinced his duty as an older brother is to humiliate me. And he always goes for a surprise attack. He's waited nearly two weeks to send this.'

Griff can't take his eyes off the image.

'And he probably figures texting from a mate's phone will throw me off track,' I add.

Knowing Luke, the photo will be on Snap any minute now. And Insta. Probably both.

Griff makes a funny sound, like he's swallowing a hiccup. 'There's a caption.' His voice is hushed even though no one's around to hear. 'Australia's top contender for ...'

Then a different sound, like he's pushing air out between his front teeth.

'Go on, I can take it!'

'For the Fat Olympics.' He makes another funny noise, somewhere between a tsk and a sigh, then passes me the phone, as though I need proof.

I turn so he won't see my hot, angry tears. 'That's it. I'm transferring to St Ant's.'

'Harls, whoever said that needs their head read. You're *not* fat. You know that, don't you?'

I shrug.

'Come on, someone's just messing with you.'

My phone buzzes again with another number I don't recognise. I click on the message.

Lose Unwanted Kilos FAST!

WTF?

Luke's upped his game a notch. He's probably set up a virtual private network just to hassle me anonymously. If only there was a whiteout for brothers. I hit delete.

I think about putting back the carrot cake, but my body has a mind of its own. I need this cake. I bring the wedge to my lips and bite off the cream cheese icing carrot.

You're so weak, the voice inside me says.

CHAPTER 5

Think Again

I think, therefore I am.
(René Descartes)

Monday's highlight: watching Carter radiating charm at lunch. He's leaning against the courtyard wall, and if I didn't know better, I'd think his confidence was holding up the bricks. We're halfway through the term and everyone's still asking him the same old questions.

'How do you like Australia?'

'Have you ever played cricket?'

'Wanna start a gridiron side?'

Before Carter can get a word out, Eden and her squad push in, calling out like entertainment reporters on the red carpet.

'When's your birthday?'

'Are you a surfer?'

'Why'd you move here?'

I know why. Carter's father is heading some overseas aid charity a few hours away, taking the train back to boring Mount Pleasant every Friday. Something about experiencing *authentic Aussie life*, Carter said.

The jacaranda's showy blooms have dropped, taking the

shade with them. But it's a box seat to all the action so Talia and I claim the spot.

'Welcome to Season One of *Everybody Loves Carter*,' Talia mutters under her breath. She reaches into a lunch bag so stylish it could double as a tote.

I'm excited by my leftover pizza, less so when the rubbery sheet of pumpkin, rocket and feta comes off on my first bite. Talia unwraps a gourmet salad roll – sprouts, cucumber and carrots in a baguette. I spy little wedges of Camembert and lean into her, my signal for her to break off an end. We nibble greedily, our eyes glued to the Year 10 paparazzi, still scrapping for a piece of Carter.

Stu hands Carter a pie. Sydney offers her wedges and Carter takes a few. The food keeps coming and I seriously wonder whether he'll ever have to buy a canteen meal. Maybe that's the answer! Maybe we're cooking partners for a reason. Maybe my kitchen wizardry will win him over.

'Eden's going in hard. Look at how she's throwing herself at him,' Talia says, reading my mind. 'Can she get any closer?'

Carter and Eden are laughing like old friends. She drapes herself around him, her hand lingering on his arm. He smiles at her then pulls out his phone.

'Subtlety is a lost art form.' The voice is mine, but the words are Nan's.

My phone beeps with a message – a yawn emoji. From Carter. I smile, guarding my screen from Talia. Knowing her, she'd blab to Eden.

'Hey, check this out.' Talia turns to me, opening her lips a fraction then cocking her head ever so slightly, like she's amused but too cool to show it. 'Does my smile look natural?'

'Uh, yeah, I guess.'

She pops the last bite in her mouth then whips out her phone. 'It should, I practised all summer.'

I nearly let out a little yelp when I remember I packed dessert.

'How about mine?' I bring the corners of my mouth up into my cheeks.

'You have a great smile, Harls,' she says, checking her feed. 'It's so big!'

Yeah, like me.

My lamington disappears in two bites.

Griff appears with a burger, hot chips and milkshake, settling into the space between us without major spillage. His burger disappears in record time. (If I was cataloguing annoying traits of Griff's, devouring food like a wild animal would be at the top of the list.) Then he turns to me and says, 'Let food be thy medicine and medicine be thy food.' (Annoying trait number two would be: Blurting out random words for no reason.)

I'm too busy admiring Carter to ask what the hell he's talking about.

'Hippocrates,' he starts to explain, passing me his sunglasses.

'Griff, why the hell are you giving me ...'

'You don't want to be blinded by his beauty,' he cuts in, nodding in Carter's direction. 'Could be dangerous, you know. Like watching a solar eclipse.'

Griff has always been a bit strange. But ever since school started back, he's been acting stranger than usual.

'Just so you know, I waited for you yesterday,' I tell him.

'For what?'

'For stud-y-ing.' I'm aiming for dramatic but end up with sarcastic.

He told me to meet him at the library so we could start our English assignment, but never turned up. Not that we would have gotten much studying done, but still.

Griff's face turns red. He sucks on his straw and cops a brain freeze, clearly trying to avoid my question.

'Yeah, sorry about that,' he finally spits out. 'I couldn't make it.'

Obviously.

He slurps up the last of his shake. 'I should have messaged you.'

He offers me the rest of his chips and I gladly accept even though I can't eat another thing.

Across the quad I spot a familiar figure. Mrs Stevens is practically galloping towards me and I'm too full to run away.

'Harley,' she says. 'Callbacks are Thursday.'

Her eyes drift to the chips but I'm not ready to part with them yet. Instead, I say, 'But I didn't audition.'

'And here's your last chance! No more hiding in the tech suite.'

She says *tech suite* like it's some glamorous setup, when she really means a simple lighting console. I got thrown in the deep end for our Year 7 musical and have never looked back. Who knew I'd be such a pro? It's all about creating emotion and mood, tracking movement and focus.

'So remember, Thursday at three-thirty!'

Before I can come up with an excuse, she's off. What makes her think I'd want to try out? I don't have a reputation to protect but I have one to build – that's even harder. And starring as the plus-sized lead in a lame Year 10 production isn't the best way to start. Then the idea of Carter and me on stage quickly takes over. After all, romance begins with opportunity. And what better opportunity than rehearsing with him after school, over school holidays – who knows, maybe on weekends too?

'Harls, you'd make such a great Tracy. You're a natural,' Talia gushes.

'What does that mean?' I snap.

'What does *what* mean?'

'A natural because I'm fat?' I bite into my second lamington.

'You're … not … fat,' Griff pipes up.

He sits up to drum the point home, staring right through me. His eyes are deep brown with flecks of cream, matching the smattering of freckles across his nose.

'I just meant you're a great singer,' Talia tries to explain. 'Geez, Harls, take a compliment, would you?'

I don't know what to think. Ever since school started back, it's like everyone's speaking a different language.

'If you're so keen on the musical, why don't *you* audition?' I ask Talia.

Talia's voice isn't fabulous, but it's not terrible either. At least she could report back to me on Carter's every move and conversation.

'No way!' Her eyes are wide. 'I'd rather lose all my teeth.'

'Gotta back yourself, Harls,' Griff cuts in as though he's the king of confidence.

I'm not really in the mood for his Dr Phil routine. Griff's words often make sense but the tone's not right. When he's not disappearing, he's offering up comments that usually miss the mark. And there's no in-between. Lately, he's either avoiding me or staring at me.

Addy and Ty stroll past the canteen, hand in hand, soon all over each other in full view. I want to look away, but my eyes are riveted, like when there's a pile-up on the side of the road. 'I think he's gonna swallow her whole.'

Talia grimaces. 'Yeah, if I keep watching these two, I'm gonna puke.'

My thoughts drift to another pair. 'So what's with you and Eden?' I pucker my lips and plant a *mwah, mwah* air kiss near her cheeks.

'Nothing, it's just a bogus greeting that masks my deep hatred of her and all she stands for.'

I laugh, but I can't shake the thought from my head: If Talia hates Eden so much, why have I hardly seen her since school started? I convince myself to forget about it. Everyone knows Eden's only interested in herself. Talia won't be able to cope for much longer.

Things always work themselves out, Nan would say.

'Aw, c'mon, Harls. That bleached skank can never replace you,' Talia adds, as though she's reading my mind. 'You know what they say. Keep your friends close and your enemies closer.'

How true.

Talia spends the next five minutes taking selfies while I watch Carter work the crowd. He's so polite, so confident, so ... everything. When the show's over, I flick through TikTok, landing on a video of a girl's glow-up. The caption:

Time to REINVENT yourself!

I couldn't have said it better myself.

CHAPTER 6

Do I Have a Soul?

It's not what happens to you,
but how you react to it that matters.
(Epictetus)

On my way to Philosophy for fifth period, I hear whispering behind me.

She's so basic, Talia says.

My dying cat is more fun to hang out with, Eden chimes in.

I wonder who they're talking about? Probably Addy. She always seemed like the odd one out in Eden's group. And what's with Talia's salty vibe? She's like a different person when she's with Eden.

I turn the corner and bash straight into Stu, sending my books flying.

'Good one,' he calls out loud enough for our whole year group to hear. He tramples my *Guide to Practical Philosophy* with his gigantic shoe as he brushes past.

When I get to class, everyone's mucking around on their phones and taking selfies but Dr Kanter doesn't seem to mind. She's wearing a tight, red skirt and a black-and-white-striped crop top with a chunky necklace that complements her tall, toned body. Her dark brown hair, streaked with magenta, is swept back with a large clip. She looks good without being try-hard.

I take the seat behind Talia at the back of the room and claim the spare one next to me for Griff, who's late as usual, operating in his own time zone. A thought pops into my head, then a pang of guilt. I secretly hope Carter walks in first. I've hardly seen him the past few weeks other than a few waves from afar and endless translation requests (the latest, 'spag bol' and 'fair dinkum,' which I'm guessing he heard on TV).

Your wish is my command.

Carter enters the room and the air crackles as though his mere presence is charging nearby ions. I'm half expecting him to run down the aisle, holding out his hand so everyone can high-five him, like a rock star about to hop on stage.

Suddenly the atmosphere seems clearer, brighter. How can someone be so *exquisite*? That was one of Nan's favourite words, usually uttered in the context of a fancy dessert. Carter's even better than dessert.

He tosses his Philosophy text on the desk next to mine.

I look around the classroom. There are at least three other free seats but he's chosen the seat next to me. *Me!*

'I think I'll need an interpreter,' he says.

I hear his words, but they don't register. Every available neural connection in my body is fixated on his perfect face. 'Pardon?'

'An interpreter, you know, for the philosophically impaired.'

'Ah, yeah, I know what you mean,' I agree, nodding too vigorously. It's like I have no control over my body. I giggle, even when he doesn't say anything particularly funny. And when I speak, the words never come out right. It's so much easier to message.

He stretches his long legs under the desk, groaning softly. The sound is mesmerising, even better than that whale music Mum made me download when I had a killer headache. I wish I could record it for my ringtone.

'You okay?' I ask.

'Just sore from the gym,' he explains. 'I went a bit overboard yesterday.'

'Everyone take a seat,' Dr Kanter urges, ushering in Addy and Paris, followed by Sydney.

'You may find it hard to believe,' she starts off, 'but the questions the ancient philosophers asked are still very relevant to our lives today.'

Griff wanders in, looking slightly dazed, like he doesn't know how everyone made it to class before him. Dr Kanter nods, as though she's in on some secret about him being time-challenged, and he smiles. Eden breezes in behind him, sucking the room's energy into her magnetic field. She stops for a skinny girl pose at the front of the class, hand on hip, leg turned outwards.

'Orthodontist appointment,' she announces, smiling as Dr Kanter signs her diary.

Heads turn, tracking Eden's impossibly rounded bum on its scenic route to a free spot in the corner, near Paris. Carter's looking too and I'm praying she's not his type. When Eden finally takes a seat, she catches Talia's eye and blows her a kiss. Talia laughs, pretending to catch it.

'Can't wait till she gets braces,' I lean forward to tell Talia, slightly sickened by their mini-lovefest. 'Perfection interruptus.'

Talia snorts. 'She just got her braces off!'

'She had braces?'

'The kind on the back of your teeth. Where've you been?' She turns around to make sure I see her eye roll extraordinaire.

Eden's smiling at us the whole time. Looks like she got her teeth bleached, too. Figures. She has such a good-looks surplus that braces don't even make a dent. If there were such a thing as a beauty transplant, I'd ask her to be my donor.

Dr Kanter scans the room slowly as though she's searching for life forms. 'Okay, everyone. Today we turn to the mind-body problem.'

'I don't mind your body,' Ty whispers to Talia, oblivious to Addy's glare.

'Moron,' Talia mutters under her breath. She turns around to flash me a smile. Not the one she practised all summer. This one has more teeth, more … attitude.

Dr Kanter paces at the front of the classroom before exclaiming. 'Let's get started! Who thinks our minds and bodies are connected?'

Stu snickers, then Ty. Soon the whole class joins in.

'Let me rephrase that,' she adds, oblivious to the words *Do I have a soul?* beaming on the screen straight over her head. 'Are your mind and body separate entities or are they somehow intertwined?'

Out of the corner of my eye, I see Griff leaning into the aisle trying to catch my attention. He's chewing on the end of his pen, twirling it around with his tongue like he always does, flashing me his notebook for approval. I give a thumbs-up to *Intergalactic Ecstasy*, the mega-detailed sketch he's been telling me about. Ever since he went to the space observatory last year, he's been raving about other galaxies. If I didn't know better, I'd think he'd actually visited a few.

'How about you, Griff?' Dr Kanter asks.

He takes the pen out of his mouth. 'Well, I've always been a big fan of Aristotle.'

Eden and Talia share a deep, throaty laugh then stop at the same moment, but I can't work out if they're laughing at Griff or if this is another dumb routine they've practised.

'I think they can't really be separate because I need my brain, which is part of my body, to think,' he says.

Nan was always saying, *Be yourself.* But this doesn't apply to Griff. I raise my hand to rescue him but change my mind. I don't have anything to say.

'This sounds kind of gruesome,' Griff continues, 'but if you cut off my head, I'd stop thinking.'

'And talking,' Stu mutters under his breath.

Carter nudges me with his knee, shooting an electric current through my leg. Is he urging me to have a go or did he shift his leg and accidentally brush mine?

'Don't be shy,' he leans over to whisper, and my hand shoots up like his brain's controlling my body.

Dr Kanter smiles. 'Yes, Harley, would you like to add something?'

'Well, I think the mind and the body are definitely separate,' I start off, not sure what I'm going to say next. 'Your mind is like your soul and when you die that part of you continues to exist. Does that make any sense?'

She nods. 'Yes, it makes perfect sense, Harley. Can you expand on that?'

'Well, for example ... my Nan died recently.'

I swallow so hard I'm convinced the class can hear it. My eyes hurt, like something's trying to push them out of their sockets. I wonder whether this is the 'healthy emotional release' that Dad's always going on about.

Griff leans forward, mouthing something to me. I think, *You okay?*

I nod, even though I'm not. I can feel the dam wall crumbling. When the first teardrop falls, it's nearly undetectable. Then others follow. I cover my mouth with my hand, trying to contain my emotions, but they escape through my fingers, announcing themselves in loud sobs. I don't know what's more shocking. The fact that I'm finally crying over Nan, or that my body can produce such frightening noises. Talia spins around in her seat and offers me her hand. I squeeze it, probably harder than I should, but she doesn't seem to mind.

Finally, the words find their way out. 'So, I'd like to think ... that my Nan still lives ... in some way.'

'I'm sorry to hear about your loss, Harley,' Dr Kanter says, as others nod in agreement. She pauses for a moment, meeting my gaze with a sympathetic smile. 'Later this term we'll study René Descartes, who also believed the mind and body are separate and distinct.'

Everyone's staring at me and I wish I'd never opened my mouth. I try to smile even though I have no idea what Dr Kanter's talking about and what it has to do with Nan.

'Descartes was famous for his statement *Cogito, ergo sum*,' she continues, as though Latin's going to help. 'Or *I think, therefore I am*.'

'Now my head hurts,' Talia mutters under her breath.

'Which simply means if I am a thinking being, I must exist,' Dr Kanter explains, and I wonder why she just didn't say that in the first place.

'I'm sorry about Harley's grandmother and all,' Ty jumps in, 'but doesn't the fact that she's so upset show the mind and body *are* connected?'

I close my eyes and grip the sides of my desk, releasing a long, smooth breath. I learned that in the 'Yoga for Relaxation' class that Mum dragged me to over the summer. I try to take comfort in my grief, pulling it close and wrapping myself up in it, like one of Nan's crocheted throws. There are so many empty spaces in each square, but suddenly I feel snug and safe, as though they've been knitted together. When I open my eyes, Carter's hand is on top of mine.

It's official: I'm in love.

The bell blares, sending Carter out the door, riding an endless wave of admiration. When I pick up my books, a handwritten note falls out of my text.

Meet me at the gym after school. C.

There's still no sign of Carter at the gym by four o'clock, so I do a lap around the building, thinking maybe he's hanging out near the back entrance. Then I do a reverse lap, in case he's coming the other way. The PE Centre is a massive brick complex with multiple spaces. 'Gym' could mean the weights room, the locker area, the basketball court. I check my phone. No message. He's not even online.

At a quarter past four I message him. My phone's on three per cent so I get to the point.

Where are you?

I stare at the screen, willing the typing dots to appear. Nothing. When I head inside, Ty's shooting free throws at the far basket and I brace myself, figuring bonehead Stu's probably not too far away. I cut across the court, tossing the ball back to Ty when it lands near my feet, relieved it ends up in his general direction. My phone buzzes with a text. I'm hoping it's Carter, telling me he's running late. Instead, it's Dad, saying how he can't wait to see me next week. Finally, he's coming home!

I pass the weights room, where some Year 9s are spotting each other's ambitious bench presses. The locker room door flies open and Stu spills out, wrestling his PE shirt over his head.

'Checking me out?' he taunts, zipping past me.

As if.

A muffled groan escapes from inside the locker room and I wonder if someone's sick. Then a crazy thought takes hold. What if it's Carter? That would explain everything! I want to fling the door open and run to him, like Florence Nightingale, his angel of mercy, but what if some other guys are in there? What if they have nothing on? I put my ear to the door then open it a crack.

'Carter?' I count to ten then try again, louder. 'Carter?'

'Caaarter, Caaarter!' comes the breathy reply. If Stu hadn't already charged out, I'd swear it was him.

I bolt down the hallway and veer sharply, taking my time to reach the door, hoping I'll hear Carter call out, *Harls, wait up! I can explain!* When I get outside, my pace quickens and before I know it, my race-walk is a jog. But I can't outrun the truth.

I haven't even hung out with Carter, and I've already been stood up.

<hr>

At home, the only thing that will make me feel better is a massive slice of red velvet cheesecake. I polish off the last crumb and collapse on my bed with instant regret. My fingers gently massage my stomach to loosen the queasy knot, but it makes me feel worse. If only there was a do-over for food.

I read Carter's note for the twentieth time.

Meet me at the gym after school. C.

I plug my phone into the charger and watch the signal gain strength, waiting for Carter's message to pop up, saying, *Sorry, change of plans.* Anything to explain why he didn't turn up. But there's nothing except a reminder to update my apps. My stomach is tumbling like a clothes dryer. I need to find out what happened. There's no way I'm going to be able to concentrate on anything until I do. Just when I finally work up the nerve to call him, he messages me.

CARTER: *i'm home*

He's not even trying an excuse. I would've thought he'd start off with *Sorry* or *My dog ran away.* Something. Anything. I don't even know what to say.

ME: *oh, okay*

CARTER: *why'd you wanna know?*

This isn't going too well.

ME: *sorry, what?*

CARTER: *you messaged before*

ME: *cos I waited for you*

CARTER: *waited?*

ME: *at the gym*

CARTER: *???*

Emergency! Assume crash position!

ME: *cos that's what ur note said*

CARTER: *what note?*

I feel sick.

ME: *the note u left on my desk*

CARTER: *?*

ME: *the meet me at the gym note*
CARTER: *ahahaha that was for Stu.*
WTF, Harley you idiot!
ME: *oh hahaha*
CARTER: *I couldn't go anyway*

My heart sinks to the floor then into the ground below where worms turn it into compost. I can't believe I thought the note was meant for me. What do I say now? Words race through my head. No matter how I string the thoughts together, they sound pathetic. I panic, opting for humour.

ME: *ok just thought maybe u were looking for a new gym buddy lol*

CARTER: *we're gonna go tmw if ur interested*

Sure, Carter and Stu seeing me all gross and sweaty. *Not.* My burp is long and loud and tastes like red velvet cheesecake. Good thing this isn't a voice call.

ME: *ah can't, have a movie date with Talia*

Date? Great, now he'll think I like girls! I panic, seeing this is going to get worse before it gets better.

ME: *gotta go!*

Before I can toss my phone, the screen lights up with a plea from Mrs Stevens. I'm still undecided about callbacks. I love singing. And I love the idea of spending time with Carter even more. But what's the point? He acts so nice in class but it's not like he's asking me to hang out after school. He only asked me to gym with him tomorrow because I put him on the spot. He doesn't want to share the stage with me. I bet he doesn't want to be anywhere near me.

Bile shoots up in my throat, propelling me to the toilet. But when I open my mouth, no food comes out – just a tortured cry like a wild animal.

There's a rap on the door. 'Mirror making you sick?' From

the other side comes Luke's laughter.

I think about opening it and vomiting on him for sheer entertainment but collapse back against the bath instead.

More door banging. 'I've got heaps on, so keep away if you're sick.'

That's the best thing Luke's said to me in a long time. I may just take him up on his offer and avoid him entirely.

CHAPTER 7

Love Shack

As people are walking all the time,
in the same spot, a path appears.
(John Locke)

By the end of the week, I'd given up on the idea of Carter ever liking me as more than a desk buddy. Then he practically insists we meet up at lunch and suddenly I'm not so sure.

'See you at the canteen in ten,' he calls out when the bell rings at the end of class, and my whole day, my whole *life*, is instantly brighter. Everyone knows you don't ask someone to sit with you at lunch unless you're tuning them.

Talia's not at her locker so I message her: *guess who's having lunch with carter.* I'm tempted to add an emoji or three but figure less is more. Then I grab my ham and cheese sandwich and duck to the loo for a quick mirror check.

The overhead fluoro lights are hideous for basic grooming, let alone self-esteem, and should be changed on humanitarian grounds. I step up to the sink, my breath fogging the mirror. A few finger strokes on the glass improve my features, making my nose shorter, my lips plumper, my eyes bigger. A sweep of my forearm across the top of the mirror reveals a mop of curls, rather than my usual waves –

the payback for falling asleep with damp hair. The colour's dull, more mud brick than auburn, the ends hugging my shoulders. I stare at my reflection, trying to find where *I* am.

When Nan took me to a photo exhibition a few years ago, she said a great portrait captured the essence of the person, while a lesser one offered only a resemblance. I study my eyes, looking for my essence. I don't see it, but then I don't really know what I'm searching for.

Is it a sparkle?

Does it change all the time?

Do other people see it when they look at me?

I focus on the good bits: great smile, straight teeth, full lips, decent hair. Well, most days, anyway. From the neck up, everything's passable. It's the middle bit that's awful. If I were an artwork hanging in a museum, people would say, 'What a lovely frame, shame to ruin it with that painting.'

Right on time, I find Carter under the Pit Stop sign at the canteen, looking very appetising. If only I could step up to the window and tell the lunch lady, 'One Carter, please.' He catches my eye and motions to the corner table.

The umbrella offers some shade but it's still stinking hot. He takes the seat opposite.

'Tackling the How to be Australian program?' I ask, nodding to his meat pie.

He laughs like I've said the funniest thing ever. 'I think I've eaten enough of these to graduate already.'

I nibble the corner of my sandwich. I'm too nervous to eat in front of him – what if I spill something, as usual? I'm in overdrive trying to come up with conversation topics. 'Hey, how'd you go at callbacks yesterday?' I suddenly remember. I'm praying he doesn't ask why I wasn't there because I'm not even sure myself.

He wipes his mouth with a brush of his hand, just like Luke always does, but Carter's version seems less gross. 'They've been pushed back till next week. Not sure why.'

I know – because no one wants to be in the dumb show. Can't Mrs Stevens take a hint?

'You're coming, I hope. Sounds like Mrs Stevens is expecting you.' His voice is calm and his eyes sincere. He'd make a good guru. 'It'll be fun!'

Before I can process his words or even take another bite of my sandwich, Eden, Talia and Paris have joined us. *WTF?* Paris gets in first but Eden wastes no time pushing in next to Carter, practically knocking her off the bench. I spy my message on Talia's phone and can't believe she didn't cover for me. I haven't told her I like Carter – she'd probably blab to Eden and then it'd be all over school – but isn't it obvious? And Talia knows the importance of the one-on-one time. She's watched every season of *The Bachelor* – and not just the Australian version, the American and Canadian ones too.

Stu and Ty quickly invade the space, tossing chips to Carter who catches them in his mouth like a trained seal. Griff spots me and hesitates, as if he's expecting me to wave him over. My nod is so slight it's nearly undetectable, but something tells me Griff will read it as an invitation. When he walks past, my stomach feels tight in the middle, like an hourglass.

'You okay?' Carter asks.

'Sure, why?'

He smiles. 'You just look like you're ... troubled.'

'Troubled!' Stu snickers. 'That'd be right.'

I need to think fast. 'I just remembered I have to do errands for Mum after school.' I roll my eyes to make it sound worse than it is. 'You know, pick up a few groceries, that kind of thing.'

By now, the entire table is staring at me. Their faces are saying *yawn,* so I'm not surprised when they're distracted seconds later by something on Ty's phone. Except Talia, who's fighting a smirk, and Carter, who seems genuinely concerned about how I spend my time after school.

'I'll go with you,' he offers. 'Our house isn't far from the shops.'

'Okay, great!' I try to tone down my enthusiasm. *Keep the man guessing*, Nan always said.

'Me, too!' Paris chirps, looking at Carter even though she's talking to me.

There's absolutely no way I'm going if she's tagging along.

Thankfully, I'm a quick thinker. 'Ah damn, I just remembered Mum's picking me up to do errands.' My disappointed look comes in the form of a shrug.

When everyone's done obsessing over the latest TikTok challenge, Ty puts down his phone. Stu whips out a football and Carter jumps to his feet. Before I can blink, the guys have fled to the oval, leaving me with the bitch squad.

I look for Griff, but he's gone. I spend the next twenty minutes listening to a fierce debate about gel polish versus shellac, and almond-shaped nails versus square and stiletto.

It's the lunch date from hell.

When I get home from school, Falco jumps on me, like he always does, then rubs his furry ear against my leg. He's been acting strange lately. Some days he lies in his bed. Other days, he sits on our front verandah like he's waiting for Nan to visit.

'You're such a weirdo.' I scratch under his neck where he likes it, noticing the grey coming through. Just like Mum's hair. When I rub his chest and belly, he collapses to the floor with a low-pitched hum that sounds like a purr.

Seconds later, he's following me into the kitchen, where I smell freshly baked cupcakes before I even spot the three-tiered stand. Before I can grab one, I hear the front door open, then familiar footsteps. Falco jumps up, trying to get in on the action.

'Missed you, Pumpkin,' Dad says, dumping his suitcase dangerously close to Mum's prized marble bench. The top tier wobbles and I let out a little gasp, my arms outstretched in case of cupcake casualties. Dad accepts my unintended hug, squeezing me tighter and longer than expected.

'Missed you too.' I tell him, because I did, even though I'm pissed off that he's been gone so long. Maybe Mum's rubbing off on me. *Oh God, that can't be good.*

I reach under his arm to snatch a cupcake. 'How was Switzerland?' I ask between licks of sugary icing. 'Did you meet any yodellers? Clockmakers? Army knife company execs?'

He laughs. 'Unfortunately not. Just some very enlightening antibodies.'

Dad's big study on autoimmune diseases means constant globetrotting to exotic destinations, though I'm guessing from how tired he looks that it's not as much fun as it sounds.

My cupcake's gone in five bites.

Luke struts in. Sniffing like a bloodhound, he zeroes in on the cupcake stand, snatching one from the top tier.

'Well, *hello*, Luke,' Dad says sarcastically.

Luke nods, cake erupting from the corners of his mouth. He can be so revolting sometimes.

Dad smiles. 'You know, in many cultures, people offer some sort of greeting when they haven't seen each other in a while.'

'My hello was implied, you know, subtle,' he mumbles before grabbing another cupcake.

Mum storms in carrying the laundry basket, overflowing with Luke's putrid trackies and who knows what else.

'Oh good, you're home, Matt. How was the conference?' She drops the basket and flicks the kettle. No hug or kiss for Dad even though he's been gone for nearly two months. Mum is the Queen of Grudges and I can't believe she's still pissed off at him for missing Nan's funeral. I wonder if that's why they've been arguing on the phone so much lately.

'Not nearly as good as our first conference,' Dad tells her with a wink, ignoring her I've-only-heard-that-a-hundred-times look.

Luke grins. 'Yeah, but were there any typos in the program?'

Mum's trying to look serious, but a half-hearted smile soon breaks through. 'My God, will I never live that one down?'

Mum and Dad met at a science and technology conference over twenty years ago. She was working for the event organiser – her first *real* job, as she always tells us. Dad was one of the speakers – the *youngest* one, as he always brags. His paper was called 'The Public Costs of Diabetes', or something like that, but Mum didn't pick up the typo on the final proof, so it appeared in the program as 'The Pubic Costs of Diabetes'. Luke and I were pissing ourselves when we first heard that but it's obviously still a sore point with

Mum.

'Kids, you should thank your lucky stars for that typo or you wouldn't be here,' Dad says. 'If your mother hadn't sent me that fancy wine and cheese hamper to apologise, I'd never have worked up the nerve to ask her out to dinner.'

'Speaking of dinner,' Luke eyes Mum, 'what are we having?'

Mum swats him playfully. 'If you mean, *what fine delicacy are you preparing this evening, Mum*, the answer would be fish.' She holds up the cookbook, pointing to the photo of grilled fish, baby potatoes and asparagus. 'Doesn't this look delicious?'

It may look delicious but, given how cooking-challenged Mum is, I doubt it'll taste any good. When she puts the book down, I flick through the pages, thinking maybe I should suggest something less ambitious.

'Carb-loading again?' Luke mutters to me under his breath.

'Fish is good for you,' Mum insists, oblivious to his sledging. 'Besides, I need to lose some weight. I can barely zip up my pants.'

'Gross, Mum.' Luke pretends to gag. 'I don't need to hear that.'

Mum's not fat, but she's trying to watch her weight because all the *damn hormones* (or *whore moans*, as Luke says) are giving her a muffin top. She'd actually be pretty if she put a bit of effort into it. Her hair's too dark and makes her look like a middle-aged vampire. She should go for a chestnut or hazelnut colour. And the grey roots running down the middle of her head like a road-line aren't helping. She's short and a bit plump so she needs to ditch the long tops she wears. They make her look like one of Snow

White's dwarves – Grumpy. Some make-up wouldn't hurt, either. What she does have are nice blue eyes and full lips. She just needs a bit of help, maybe a fresh new wardrobe and a makeover … but I'm not about to tell her that.

'Fish is great,' Dad chimes in, I bet just to get on Mum's good side. 'G, how's the packing going?'

What the hell? Now she's *going away?*

'It'd be going better if I had help,' Mum snaps.

Dad flinches, clearly not expecting the sudden mood shift. Luke and I are used to it and don't budge.

Mum sighs deeply. 'It's just too much, I can't do it on my own.'

Dad strides over to her, arms outstretched. Mum reluctantly accepts his hug, jumping when his phone rings.

'Sorry, I really need to take this,' he says sheepishly, slipping into the next room.

I think back to Mum's shouting match with Dad last week. When she wasn't yelling into the phone, she was crying. Something about whether she should rent or sell Nan's house.

'I can help you,' I tell her, figuring maybe she just wants some support, but her glassy eyes say she's holding out for a better offer.

Dad walks back into the kitchen, looking even more exhausted than before. He leans into Mum, mumbling, but I can hear every word. 'I know this isn't great timing, but I need to go to Washington the week after next.'

The cupboard door slams shut. 'Tell the president I said hello!' Mum growls. Another slam, their bedroom door.

Dad parks his phone on the bench with a loud sigh.

I pat his back gently. 'Welcome home.'

Then I snatch another cupcake and head to my room.

A terrible dream wakes me just after midnight. I'm enjoying a romantic dinner with Carter at a fancy restaurant – the kind where a waiter comes up to wipe the crumbs off your table – and Dad walks in with some blonde who looks half his age. When his eyes meet mine, I bolt up in bed. The clock says 1.35 am.

Luke's room is pitch black except for the stream of blue light coming from under his covers.

'What the hell?' he shouts when he sees me in the doorway. 'You scared the shit out of me.'

'Shhhhh, not so loud,' I whisper. 'I have something important to tell you.'

He grunts.

I take a deep breath. 'I think Dad's having an affair.'

'Are you sleepwalking?'

'I'm serious. Think about it. He's travelling all the time, like he wants to be anywhere but home. Plus they've been fighting a lot lately.'

'Anything else, Doctor Hastings?' Luke laughs.

'They hardly ever hug or kiss.'

'You're just like Meika, overthinking everything.' He puts down his phone. 'Dad's just busy with work stuff. And Mum's probably missing Nan. They're just stressed.'

'But what about?'

'Get. Out. Of. My. Room.'

'I just think ...'

'Now!'

I flop back into bed, wondering why I wasted my time talking to Luke. He can live in denial if he wants but I'm choosing reality.

I bet Dad doesn't even go to any conferences. He's probably shacking up with *her* in some fancy hotel. That would certainly explain his 'urgent business' in Washington. I wonder what she looks like and what she does for a living. Other than steal husbands, of course.

My screen lights up with a message from Carter.

wish you had come to the shops

I'm wide awake now. I have to choose my words carefully.

Paris is fun to hang out with

I hit send. His reply comes through in less than two seconds.

in small doses

I smile. Is he flirting with me?

'Harley go to bed now!' Mum's standing in my doorway, scowling, as usual. What's she doing up?

'I am!'

My fingers bang out a reply but it's missing something. A smiley face? So predictable. A love heart? Way over the top. Think, Harley, think! I have to be quick or it'll look forced. I thumb the first thing that comes into my head.

hahaha next time x

The minute I hit send, I regret it. A kiss? I've only known him a few months. Too much, too soon. His reply is taking forever. I probably scared him off. My screen lights up and I force myself to look.

The best part? The heart's red. There are endless colours to choose from and he picked red.

I smile myself to sleep.

CHAPTER 8

You Reap What You Sow

To find yourself, think for yourself.
(Socrates)

The night before he leaves for Washington, Dad pokes his head in my bedroom. 'You still up?'

'Yep.'

He's standing alongside my Ed Sheeran poster, the one with the guitar hanging over his shoulder. 'Why the long face, Pumpkin? Is it Nan? School?'

'It's life.' I don't have the energy to tell him how badly every aspect of my life sucks. Ever since Nan died, nothing's making sense.

He leans against my desk. 'Ah, I see. Teen angst.'

'Whatever.'

'Yeah, that's the secret password.'

Ugh. I'm not in the mood.

'Go on, don't hold back. I know you want to smile.'

'Dad, now you're just being lame.'

He taps his fingers on my desk and I wonder if he even realises he's doing it. 'You know, it's easy to repress all the negative stuff in life, but it's always healthier to acknowledge it.'

'Okay, I acknowledge my life sucks.'

'I have an idea. Here, pass me your laptop.' His hands are outstretched, eager, but his voice is low and soothing, like a yoga instructor. 'How about journalling your feelings?'

Within seconds of wedging himself into my chair his fingers are sailing across the keyboard.

'Here's another idea,' I tell him, 'why don't I just wear a bullseye?'

Dad sighs and takes his glasses off, carefully wiping each lens with his shirt. 'Just trying to help.'

All my friends think he's attractive – nice face, wavy brown hair, green eyes and cool specs. Talia thinks he's totally hot for forty-nine, though I wish she'd never told me that. But today, cramped in my chair, he looks awkward, not his usual, confident self. That's no surprise after Mum's passive-aggressive *Welcome home*. I guess it wouldn't hurt to show some support. Most kids go to their mothers for help, but ever since I was little, I've gone to Dad. Now that I'm older, I don't need him as much. Maybe that's the issue.

I'm not really into journals, but I'm struck with a good idea. I rummage around my bedside table drawer like it's a lucky dip. One honeysuckle body spray, bookmark and packet of throat lozenges later, I unearth what I've been searching for.

'Here it is!' I inspect the leather notebook, a birthday gift from Nan that I'd forgotten till now.

I run my hand over the gold-embossed circle that takes up most of the cover. It's divided into eight sections, like a pizza, each featuring symbols that resemble the Egyptian hieroglyphics we studied in History last year. I wonder if it says something. I pick up a pen to get started.

'Great, I'll leave you to it,' Dad says, extracting himself

from my chair with some effort. He gets as far as my door then turns around. 'But remember, it's about getting in touch with whatever's in your head, you know, validating your feelings.'

I nod.

'So, when the words hit the page, just let it all go.'

'I will, Dad. Thanks.'

My thoughts are jumbled so I try a few pen-tapping beats instead. I close my eyes and see Nan in her favourite place – her garden – nipping the dahlias to make them bloom or plucking rosemary for her lemon chicken dish. Near the back door are the pink-and-white camellias she'd let me clip for her favourite crystal vase. Nan taught me how to make the soil pH just right for the Japanese maple and how cutting back the roses could boost growth the following season. 'Gardening is hard work,' she'd always say, pointing out the trees that had been growing for over fifty years, their roots deep and strong, 'but the rewards are endless.'

I crack open the journal, taking a few moments to fan the stiff pages. It doesn't take long for the words to come. In my neatest writing, I make a long overdue entry from the start of the year.

Harley's Year 10 Wish List

Get a job.

Get a boyfriend.

Get a life.

When I first came up with the list, I wasn't even sure that I really wanted a boyfriend. Then Carter arrived and something changed. Something deep inside me that I don't even understand. There's a voice that builds me up, telling me anything's possible. But there's another voice, one that's much louder, that hisses and tears me down.

A boyfriend means the first voice wins. I need it to win. And I need to win before the biggest night on the Year 10 calendar later this year – the formal. It's actually a semi-formal at the end of the year but everyone's already super-hyped, treating it like a rehearsal for the real deal in Year 12. I have so many good ideas for transforming our ugly school hall but why waste my time? It's not like I'll have anyone to go with.

I revise my wish list to reflect my new priorities.

Get a boyfriend.

Get a job.

Get a life.

All good things come to those who wait, Nan's saying in my head.

But I can't wait – I have to step up. I have to work for this. The term's over in two weeks so I better get onto it.

Then I remember something else Nan always told me, and before I know it, the words have found their way to the page.

You reap what you sow.

Dad pokes his head in my door. 'Griff's here.'

What?

Griff walks in and plops down on the end of my bed, like I'm expecting him. I can't even remember the last time he was in my room.

His hands are clenched. He holds them in front of me, palms down, and I choose 'left'. When his fingers open, my earring's there, the one I thought I lost ages ago. How random.

'It was under the sofa cushion,' he explains.

'Thanks but you could've just given it to me at school tomorrow.' The minute the words are out of my mouth, I wish I hadn't said them. I hope it didn't sound ungrateful.

'That's okay. I was out walking anyway.'

I laugh, thinking he's kidding, then realise he isn't. 'At this time?'

He gets up to leave. 'Yeah, I've been doing that a lot lately. It helps clear my head.'

Only Griff would be out walking at nearly ten at night. Maybe he's on to something. I consider joining him sometime, but really I do my best thinking in bed.

'Anyway, I should be getting home.'

'See you tomorrow,' I call out when he's halfway through the door. 'And thanks again.'

I pick up my journal and write the thought I can't shake.

What is going on with Griff?

CHAPTER 9

Truth Be Told

*We ought so to behave to one another as to avoid
making enemies of our friends, and at the same time,
to make friends of our enemies.*
(Pythagoras)

The last day of term calls for a celebration but Griff bails on our plans to meet up at The Mount, so I go with Plan B – ice cream with Talia. I figure one little treat at Scoop won't hurt. Besides, I've already told myself I need to go on a diet. Tomorrow.

When it's our turn to order, Talia leans over the front counter, her smile bigger than usual. I crane my neck and spot Ty grinning back at her. Two thoughts pop into my head: *I wonder when he started working here.* And *I can't believe Talia would waste her time with him.*

He's wearing Scoop's cringey uniform: white sailor shirt with navy blue stripes along the wide collar and a matching scarf knotted around his neck, like a Navy reject. The weird little white cap isn't helping. It looks like a paper plane landed on his head.

'Nice hat,' I say when he finally makes eye contact.

He adjusts the headgear, as though he's finally seeing it

for what it is. A human rights violation.

Note to self: check uniform requirements before accepting any job offer. Not that I've had time to look. I've spent most of my free time lately either daydreaming about Carter or obsessing over the formal even though it's over six months away. Some girls at school are already talking about dresses, so the pressure's on.

Ty starts preparing a sundae for us to share, adding a bit of everything – M&Ms, snakes, berries, banana, caramel sauce, whipped cream. He's obviously trying to win over Talia with his tower of sugar. She fake gasps, leaning over the counter, thrusting her boobs at him. I've seen this show before and have no interest in re-runs so I claim a table by the window, and dig my spoon in.

'Oh, don't wait for me or anything,' Talia grumbles when she sees the dent I've made. I'm an overachiever when it comes to food.

Ty's lurking behind her, pretending to clear trays. He darts over, wielding a damp cloth and wipes our table, slowly, rhythmically, smiling at Talia the entire time while she giggles and bats her eyelashes. Maybe she should see a doctor. Symptoms: profuse smiling, unexplained laughter, fluttering eyelashes. Diagnosis: serious crushing.

'That'll be all, thanks,' I manage to say with my mouth full, waving Ty away with my spoon.

Talia flicks her spoon around the bowl, scooping up all the green M&Ms like she always does. We've shared too many sundaes here to count, but I wonder how many more there'll be. Some days, Talia and I seem as close as ever. Other times, it's like I don't even know her. There's the Talia who cried over Nan, the one who makes me laugh, who builds me up, who shares her lunch. Then there's the Talia with attitude, the one who seems to care more about what she looks like, and who she hangs out with, than anything or anyone else. Somewhere in the middle of the two Talias is Eden. Half the time Talia acts like she's her best friend. The other half she's cutting her down to size.

It's time to finally clear things up. 'What's your strategy with Eden, by the way?'

She hesitates, giving me plenty of time to indulge in a mouthful of peanut butter and fudge – the perfect combo.

'No strategy.' She shrugs. 'Just a survival tactic.'

'Huh?'

'Well, I still love taking the piss out of her. It's a hobby that demands time and energy, but the emotional payoff is huge.'

I giggle. There's the Talia I know and love.

'Harls, the stakes are getting higher each year and we're running out of time.' She leans in to whisper, smiling at Ty when she catches his eye. 'I figure if we can worm our way into her airbrushed little world, it can open doors for us.'

I'm not sure where these doors lead but I figure there's no harm in going along for the ride. It's not like I have much else to do. 'Well, if anyone can do it, you can.'

'We can work out a strategy over the break,' she says.

'At a sleepover ...'

'Definitely a sleepover.'

We clink spoons and dig back in. With no M&Ms in sight, Talia turns her attention to the berries. 'Can you believe Eden's already planning her party?'

'You mean the I'm-better-than-you-because-I-live-in-a-mansion bash?'

'The one and only.' She traps a strawberry, coaxing it onto her spoon. 'Only Eden would take half a year to plan an event, but at least it gives us time.'

I dip my spoon into the gooey fudge. 'Time for what?'

'For figuring out how we're gonna score an invite,' she says, watching me eat. 'Geez, Harls, try to keep up.'

There's that attitude thing again.

'The ratio's always crazy good, not that I've ever gone,' she adds, mindlessly picking through the sundae.

'That's because Eden has no girlfriends,' I remind her. 'Except the Skank Squad.'

'Seriously, Harls. We *have* to go to this bitchfest.'

'Bitchfest?'

'Yeah, all women are bitches when you really think about it. It's just a matter of what kind.' Talia rolls her eyes when she sees I'm not following. 'Like Paris. She's the fashion bitch.'

'What about Addy?' I ask.

'She's the cool girl bitch.' Another eye roll. 'Acts like a bro … loves sport.'

She's right. Addy's the odd one out in Eden's squad. 'Oh, I get it, let me try.'

'All right. Sydney,' she suggests.

'Easy, Sydney's the …' I draw a blank, unable to think of anything to say. 'Sydney's the boring bitch.'

Talia laughs, patting me on the shoulder. 'Now you're catching on.'

'Wait a minute!' I blurt out. 'What's Eden?'

'That's easy. She's an *actual* bitch.'

My projectile lands smack in the middle of the table, a misshapen ice-cream blob with some Crunchie pieces breaking through. Talia covers her mouth, trying to swallow her laugh then snorts, making me laugh even harder.

'So, if they're all bitches why do you even want to go?'

I finally manage to ask. 'They'll just be standing around posing. You can watch them do that at school.'

'I know, but it's time we up our game.'

Talia sighs heavily when she sees I'm not following. 'Harls, if life is a game of chess and we're the pieces,' she starts to explain, 'then we need to start moving.'

'Okaaay.'

'This term's already over and what did we accomplish? Nothing!'

She's right. I have more chance of being prime minister than working through my wish list. I have the time and motivation, but I'm missing a key piece of any strategy.

Opportunity. And confidence.

Okay, two pieces.

Talia leans forward, her face hard in concentration. 'An invite to Eden's party would advance us on the board.'

'Do you think Carter will be there?'

'Uh, let me think.' She taps her dusty-pink gel nails on the edge of the laminex table. 'Yaasss!'

My brain skips from Carter to *Hairspray*. The cast is being announced this afternoon, conveniently after the term's over so no one can complain. Planning starts Monday and goes through the holidays. All that valuable bonding time with Carter – lost! I don't want to admit it, but I should've tried out.

I did go to callbacks. Sort of. I hovered outside for ages, but no matter how hard I tried, I just couldn't step through the door. What if I made a fool of myself in front of everyone? Especially Carter. Worse, what if I auditioned and ended up in the chorus, my voice drowned out by people who can't even sing? I figured maybe Mrs Stevens would see I was a no-show and shout, *Go find Harley!* Someone would fly out the door and I'd just happen to be standing there. But no such luck. The voice inside my head, the one that's always tearing me down, won.

'Come on, spit it out,' Talia urges, reading my slumped body language.

I take a deep breath. 'It's nothing. Really.'

Her eyes are locked on me, forcing the words out.

'I'm just thinking about the play. And if I'd gone for Tracy, then maybe Carter and I would've had a chance to ...'

She puts down her spoon, her eyes twice their normal size. 'Seriously?'

A chunk of cold sugar hits my brain when I swallow, sending a sharp pain through my skull. 'Thanks so much for your support.'

'Sorry, I didn't mean ...'

'It's just that we get along so well. He's so nice and he's always paying attention to me, so I thought ...' When I hear myself speak, the absurdity of it all seems so obvious.

Talia leans forward, looking me in the eye. 'Did you ever think maybe he's just being, you know, nice?'

Yes, I did think that.

She laughs as though the idea of Carter and me is crazy, unnatural even. Like different species mixing. Whatever happened to nice, caring Talia? The one who sat up with me all night when I was sick at Year 7 camp. The one who told me to get the cool turquoise earrings at the markets even though she spotted them first. The one who put together the best scrapbook ever for my birthday last year, bursting with selfies and cringey poems, all our friendship bracelets from middle school and ticket stubs from nearly every movie we'd seen.

'I dunno, I just get a funny feeling when I talk to him,

that's all,' I try to explain, wondering why I'm even bothering. I take another bite, pleasantly surprised to get a megadose of caramel.

She circles her spoon inside the bowl, cleaning up the last toppings along the edge. 'I hate to break it to you, but he goes for skinny chicks.'

I cross my arms. 'Oh, thanks heaps.' Obviously, Talia's the mean bitch.

Her spoon drops into the bowl with a loud clank. 'I'm just saying, Sydney saw a photo of him with his arm around some girl and she was a total stick.'

My stomach drops. 'Maybe he has a sister.'

She sighs loudly. 'Who he makes out with?'

'Maybe she's an old girlfriend.'

Talia's breath comes louder and faster. 'Or a *current* girlfriend.'

'And how's that gonna work with an ocean in the way?'

I think back to my mini-breakdown in Philosophy. I can still feel the touch of Carter's hand on mine and the rush of adrenaline that followed. Suddenly I realise I was ridiculously lucky to be partnered with him in Food Tech. It's not much of an opportunity, but it's all I've got.

'What's the matter with your hand?' Talia asks.

'Nothing. Why?'

'You keep rubbing it, you know, like *'Out, damned spot!'*

'Just a cramp,' I lie, impressed she actually remembered something from *Macbeth* last year.

'Maybe you have RSI.'

'From what?'

'From this.' She cranks her arm from bowl to mouth, faster and faster.

Guess that makes me the fat bitch.

I feel a headache coming on. I don't know if it's all the sugar, or the toxins in Talia's words that hang in the air like subtitles waiting to be translated. I know she's just trying to help me, but why the superiority vibe? Ever since she got back from Italy, she's been acting like she's better than everyone – even me, her best friend. The roll of fat that sits around my waistband suddenly feels bigger, but I pull the bowl back towards me anyway, studying the unappetising soupy mix in the bottom. When I take a mouthful, I hate myself for being so weak.

And I hate Talia a bit, too.

———

Later that night, when I'm getting ready for bed, Carter's name pops onto my screen.

CARTER: *hey*

ME: *hey* :-)

CARTER: *great news*

ME: *ooh what?*

CARTER: *i got link*

Can't say that I'm surprised.

ME: *that's great, perfect casting*

I wonder who got Tracy. Probably Sydney or Addy. Eden would never agree to a fat role.

ME: *who got tracy?*

CARTER: *talia* :-)

What the hell, Talia auditioned? A train is running through my head and my heart's tied to the track. Talia swore she'd never audition. I just told her I had second thoughts about callbacks and she didn't bat an eye. Nothing's making any sense.

I message Talia. My hands are shaking so much it's hard to type a simple sentence.

ME: *hey, congrats, didn't even know you auditioned*

Because you never told me. What else haven't you told me? I'm not sure what hurts more. Me being too weak to audition or Talia being so shady.

She replies straight away.

TALIA: *i didn't!*

ME: *???*

TALIA: *i was just singing with my headphones on at lunch and mrs s came up and begged me to go to callbacks*

TALIA: *thought i told you*

ME: *nuh*

So much for never auditioning. I hope all her teeth fall out.

TALIA: *didn't think I sang very well at all*

TALIA: *then I just got the email :-)*

I cannot believe what I'm reading.

TALIA: *she probably wouldn't have asked if you tried out*

There's so much I want to say but I try to stay positive.

ME: *well, that's show business!*

Then I start to build a wall around my heart, brick by brick.

I pop on my headphones and skip through my playlist, quickly settling on some R&B. I crank the volume up until my ears vibrate.

When I close my eyes, the whole awful day runs on playback like a bad movie. Talia low-key stabbing me in the back, tearing me down all afternoon. It's like she's been rewarded and the prize is Carter. The thought of them frolicking on stage makes me feel sick.

The song cuts out without warning. I figure my phone's

flat and plug it in, surprised to see there's plenty of charge. I hit play and the music app shuts down and my screen goes black. A message pops up.

You are my everything.

That was Nan's last message to me, the night before she died. How did that come up now? I haven't even clicked on it since then. It's been too painful.

But I can't stop myself now. I scroll to the start of our thread about six months ago when I showed her how to send a text. Her first? An upside-down selfie. I take in her bright blue eyes and beaming smile and the tears come.

Then her countless questions. *What does a colon, a dash and a bracket mean?*

A smile, I told her.

:-) she'd replied.

Another message. *How do I find the little thumbs up?*

I keep scrolling. Half her messages are lol or lmao. I'm smiling and crying at the same time, remembering how she'd make up her own acronyms, like *WDYDT*, which I finally worked out meant, *What did you do today?* And how she thought meme was pronounced mee-mee.

My body soon takes over, convulsing with noisy sobs that suck the oxygen from my lungs. I cry for Nan, for Talia changing, for a lost opportunity with Carter. For me.

My throat feels cracked. There's no saliva, just a bitter acid taste, like vinegar.

I ditch my phone for my laptop, figuring I'll distract myself with boring schoolwork. I click on the Philosophy link and see Dr Kanter has already uploaded the assignment for next term.

Reflecting upon our class discussion, explain (in 500 words or less) how you can be certain of your existence. Start a conversation with classmates below to refine your arguments.

Ugh.

I scroll through the thread, topped by posts earlier today from Sydney, Stu and Talia. When I'm halfway through, my name leaps off the screen, like an easy answer in a Find-A-Word puzzle.

Blood's pumping through my body and I blink, praying my eyes are playing a trick on me. I read the last entry in today's thread, logged by *Guest* at 6.38 pm.

I eat, therefore I am. (Harley)

The words on the screen blur through my tears. Who would do this? And why? Luke's always throwing shade my way but he wouldn't sink this low. And he couldn't even access this chat ... unless he knows my password. I message Griff, but the post is already down by the time he logs on. That doesn't stop him from offering some useless advice: *Stop stressing over stuff.* What the hell does that even mean? Talia brushes off the post too, saying it's obviously someone's idea of a joke.

I shut down my computer and turn off my phone. I close my bedroom door and stand in front of the mirror, my eyes fixed on my image as I strip off my clothes.

My flaws announce themselves immediately. The rolls of flab on my hips. The cottage cheese lumps on my legs. The bulges on my inner thighs. The chins I carry, like excess baggage. My head is too small for my body. I rotate it left to right, mouth open, like a clown in Sideshow Alley.

I'm not an elephant. I'm a whale.

Within minutes, the room is spinning. I bolt for the toilet. My stomach is being squeezed like bagpipes. The sundae erupts with such force that I nearly knock my head on the cistern. I slump against the cold tiles, my head resting on the bath until another projectile comes moments later. No amount of teeth-brushing gets rid of the vomit taste.

I stumble back to my room and scrawl an entry in my journal.

I'm fat. I'm fat. I'm fat.

I'm ugly. I'm ugly.

I'm nothing.

I flip through the blank pages, imagining them jam-packed with exciting news – coming home from school, jotting down all the cool things that had happened. That's when it hits me. I have two weeks holiday to change my life. To become someone else.

Someone *better*.

Maybe 2019 will be The Year of Harley after all.

New Harley.

My phone lights up with another old text from Nan.

I believe in you.

AUTUMN

CHAPTER 10

Odd One Out

There is no reality except in action.
(Jean-Paul Sartre)

I make it to school early, hoping to catch up with Griff. I've been wanting him to help me figure out how Nan's texts are suddenly popping up, but he was away all holidays. Worse, he wouldn't tell me where. What's the big secret?

I thought maybe Talia the Traitor could help, and we'd fix all the weirdness between us at the sleepover we talked about, but it never happened. Then I saw the photos on Insta. Talia and Eden at the coast on the weekend, bodyboarding and sunbaking. The two of them getting dressed up, taking photos, watching movies.

Why didn't Talia invite me?

I know why. Because she cares more about being popular than spending time with her bestie.

Fat ex-bestie.

Before I even get to my locker, Ty appears out of nowhere, blocking my path. His stare is intense. 'Tell Talia I like her.'

Great. I'm trying to reinvent myself and no one notices. And Talia does nothing and someone likes her.

'Snap her!' I snarl at him, pushing past. 'Better yet, why

don't you get Addy to?' I call out over my shoulder, in case he's forgotten he already has a girlfriend.

He quickly catches up, tugging my arm, like a child with his mum, but this kid's nearly six feet tall. I've never noticed his eyelashes until now. They're unbelievably dark, like black tar, and super long. The closer I look, the more I think he's actually not so bad looking. Then he opens his mouth and ruins it.

'Addy dumped me.'

'Thanks for sharing.' Sarcasm is my default mode.

'And I think Talia's into me,' he adds.

After flying solo all holidays I thought I was ready for social contact, but my run-in with Ty has given me second thoughts. I race off, seriously doubting she's into him but he easily catches up.

'Come on, Harls.'

There's something different about his voice. It's a far cry from his usual tough guy routine.

He tries again. 'What kind of wingman are you?'

Wingwoman. Ty's never uttered a positive word in my direction and he thinks I'm going to run offence for him?

Talia's already landed the lead in the musical. At this rate, she'll get a boyfriend before me, too. What about my wish list? Somehow I doubt she'd be my wingwoman for Carter. The thought of them dancing and laughing at rehearsals is still taking up most of the available space in my brain.

'Just do me this favour, wouldya?' Ty's voice is strained.

When I stop to look him in the eye, he's not Ty anymore. He's just a guy who needs a bit of help.

'I'll see what I can do,' I tell him, wanting to end the conversation.

What would Rory on *Gilmore Girls* do at a time like this? I spent the first few days of holidays binging the series, which did make me feel better. Then I thought about channelling my boredom into something constructive, like helping Mum go through Nan's things, or tidying up her garden. I barely had the energy to operate the remote, so I filed those tasks away with other ideas that seemed good at the time, like reorganising my room and learning calligraphy. Besides, Mum and I would probably just end up fighting if we had to sort all of Nan's belongings.

The upside of being alone for two weeks? I could rest, think, dream. The last one was easy. My dream is to have the body of Kendall Jenner (at least her legs), confidence to spare, parents who don't fight, and the undying admiration of at least half my year group.

But dreams don't just happen. They begin with baby steps. That's why I'm focusing on small, simple changes … starting with a new haircut. I was so desperate I nearly cried when the salon couldn't squeeze me in over the break. But New Harley has a positive mindset. Now I have more time to find a fresh cut – easy with my new app. I've already uploaded my photo so I can try hundreds of looks.

All this thinking over the holidays has made me reevaluate my priorities. The result: a slightly revised wish list. I was so psyched I even recorded it in my journal.

Get skinny.

Get a boyfriend.

Get a life.

I power towards my locker, fuelled by this new mantra. When I turn the corner, a few Year 8 girls are pirouetting towards me. They're tiny, like someone threw them in the clothes-dryer for too long. Across the quad, Eden, Paris and Sydney pose like newly-opened Barbie dolls, their legs positioned at odd angles to showcase their toned thighs. Paris's annoying squeal pierces the air.

When Talia runs up, they shower her with air kisses, luring her into their triangle of popularity. I offer Talia a half-hearted wave and she catches Eden's eye, like she needs approval before returning the greeting. Well, if she wants to take orders from a stuck-up, fake-tanned, bleached-blonde dictator, so be it.

Griff's at his locker, juggling a milkshake and a blueberry muffin that I want to snatch and eat whole.

'Hey, you're alive,' I joke. 'I thought maybe you were abducted by those alien life forms you've been sketching.'

'Something like that.'

When he finally looks at me his eyebrows are scrunched. 'You're wearing make-up.'

WTF? How about, *Sorry I disappeared without warning and haven't even answered your messages?* With Talia acting strange lately, I can't risk losing Griff too. So I bite my tongue on that one.

Instead, I say, 'Yeah, so? Everyone does.' I try not to sound too defensive, but I don't think it works. It's not like I packed it on, anyway. It's just a bit of mineral powder and mascara and a new lip gloss in a shade called 'Fearless'.

New term. New Harley.

'Wanna catch that new movie this weekend?' he asks.

'Sorry, can't,' I tell him. 'Mum's been whinging about cleaning for ages, and I promised I'd help.'

Griff's eyes look glassy. Tired.

'How 'bout the next Saturday?' I suggest. I wish some rom com was playing, not another action flick, but at least it's better than sitting at home. 'The show at seven?'

Mount Pleasant's so small there's only one movie playing

at a time. B.O.R.I.N.G. But it'd be good to hang out with Griff.

'Okay,' he mutters.

Something's off, but I can't put my finger on it. I want to ask him where he went over the holidays. I want to tell him how Talia's changed, how trying to be popular is making her an entirely different person. But the bell rings first.

In Food Tech second period, my stomach rumbling peaks at 8.6 on the Richter scale.

Stu can't help himself. 'What the hell is that noise?' He's holding his hands over his head like there's an air raid. 'Have you not eaten in, like, ten minutes or something?'

'Why don't you go look for your hair?' I snarl.

'Here, have this.' Sydney tosses me a muesli bar. 'I hate these things, but my mum keeps packing them.'

'Thanks.' I open the stubborn wrapper with my teeth, trying to process Sydney's random act of kindness. The moment the yoghurt-topped oat crunch combo hits my tastebuds I want more.

'Time for spring rolls,' Miss Zhang announces, and the thought makes me even hungrier.

Where's Carter?

I line up the sauces and oils at the edge of our workbench, instantly lost in a daydream: Carter steps into class with a bouquet of red roses. Eden snatches a flower as he walks past. Talia and Addy do the same, then the other girls, leaving only a single stem by the time he reaches me. He smiles, twirling the last rose between his fingers. I smile back, not my usual smile but the one Talia practised all summer. Stu plucks the rose from my hands when I'm not paying attention, placing it between his teeth. Before I know it, he's spitting thorns at me like machine-gun fire but they ricochet off me, hitting Eden and Talia in the crossfire. Carter rips open his shirt like Superman. There's a red heart tattooed across his chest with a single word inside: *Harley*.

'You'll find that everything else you need is in the fridge,' Miss Zhang adds, wrecking my daydream.

But I don't care because reality's even better – Carter in 3D, tossing his folder on the workbench, where it overlaps with mine. I wonder whether that's somehow symbolic. Our lives intersecting.

'Reporting for duty,' he announces with a salute.

'Perfect timing. Why don't you grab the wrappers,' I suggest, double-checking the recipe, 'and I'll get the meat and veg.'

'Wrappers? Aren't we gonna eat them here?'

'The *spring roll* wrappers. Geez, you really do need help in the kitchen.'

Talia and Eden are huddled at their workstation, playing with their food, giggling about I'd love to know what.

'Girls, cut the shenanigans or I'll separate you pronto,' Miss Zhang cries out.

They ignore her. Eden rolls the stack of wrappers into an Olympic torch, holding it up for Talia who whips out a lighter.

'That's it!' Miss Zhang snaps. 'Talia, you work with Sydney and Paris. Eden, go with Harley and Colt.'

Oh, please God, no!

Eden practically flies across the room like her name's been called out on *Millionaire Hot Seat*. She rips out her earphones and runs straight into Carter's double high-five.

'Harley, be a good girl and chop the cabbage,' she says in a throaty voice. 'Carter and I will get the pan ready.'

There's a stabbing pain in my stomach, like someone tied my intestines in a bow then pulled the knot too tight. Carter doesn't seem to mind Eden monopolising his attention but he's probably just being nice. Come to think of it, I've never seen him in a bad mood.

I start preparing the spring rolls. There's no way I'm going to let her ruin our dish.

'Can you dice this, Eden?' I ask, passing her the ginger. 'It's cutting. You should be good at that.'

'I'm good at everything,' she tells Carter with a not-so-subtle wink.

He smiles and glances my way. I could be imagining things, but I swear I detect a subtle eye roll.

'What should I do?' he asks.

'You just sit there and look gorgeous,' Eden says, and I want to vomit in her cropped blonde hair.

'Here, follow this,' I suggest, pointing to step three of the recipe.

Carter measures the fish sauce, brown sugar and rice wine vinegar with the concentration of a Nobel Prize-winning scientist. Meanwhile, I shred the veggies and squeeze the limes, then toss all the ingredients together.

My stomach rumbles so loudly I nearly expect the class to evacuate.

I'm not hungry, I'm not hungry, I keep trying to convince myself.

I road-tested diets over the holidays. Each time I started, I was ready to take on the world, but before I knew it, I was waving the white flag. My vegan experiment only lasted a few hours, the soup diet made me crave solid food and the fruit cleanse gave me serious anger issues.

Problem is, I like everything about food – eating it, cooking it, serving it. I love setting a fancy table, lighting candles and making cool napkin designs, although these touches are lost on my family. Mum whinges that she can't see in the candlelight and Luke shovels down his food then bolts from the table. I make a mean beef stroganoff and my cassoulet is to die for. One night, Dad actually paid me twenty dollars to cook him his favourite meal and my signature dish: Moroccan lamb and couscous.

I spoon the mixture on the spring roll wrappers while Eden watches, as though cooking is a spectator sport.

'Just a reminder,' Miss Zhang calls out. 'I need everyone to bring in their recipes next week. I want to get an idea of what you're all thinking for the bake-off.'

Eden pops in her earphones then starts sealing the wrappers, pressing the edges so hard that the insides are oozing out. I'm tempted to take over, but can't be bothered fixing her mess. I have more important things to do, like making Carter fall in love with me. When she's done destroying our spring rolls, she turns her attention to her playlist, singing with her eyes closed like she's caught in the moment. She's so fake.

Carter lights the burner. 'You know, I could use some help in the cooking department,' he tells me. His eyes are impossibly blue.

'Ah, don't worry, you're not that bad,' I tell him, adding a drizzle of oil to the skillet.

He's waiting beside me, armed with the spring rolls. 'Oh, okay,' he hesitates, 'it's just I was just hoping you could ...'

I could what? Lend you my Maths notes? Give you singing lessons?

'Show me a few tips for the bake-off,' he continues. 'If you're free, that is.'

Nervous energy takes over when the invitation finally clicks, and I smile a little too brightly. 'Oh, right! I mean, sure.' *Breathe, Harley, breathe.* 'Happy to help.'

'This weekend's out,' he says, 'but I can do next Saturday if you're up for it, maybe catch a movie afterwards?'

I quickly take my pulse under the table because I'm pretty sure I'm about to have a heart attack. 'Uh, just let me think for a sec,' I say, super casual, like I'm ordering a pizza.

I count to three, mulling over my imaginary commitments. Nan always told me to play hard to get, like Audrey Hepburn in those old movies we loved to watch together. But I've never really had an opportunity until now.

Damn! My haircut! Then I remember I booked for eleven – plenty of time.

'Yeah, I think that'll work,' I tell Carter.

He smiles. 'What time are you thinking?'

Breathe.

I do some quick mental maths. Allow two hours for a cut and colour then time to go home and get ready. 'Maybe around three-thirty?'

'It's a date.'

A date! My wish list is about to come true.

When I get home, I write the date down in my journal and underline it twice. Carter coming over is just the start. Soon we'll be going to the movies, or maybe having a nice romantic dinner, if that's possible in any of Mount Pleasant's three restaurants. Then there's Eden's event. It's not till the end of next term but that's okay – more time for New Harley to emerge fully formed. Everyone will see us together and we'll be the talk of the school. *Look at Harley and Carter, don't they make a great couple?* Before I know it, he'll be looking hot in his suit, slipping a wrist corsage over my hand, and we'll be dancing the night away at the formal. If I didn't have to drop a few sizes, I'd start shopping for my dress today.

My eyes follow the gigantic ladle of chicken curry Mum's about to whack into my bowl.

'Whoa, way too much!' I can tell it's full of coconut cream and all that fat is the last thing I need. And dining one-on-one with Mum is the second last thing I need.

She ignores me. 'How's your job search going?'

'It's not,' I tell her, sniffing my bowl. 'There are no jobs. Anywhere.' I slosh the curry clockwise, mentally committing to eating only half.

'How's *your* job search going?' I add, trying to make conversation. She doesn't need to reply. The grim look on her face says it all.

I switch topics. 'Where's Dad?'

She's staring at the salt shaker, a world away. 'He's at a meeting, I think.'

'Geez, Mum, you don't even know where Dad is?'

'Your father is not a child, Harley,' she grumbles, serving herself the smaller portion I wanted. 'I don't have to keep my eye on him every minute of the day.'

True, but he just got back from Washington last week. I'd think they'd want to see each other.

'And Luke?'

'At Meika's.' She sighs, taking a bite.

Falco is rubbing against me, his tail thumping my leg like

a metronome, so I sneak him a piece of chicken.

'Harley, eat up,' Mum insists, shooing Falco away.

I stab a piece of meat with my fork, figuring I can enjoy the taste without any major calorie damage. The sauce splatters all over the placemat.

'For Chrissakes, will you stop picking and eat properly?'

Mum hasn't worked since Christmas. I hope she finds another job soon, so she can start bossing other people around instead of me.

I bring the fork to my lips. The intoxicating aroma of spices hits me first, then the sweet, creamy sauce and tender chicken. It's Harmony Day in my mouth and I surrender. Within minutes, there are only a few stray vegies in my bowl.

The voice is loud and clear. *You're disgusting.*

Later that night, I spend half an hour with my head over the toilet, hoping that if I heave long and hard enough, the voice will come up too.

Oh, my poor darling, Nan would say.

I glance down at my phone, wishing one of her old messages would pop on my screen. I don't care how, or why. I just want to see her name, like she's still here. With me.

But there's just a message from Talia.

Eden is evil

CHAPTER 11

Food for Thought

I know how men in exile feed on dreams of hope.
(Aeschylus)

For two weeks I've been asking Talia what she meant by her Eden comment and she still can't explain. On the bus ride home, I try again.

She sighs loudly. 'Let's just say the more I get to know her, the more I'm convinced she'd do anything to protect her turf.'

That's probably true. Eden's like a boxer who conditions herself, watches what she eats and exercises. She's already won the title. Now her job is to fight off the people waiting in the wings to take it off her. Like Talia. I'm getting a vibe that she'd do anything to be on top.

The trees on the median strip blur past, the stream of burnt orange and magenta reminding me that winter will soon be here. There's a dull, throbbing ache in my head and my heart. A strange sort of emptiness that I don't know how to fill. I focus my energy and make a pact with myself.

I don't want to be Carter's bro. I want to be his girlfriend. I'm not sure how I'm going to make it happen, but I know when. Tomorrow!

Lately, I've been analysing every moment for hidden meanings. Carter's beaming smile, all the attention he pays me when he could so easily find someone else to talk to. We've been Snapping more and more. Carter's first: half his face, eye and mouth wide open with a spider on the wall behind him. I replied with an artsy animal shot: Falco on the foot of my bed snoozing in the soft glow of my fairy lights. We've graduated to messaging on the weekend. Surely that means something.

'I think Ty likes me,' Talia announces the second we step off the bus. She flashes a new smile, subtle, less teeth. It says: *Someone likes me and not you.*

After our conversation last week, I wonder if Ty worked up the guts to say something. I decide to play it safe. 'What makes you think that?'

'Oh, it's just little things,' she begins to explain, swinging her backpack at the pedestrian crossing. 'He's always trying to make me laugh or offering me gum.'

Gum? If someone asked Talia the time, she'd think they liked her too. But when Carter's nice to me, she acts like it means nothing.

'Haven't you noticed he can't stop staring at me?' She picks up her pace, a girl on a mission.

'Uh, now that you mention it ...' I start to say but change my mind. Why should I tell her about Ty? That's the one thing Talia and I have in common lately – no boyfriends – and no one wants to be a third wheel. Besides, I have a feeling she'd be unbearable if she hooked up with someone.

The girl standing next to me isn't the same Talia who threw her arms around me on the first day of school. That seems like a lifetime ago.

'I bet everyone would call us T and T, you know, for

Talia and Ty,' she chirps. 'Or TNT 'cos we'd be explosive.' She giggles at her own joke.

I head to the bakery like a homing pigeon, lured by the smell of chocolate ganache and freshly baked bread. Talia's still going on about Ty when she catches up with me.

The display case has every pie, cake and doughnut imaginable. They should offer a sampler plate.

'He wants pics,' she mutters under her breath when I'm nearly done scanning the top shelf.

'Pics of what?'

Talia laughs. 'Of *me*. Obviously.'

I guess Ty does like her. Or at least her body.

'You're not going to, are you?' I whisper.

Her brown eyes look gun-metal grey, like the storm clouds that have just rolled in, casting a shadow over the front half of the bakery.

'Nah, probably not.' She gestures to the custard tart for the shopkeeper. 'It's just a game.'

Transformation complete. She *is* Eden.

I've tried so hard to forget our conversation at Scoop. And to ignore Talia's little half-waves whenever she's with Eden, and her I'm-better-than-you vibe. Now she's really starting to piss me off.

The lemon meringue pie taunts me from the bottom shelf. Every molecule in my body screams, 'Eat it now!' but I can't. Not with Carter coming over tomorrow. If I was Superman this would be my kryptonite. But I'm not Superman. Or Superwoman. I'm a girl still eating too much, praying for a miracle. Before I know it, I'm ordering the pie, telling myself one nibble won't hurt any. Besides, it's not like I'm going to sit across from Talia, watching her eat.

Since the curry crisis a few weeks ago, I've tackled this

challenge scientifically. Nearly every article I've read says reducing portions is the best, and safest, way to lose weight. So that's what I've been trying to do the past few weeks, even using smaller plates to trick myself. I read that online somewhere too.

But I can't work out how to deal with being hungry all the time.

The dark clouds part without the rain they promised, making our choice of an outdoor table easy. My lungs fill with crisp autumn air but there's enough bite in the late afternoon sun to keep us warm. Talia dumps her backpack and grabs a seat, while I dig around in my bag for a hair tie.

She takes her first bite, eyeing my ponytail. 'You growing it long?'

'Nah, opposite.' I savour my first taste of the tangy but sweet lemon centre. 'I'm going shorter. Tomorrow, in fact.'

'Really?'

'Yeah, finally got in at Hairbrain.'

Her mouth opens at least three seconds before the words come out. 'Why the change?'

A random shiver runs through me. Something's telling me, *Be careful*.

'Dunno, just thought I'd try something new.' I contemplate a second nibble but that would lead to a third, then a fourth and I know how that story ends. I tease Talia with possibilities. 'Who knows? I may even go for a fringe.'

She grips her fork like a shovel, scooping up another bite. 'You have such a good face, Harls,' she says between chews, but her eyes tell me she's impatient, or bored. Maybe both.

Suddenly, I'm fifty-fifty on this haircut idea. There's no New Harley without change. But a haircut's a risky proposition with a high margin of error.

Talia leans forward. 'You should have a shorter cut to show it off, plus fringes are the in thing now.'

The more excited she seems, the more worried I get. What if she wants me to look bad?

Eden's name flashes on Talia's phone and she quickly thumbs a reply, probably messaging: *Harley's cut soon to be on* Botched! I bring another mouthful to my lips, her eyes following my hand. She's taken the fun out of eating.

'What?' I snap, then immediately regret it.

'Nothing, it's just ... I'm surprised you're eating that.' She nods at my plate.

My fork drops, startling Talia and the woman at the next table. When she finally speaks, her voice is so soft I have to lean in to hear.

'It's just that you're always going on about your weight, which is bullshit by the way, but ...'

Her lips tighten into a thin line. Obviously, I don't look fine.

'Go on.'

'I just mean if you, uh, lost a kilo or two, you'd get a bit more definition. You'd cross.'

'Cross what?'

She sighs gently. 'Categories. You wouldn't just be nice, funny Harley. You'd be nice, funny, *hot* Harley. So think of that pie as your enemy, not your friend.'

Takes one to know one.

She flicks her hair over her shoulder before taking another bite. Guess she's made friends with her custard tart. 'There's only one other thing standing in your way.'

The knot in my stomach tightens. 'Which is?'

'Well, Griff's a great guy and all,' she starts off, wiping the corners of her mouth, 'but he *is* a bit odd.' She takes her time meeting my gaze. 'You can't deny that, Harls.'

A sudden breeze sends a single leaf pirouetting onto our table. My eyes track the fine veins running through its cracked surface. It's the type of leaf Griff would photograph.

'He's not odd, just different.' I rub the leaf, feeling it crumble under my touch.

Talia sighs. 'Well, his *differentness*, or whatever you want to call it, isn't going to help us any.'

'What does that mean?

'It means he'd never get an invite to Eden's party. And being friends with him, you won't either.' Her eyes narrow to slits. 'So, you need to lose him. And the sooner, the better.'

Guess Talia sucking up to Eden has finally paid off. She's probably scored an invite and now she thinks she can tell me what to do. *Not going to happen.* Then I remember Griff ignoring me for no reason, hovering when I was eating lunch with Carter that day, waiting for me to wave him over to join us. But I didn't.

Maybe deep down inside I know Griff's a bit strange. Maybe Talia's right.

Her shoulders collapse in a giant exhale. 'I haven't even hooked up with anyone yet!'

She lets the statement hang in the air, waiting for my reaction. But I'm over it already and don't trust my face.

'Though I bet I will soon,' she adds. 'Did I tell you, I think Ty likes me?'

'Uh, yeah, like five minutes ago.' I stare at my plate, desperately wanting another bite. 'Well, guess who I'm hanging out with tomorrow.' I try to hide my excitement.

Talia's eyes practically bulge out of her head. 'Who?'

'Carter.'

'Bullshit!'

The thunder cracks without warning. The storm clouds have blown back in. I push away my plate.

'Seriously, he's coming over tomorrow after my haircut for a baking lesson, you know, for the bake-off and then ...' My smile is as big as my shrug. 'Maybe a movie.'

Trump that, bitch!

The smell of freshly baked banana bread hits me when I walk in the front door. I follow the scent into the kitchen, where I go through my normal routine. Quick hello to Mum, backpack in the corner, mobile on the charger. I push away the piece she's waving in front of my nose – more of a slab than a slice. She brings the plate to the table, expecting me to join her.

My hunger pangs notch up a level but Talia's words are still playing on my mind. I open the fridge door. There's nothing but last night's leftovers, a wedge of cheese, a packet of Hokkien noodles and some grotesque eggplant casserole that I wouldn't eat if I was starving to death.

I remember reading that green tea boosts the metabolism, so I flick on the kettle and make a cup. I need all the help I can get.

'I HAVE to find a job,' I tell Mum, scrolling through Seek. Nothing. No dog walking, or letter-dropping. I'd even babysit.

'Speaking of jobs, guess who found one?' She does a little happy dance in her chair.

'That's great, Mum! Where?'

'The new events management place in town. Part time. I start next week.'

Without Mum being home all the time trying to force-feed me, I reckon I'll be a size smaller in no time. I feel lighter already.

'It takes time,' she tries to assure me. 'So don't give up!'

The second I park my tea on the table, she pushes the plate towards me. Again with the banana bread.

'Please, Mum, stop! I'm trying to lose a few kilos.'

'Honey, I don't know what you're going on about. There's nothing wrong with being statuesque.'

Statuesque? What does that even mean?

'Your weight is fine!' she says with enough force that I nearly believe her.

Now that I've seen and smelled the banana bread twice, I can't stop thinking about it. I hardly touched my lemon meringue pie and only had a tin of tuna for lunch. No wonder my stomach's doing backflips. I tear off a corner for a nibble. Then another piece, this time larger. Mum's babbling about her job that hasn't even started yet, but I can only hear the banana bread calling me. In less than a minute, the plate is empty and the voice kicks in, louder than ever.

You're REVOLTING!

'Oh, Mum, I forgot to tell you!' I flick the voice from my head. 'Remember the new boy at school, Carter?'

Her blank stare says she doesn't.

'The guy who's seriously hot?' I sip my tea slowly, wondering why things that are good for you have to taste so gross. 'My cooking partner?'

'That rings a bell,' she says, heating a slice of leftover quiche in the microwave.

The smell of melted cheese and onion make me even hungrier. Is she trying to torture me?

'What about him?' she asks.

I grab an apple from the fruit bowl. I need something healthy to counteract the banana bread.

'Well, he's coming over tomorrow to practise for the bake-off.'

Mum smiles, but I can tell she has no idea what I'm talking about.

'I'm just saying, tomorrow's a big day, Mum. I'm using my birthday money for a totally new hairstyle, maybe a make-up lesson too if they have time, then cooking with Carter and ...'

'New hairstyle?' she cuts in, strange because I would have thought that Carter was the headline.

'Didn't I tell you?' I sip my tea again, convinced I had. 'I'm going shorter, with a few foils, maybe a fringe.'

Before I know it, I've polished off another slice of banana bread.

'A fringe?' Her eyes practically bulge out of her head like a cartoon character's. It's not like I told her I was about to shave my head and tattoo an emu on my scalp. 'Are you sure that's such a good idea?'

I open my mouth but no words come out. The green tea and walnuts are doing battle in my throat, working their way to my stomach where the nibble of lemon meringue is already protesting. My body is a massive garbage bin.

I gently massage my belly flab, like I'm soothing a baby. But this baby's fussy. When it's not crying, it's spitting up. The thought lingers, making me want to spit up too.

'What's the matter?' Mum calls out, but I'm already halfway down the hallway.

Seconds later, I'm crouching over the toilet, bracing for the inevitable.

I give up after ten minutes and take matters into my own hands. Or should I say fingers. Two do the trick.

* * *

I skip dinner and collapse into bed, feeling like a steamroller has flattened me, but my brain kicks into overdrive before my head even hits the pillow. I replay every conversation with Carter, searching for some connection, for a glimpse into the future. I concentrate with all my might, willing a message from Nan to appear. Nothing. I flick through my journal, the same word claiming space.

Carter. Carter. Carter.

Except for his name, *You reap what you sow* and some not very good haircut sketches, all the pages are still blank, begging for a plan. A fast-acting one. My phone soon buzzes with possibilities.

CARTER: *hey, what's up*

ME: *nothing much, just having an early night*

CARTER: *ur in bed?!*

ME: *haha yeah I need my beauty sleep lol*

Why the hell did I say that? It's like I vomited out all my commonsense.

CARTER: *haha my girlfriend says the same thing*

An earthquake strikes my skull. Girlfriend?!? Talia was right!

My thumbs fumble, unable to come up with anything that can make sense of those two words. *My girlfriend.*

The longer I take to reply, the worse it looks. I type the first thing that comes into my head.

ME: *yeah us girls are high maintenance haha*

I have no idea what I'm saying but I keep typing.

ME: *how long u been together*

CARTER: *about 2 years*

Two *years?*

It has to be someone in America, and in an odd way I'm relieved. If it was anyone in Mount Pleasant, especially if he dropped Eden's name, or Talia's, I would've vomited again.

I see the three dots on the screen and wait for details. Then nothing. WTF?

ME: *that's a long time*

CARTER: *yeah I don't think it's gonna work with an ocean in the way*

Ha! That's what I told Talia! She might have the musical to cosy up to him but I bet he's never confided anything like this. Things are looking brighter. I have a sudden urge to break into song, maybe 'Tomorrow' from Annie.

ME: *well time will tell I guess*

What the hell? Now I'm sounding like his mother. I double text but don't care.

ME: *things will work out somehow if they're meant to*

CARTER: *ah ur a hopeless romantic*

ME: *guilty as charged haha*

***

Later that night, I'm jolted awake from a great dream where Ed Sheeran pulls up to school in a limo, sings and dances his way to my English class, then bends down on one knee, begging me to star in his next music video. I reach for my phone, surprised it's only eleven-forty-five. Even with the pillow over my head I can still hear Mum and Dad. I've hardly seen them in the same room lately – it's like they're going out of their way to avoid each other. But tonight, it sounds like they're hurling all the words they've stored up. I can't make out what they're saying, just Mum's high-pitched shrieks and Dad's words cutting in low and slow, like a bass line.

Judging from Mum's crying, I reckon she's discovered what I've suspected for ages: Dad's having an affair. I wonder if she knows the woman. Poor Mum. And poor me. Because she's going to be even more unbearable if they split up.

Just when I think my life couldn't possibly suck more, my phone lights up.

Things always work themselves out, Nan's message says.

CHAPTER 12

She Will Be Loved

One must wait until the evening
to see how splendid the day has been.
(Sophocles)

When I walk into the kitchen on Saturday afternoon sporting my new haircut, Mum doesn't blink for an entire minute. 'I didn't think you meant *that* short!'

'What's your problem?' I can't help but snap back. Well, I think it looks good. Correction: I think it looks *great*.

'It's not even that short!' I insist, checking out my new style in the glass splashback. The layered cut falls nicely just below my jaw. But the best part is the sideswept fringe. Bonus points for disguising my bloodshot eyes.

I hardly slept last night. I wanted to wake up Luke and tell him about all the texts I've been getting, but I knew he'd just yell at me to get out of his room. After an online chat that dragged on forever, even the tech couldn't work out how Nan's messages keep appearing. So much for nerds being smart. Though now that I think about it, I was probably pouring my heart out to a bot.

Mum drops a peppermint teabag into a mug, but I'm tempted to recommend the relaxation blend instead.

'And why'd you pick that colour?' she asks, stirring in two teaspoons of sugar to satisfy her sweetening disorder. 'Warm tones go brassy.'

Hunger's not helping my mood any but what's her excuse?

I opted for *Golden Chestnut* with just a few highlights. Caramel. I think it looks fabulous. Everyone at the salon thought so too.

'Maybe you're jealous because your hair's getting thinner,' I snarl, grabbing a handful of grapes from the fridge. Admittedly, a low blow, but I plead self-defence.

She stirs her tea, glaring at me. 'That's lovely, Harley. Throw menopause in my face, why don't you. I have no control over it by the way.' She takes a sip, wincing at the temperature. 'Just wait till your hormones blindside you.'

They already have. When I think about Carter, which is nearly every minute of every day, my heart races and a weird sensation buzzes through my body, like there's an electric butterfly fluttering inside me. Maybe the mind and body are connected after all.

If only they were. I'd tell my body to shut up with all the rumbling, growling and gnawing. Today's menu: an egg for breakfast then a Coke Zero and a few biscuits at Hairbrain. I haven't eaten much all week. I've been too nervous, thinking about today. And good thing, because I'm sure my stomach is slightly smaller.

Luke zips past Mum on his way to football training. He grabs a banana and does a double take when he spots my hair. 'Who hacked your hair?'

'Asshole.'

'Her hair looks just fine,' Mum says, her protective instinct making a surprise appearance.

Hardly the endorsement I was looking for but I'm just glad Luke's leaving. I don't want him around when Carter's here.

Mum takes out a plate of leftover chicken from the fridge. When she removes the plastic wrap I smell lemon and rosemary. Nan's recipe.

'Mum, Carter's going to be here any minute, so please just chill, okay?' I'm seriously considering ripping into the chicken like a wild animal, but opt for a pear instead. 'No hovering and not too many questions.'

Her eyebrows arch.

'And no dumb jokes.'

Mum smiles. 'That's Dad's territory.'

I'm surprised she can smile after their mega-fight.

I hear Luke close the front door. Instant relief.

'Don't worry, I have a few errands to do,' she tells me, checking her pockets for her car keys. 'I bet you'll find this hard to believe, but I do remember what it's like to have a crush on a boy.'

'Who said I ...?'

She pinches my cheeks like Nan used to. 'It's written all over your face.'

I polish off the pear in no time. 'Is that how you felt when you met Dad?'

She hesitates. 'That was a long time ago, honey. It's hard to remember what I felt.'

'Geez, Mum, that doesn't sound great.'

She holds out the plate of chicken and I cave, taking the smallest piece. I don't want my stomach to be grumbling when Carter's here. I count to twenty between bites so I feel fuller quicker. I read that online somewhere.

'When you're young, everything's so new,' she continues,

settling into the conversation. So much for her errands.

'But with marriage and motherhood, you quickly get into a routine, the rhythm of daily life. Then your dreams ...'

'Sorry, Mum, I'm kind of in a hurry,' I cut in, checking my phone. I'm praying when she starts her new job next week, she'll be too tired to dole out useless advice.

She smiles weakly, patting my hand. 'Maybe you're right, honey. Maybe my hormones *are* holding me hostage.'

My phone lights up with a message from Talia. First, her face, all puckered up. Then the text:

I kissed a boy and I liked it! ☺

I'm happy for Talia, though I can't work out what she sees in Ty. But a part of me wishes it was my message. I want to be the first at something for once. Every day the world seems to throw more shit my way. I try to blast through it, but I have no weapons, no protection. Carter is the only good thing in my life.

'Okay, I'm off,' Mum sings out. 'If I don't see you, have fun.'

I follow her to the hallway before she develops another personality. When she opens the door, Carter's hand is in the air, ready to knock. He smiles, reeling her in with his *Carterness*.

'Hi, you must be Mrs Hastings,' he says, quickly extending his hand. 'I'm Carter.'

'Well, *hellooooo*!' Mum grins like a tween crushing on Harry Styles. She stands back, taking a moment to absorb his full glory. 'Oh, here's Harley,' she says, pushing me in front of her as I approach.

Falco practically flies through the air to greet him. 'Who's this?' Carter asks, stooping down to pat him. He lets Falco lick his face, and suddenly I wish I was a dog.

'This is my jackshit, Falco.'

He laughs, stroking him from head to tail. 'Hey bud.'

The sound that comes out of Falco's little body is somewhere between a wheeze and a moan. My thoughts exactly.

Carter's eyes finally drift up to me. 'Nice hair,' he says, like he really means it.

My heart is pounding through my chest. 'Thanks!'

'See you two later,' Mum calls out. 'Must dash!'

Dash? Mum's suddenly channelling a BBC character. Just when I think she's gone, she pokes her head back in the doorway, flashing me a look that says, '*OMG, he's fine!*'

'Do you want a drink or something?' I ask Carter, leading him to the kitchen.

'No, Bob's your uncle.'

'Pardon?'

His cheeks are instantly red. Strange, I didn't picture him as the blushing type.

'Isn't that what you'd say?' he asks. 'You know, "It's all good?"'

'You can just say, "It's all good!",' I tell him, trying not to laugh – I don't want one of Talia's snorts to escape – but he does anyway, and his laugh is so big and free, I reckon it'd drown out any noise I make.

'Your mum's nice,' he tells me, pulling out a stool at the breakfast bar.

'Occasionally.'

'Where's your dad?'

'Not sure, I haven't been home all day. He's probably in the granny flat,' *avoiding Mum*, 'pretending to work, or in some alleyway playing sax.'

Carter laughs. 'Like Lisa Simpson.'

'Yeah. Come to think of it, he's a lot like Lisa.'

'Short and yellow with spiky hair?'

'I was thinking overachiever, vegetarian, loves jazz and blues.'

He laughs. 'Talia told me he's some big scientist.'

Talia? What else has she been telling him? A truckload of ideas drives straight through my brain. Does Carter Snap Talia? Has he been to her house? What about Eden's? Have Carter and Talia been 'getting into character' at rehearsals? It's not like I'm being paranoid. Celebrities fall in love on set all the time.

I push the thoughts away, trying to focus on the moment. Carter is here, standing in my kitchen, wanting to know about my family.

'Yeah, Dad travels a lot, speaking at international conferences.' *Sleeping with other women.* 'Mingling with germs and lab rats. Crunching data. That kind of thing.'

'That's cool.'

'I guess.'

Carter looks around the room like he's never been in a kitchen before. 'Where do we start?'

'Ve start at ze beginning,' I say, suddenly feeling the need to speak with a German accent.

He laughs again. 'You mean, with a cake mix?'

'No mix here, we're baking from scratch. These are going to be the best muffins you've ever tasted.'

'Amen,' he exclaims, and I think what a weirdly cool thing that is to say.

I quickly gather all the supplies, flying between cupboards and back to the bench in record time, like a MasterChef contestant. Then I call up the recipe for raspberry, white chocolate and macadamia muffins on my phone so Carter can follow the steps. I've made them so many times that I could bake them blindfolded.

Now that'd be a good baking show: *Blind Baking!*

They're the perfect choice for the bake-off at the end of this term – easy to make and unbelievably delicious. Today's only a trial run, so I figure a dozen muffins will do.

When I turn around, Carter's standing at our kitchen table, studying the montage of family photos under the glass top. That was Nan's idea. I can still hear her: *No point hiding them away in a book somewhere. May as well throw them out.*

Well, I wish we *had* thrown them out because I look hideous in every single one of them. It's like Mum picked the ugliest, most embarrassing photos and shoved them under glass. Luke looks like a model. Of course.

'So cute,' Carter says, studying my kindergarten photo.

'Yeah, pigtails never go out of style.'

'My sister wears them all the time.'

'You have a sister?' I cream together the sugar and butter, suddenly realising I know virtually nothing about his family.

'Yeah, and a brother. Twins.' He walks around the table, taking in the rest of the photos. 'Caroline and Mike, they're eleven.'

I wonder if the mini-Carters are as gorgeous as the real deal, but I doubt that's possible.

'Your brother's the school captain, right?'

Ugh, can we not talk about Luke?

'It must be nice to have an older brother looking out for you.'

I try not to react but I can feel my eyes widen. 'Uh, Luke tends to look out mainly for himself.'

'I bet he cares about you,' Carter tries to assure me. 'Guys find it hard to show feelings sometimes.'

Wait, what? All this time, I've been thinking maybe he's just polite. But now I'm realising, maybe he's just shy.

'Here, let me do that.' Carter brushes my hand as he takes the sifter, sending shockwaves through my body from head to toe. Our sleeves are practically touching, activating every nerve ending in my body.

I toss in the white chocolate chips and macadamia nuts, watching his biceps flex as he blends the ingredients to perfection.

He smiles. 'Okay, now give me another job.'

Oh, shut up and kiss me.

That's what I want to say. Ever since I heard the line in a rom-com flick I saw with Talia last year, I've been dying to use it.

'Here, you can toss these in,' I offer instead, passing the bowl of crushed raspberries. 'But only half.'

He dumps the berries in one go, stirring hard, like he's mixing concrete.

'Whoa, here's a tip.' I resist the urge to laugh. 'You're meant to take your time and fold them.'

'Fold them?' He looks so adorable when he's confused.

'Yeah, like this.' I take the spoon and gently lift the ingredients from the bottom of the bowl, up and over, with a delicate motion.

'Sweet.'

'It's all in the wrist,' I explain, and he finishes the job in no time.

'Okay, time to fill the trays,' I tell him, passing him another spoon. 'They just need to be about two-thirds full.'

Carter hums a familiar tune as he spoons the mixture into the muffin papers. I can't remember the name of the song because every brain cell is focused on sucking in my stomach while trying to look relaxed.

When I head to the fridge with the leftover berries, he spins around and *kapow!* the messiest, loveliest collision imaginable. The berries fly out of my bowl, most of them landing on my shirt.

'Whoa!' he blurts, diving to salvage some berries from the floor. He grabs a sponge from the sink and circles it over my shirt – right on my flabby belly! – making me squirm. 'Stand still!'

'Caaan't,' I finally manage to say between giggles. 'Ticklish!'

He checks me out head to toe then back again, assessing the berry damage with a huge grin. 'We need to get you cleaned up.'

His hand grips my shoulder, sending me into sensory overload. For a second, I think he's about to escort me to the bathroom to give me a sponge bath and I can't breathe.

'How about I get the muffins in the oven while you get changed?' he suggests.

'Okay, I'll just have a quick shower.'

'Then we can catch a movie if you want.'

'Great, I'll just have a quick shower.' *Shit, I already said that.* 'But I'll leave the door open in case I smell something burning.'

'Very funny.'

Rather than risk unsightly frizz with a second hair wash, I dump my dirty clothes on the bathroom floor and gently wipe the sweet-smelling fruit from my skin, before flying across the hallway in a towel, praying Carter doesn't see me. I snip the tag off my new shirt. The bright green was so flattering when I tried it on in the shop but now I look hideous, like Kermit the Frog's fat cousin. My pulse triples when I realise I've wasted over ten minutes staring at the row of ugliness in my wardrobe. I imagined this day so many times, each with a different outfit, that I can't remember any of them. I need to quickly pull together a fashion statement that says 'movie casual' without being too try-hard, like: Effortlessly stylish chick catches flick with new boy in town. Stay tuned!

My capri pants could work, assuming my thighs don't exceed the load for stretch fabric. I reckon I've lost a kilo, maybe more, but that's nothing. I'm not game to hop on the scales to find out for sure. What if the fat's simply shifted? I hold my breath, working the pants over my dimpled skin. The button fastens easier than I remember. *Progress!* When I summon the courage to look in the mirror, I can't believe what I see. My thighs are still big, but not as chunky as usual. It's like someone has let out a bit of air from two balloons. I inspect myself from every angle in the mirror. Could be worse.

Finding a top takes forever. I settle on a free-flowing lavender blouse to minimise my hips. A studded boho belt creates a decent waistline and my amethyst necklace caps off my outfit perfectly. After I've ripped through my entire room, I find my handbag under my bed, camouflaged by a giant dust bunny. I give it a quick wipe before tossing in some lip gloss and a pack of gum.

One last mirror check. Nan always told me to walk tall, like someone was pulling a thread through the top of my head. I practise as I strut towards the mirror, feeling lighter with each step. My heart is racing in my chest. I can't believe I'm going to the movies with the hottest guy at school!

The scent of warm muffins wafts down the hallway. I

nearly don't recognise the kitchen. It's spotless. He cleans too?

'You look good,' he says, and I smile. I *feel* good.

He picks up a muffin and walks towards me, his eyes serious but the slight upturn in his mouth hinting otherwise. 'You gotta taste one, Harley. They're *to die for*, as my little sister would say.'

'No, that's okay. I believe you.'

He traps me against the kitchen bench, moving his arm like a muffin plane is about to land in my mouth. I veer sharply to the right, my lips just missing it, but he's still dangling the muffin in front of my face. 'Come on, Harley. Sink your teeth in. I know you want me.'

How true.

I'm lost in his full, perfectly formed lips and forget to protest. He peels off the muffin paper and I instinctively open my mouth and nibble the still-warm sweetness. I flick the morsel around my mouth, trying to extract the most taste in the shortest amount of time. When he turns, I spit it in the bin. I've been so good lately, there's no way I'm going to ruin it now.

'We should get going,' I tell him, placing the muffins on a plate. I hide my chewed one behind the fruit bowl. 'Movie's at seven.'

'Sure thing.'

My phone buzzes and I read Griff's message: *pick u up at 6.40*

'Shit!'

'Problem?' Carter asks.

'Oh, nothing. I just forgot to cancel something with Griff.' *Because I forgot we were even going.*

'Hey, if you have other plans, that's okay. I get it.'

'No, all good.'

Griff and I can see a movie anytime. Besides, he didn't even seem that excited about going.

I message Griff: *Soz, feeling sick.*

He'll understand. Griff always understands.

I hear a car door slam then familiar footsteps in the front entry. My heart sinks. Why is she back so soon?

'Hello again, Mrs Hastings.' Carter stands like royalty has just entered the room.

'Please sit,' Mum tells him, flicking on the kettle. 'And call me Gina.'

I grab my handbag. 'We're going to catch a movie.' I flash her a look that says, *Stop talking now*, but she ignores me, as usual.

'Have you eaten yet?' She starts unpacking plastic containers from the fridge, slightly panicked, like we're going off to war without provisions. 'Here, let me heat some leftovers.'

'Please don't go to the trouble, Mrs Hastings. I mean Gina,' Carter stumbles. 'We're happy to walk.'

I love that he says 'we' ... like we're already a couple! My brain quickly catches up. Walk? Does he mean a nice, *romantic* walk?

Carter holds out his arm, ushering me towards the front door, and I catch Mum winking at me. When my hand touches his well-defined bicep, every hair on my arm stands to attention. I feel lightheaded. The second we step into the entry, my foot catches the fringed edge of the Persian runner. Suddenly, I'm airborne.

Carter lunges to grab me, his powerful grip making me feel so safe, so secure. Every cell in my body relaxes in his strong hands.

He smiles. 'Gotcha!'
Yes, you do.

121

CHAPTER 13

Showtime

Stretching his hand up to reach the stars,
too often man forgets the flowers at his feet.
(Jeremy Bentham)

With movie tickets in hand, we head straight to the refreshments bar where I'm surrounded by temptation. Fluoro-coloured lollies, five types of gummies, and endless chocolates including the peanut clusters that Griff and I always share on movie nights. There's even hot food – pies, pasties and pizza – in the revamped café. I can name every aroma and want to raid the display case.

'How about some raspberry swirls?' Carter jokes, as though I need to be reminded of the muffin incident. I ignore the pleas from my empty stomach and summon my willpower.

He tries again. 'Chocolate?'

'No thanks.' The way I look at it, I have a choice. Maltesers or thin thighs. I'll take thin, or at least *thinner* thighs, thanks very much.

My eyes linger on Carter. 'Just a Diet Coke,' I tell him, though what I'm really thinking is, *Your chromosomes are arranged so beautifully.*

We make our way through the busy foyer, juggling our refreshments. I scan the crowd, hoping to bump into someone from school. Anyone. Then the rumours will fly.

You'll never guess who I saw at the movies together. Harley ... and Carter!

We claim the last table, which is barely big enough for our drinks let alone all the food. Carter shakes his head in disbelief when I decline his offer of chips. 'You can't be full after one measly muffin.'

'I had a massive lunch before you came over.' Yeah, really massive. A few biscuits at Hairbrain, a pear and a bite of chicken.

I point my knees to one side to minimise any thigh bulge. Last week I watched a TV program where models shared their secrets for minimising their flaws, not that I could see any. Who knew I'd need these tips so soon?

Carter attacks the Margherita pizza while I nurse my Diet Coke. I would have thought he'd be a Meatlovers kind of guy.

'Okay, favourite song,' I ask. Conversation launched.

'Probably *You & Me*.'

'Pardon?' I croak, nearly choking on my drink.

'*You & Me* ... you know, Disclosure? The Flume remix?'

The song pops into my head and my throat relaxes enough to swallow. 'Mine's *Runaway*.'

'Ah, Kanye,' he nods.

'Nah, The Corrs.'

'Who?'

'Irish siblings ... mid-nineties,' I explain. 'Mum always plays them.'

'Interesting.' He takes a swig of his drink.

I can't take my eyes off his Adam's apple, bobbing up and

down, up and down.

'Favourite holiday spot?' I offer. Probably lame but I'm too distracted to think properly.

'Hawaii. You?' He takes another swig.

'Port Douglas. Movie?'

'*The Dark Knight.* But *Superbad* for comedy. Don't tell me. *The Notebook.*'

I laugh. 'Nah, *Sabrina.*'

'The teenage witch?'

'Noooo,' I laugh harder. 'Audrey Hepburn. One of those black and white films from the 1950s.'

He leans in with a big grin. 'Ah, you like the classics.'

My body twitches like it has a mind of its own. 'Yeah, my Nan always said I had an old soul.' Thoughts of Nan take over until there's nothing in my head but her and me. I pray I can keep it together.

'Favourite TV show?' There's energy in Carter's voice, like he's really getting into it.

I catch the time on my phone. 'The movie!' I blurt out, pulling him up by the arm; boldness is my new superpower. The moment my skin touches his I feel so alive, like a bright light has just burst inside me. I should jot down all these feelings for my English assessment.

The ads are still playing when we head into the theatre. I point to an empty row about two-thirds back and Carter holds out his arm for me to go first. Such a gentleman. I try to get comfortable in the seat but my limbs feel awkward, like they're not attached to my body, and I'm not sure what to do with my legs. Do I cross them or keep my feet flat on the floor? And who claims the armrest? Is it too forward if I do? There are endless options and I don't want to stuff up. It's much more relaxing going to the movies with Griff.

A cartoon hippo dances across the screen, a giant 'H' emblazoned on its tutu. It's teetering on a tightrope, juggling a massive popcorn bucket, slice of pizza and large drink.

'Popcorn! I knew I forgot something! Carter's nearly in the aisle when he backtracks and asks, 'Do you want anything else?'

Yeah, you, I'm thinking, but instead I smile and say, 'Nuh, all good.'

He bolts down the aisle like a superhero saving the day, which he has in a way.

I settle into my seat. The hippo's so big that it falls off, spilling everything on its tutu and nearly taking out the poor monkey family swinging in a nearby tree. I wonder if fat people could sue for discrimination.

There's an outburst a few rows in front of me. 'Look, it's Harley!' a familiar voice calls out, pointing at the hippo which is now belly up under the tightrope. Then there's a high-pitched squeal of laughter. Paris.

There's a sharp ache in my stomach, as if someone has stabbed me. Eden's spiked hair casts a jagged silhouette on the screen, like a baby stegosaurus. She holds up her hand to high-five Paris. On her other side, a girl says something. All I can make out is my name, followed by giggles, then a snort. Talia.

I want to run to the foyer to find Carter and tell him I need to go home. That Mum called and there's a problem. Maybe I could say that Falco ran away – anything to get out of here. But I can't. My brain's shouting 'Run!' but my body won't budge.

I pray they don't turn around and see me. I slow my breath, close my eyes and imagine I'm floating up high, out of their reach. From above, their words seem small. Powerless. I'm not going to let anyone spoil tonight. Especially them.

Carter returns, balancing a huge tub of popcorn nearly the size of the bucket Mum uses to mop the kitchen floor. He holds it in front of me until I pop a few kernels in my mouth. I savour the perfect balance of salt and butter, each ingredient bringing out the best in the other. My intestines respond instinctively with a sharp ache. I press my fist into my stomach to remind it who's in charge.

Carter is relentless with the damn tub, offering it to me every few minutes like we're locked into an alternate feeding cycle. I toss a few kernels in my mouth, wedging the rest between my seat and the empty one next to me. We take turns in perfect rhythm until the movie's action-packed opening sequence screws up my timing. When our fingers tangle in the tub, I feel a tiny zap of static electricity, like when Luke and I used to run around the carpet in our socks then touch the TV.

'We're electric,' he leans over to whisper.

Yes, we are.

I'm not a big Chris Hemsworth fan, but this movie's making me have second thoughts. It won't be nominated for an Oscar but it's not bad, in a heart-pumping, special-effects overkill kind of way. I smile, seated alongside my own Chris Hemsworth, the perfect first boyfriend. Is that what this is? Is that why he suggested the movie?

The second the closing credits run, I eye the exit, mentally planning my escape before the hyenas strike. Carter's hand brushes mine as we head up the aisle. I want to grab it – to interlock my fingers with his, to feel skin on skin. I float outside my body just thinking about it. Nan always said that her favourite movie star, Clark Gable, was so handsome that all the women *swooned*. I feel like I could pass out at any moment. Maybe that's what swooning is.

Before I'm even halfway up the aisle, my perfect evening ends.

'Harley?' Paris's voice sounds cracked, unnatural. Even for a hyena.

You can do this. I take a deep breath and turn around. 'Hey,' I offer casually, scanning the three of them. Talia's eyes dart away. Gutless.

I try to look relaxed, like Carter and I go to the movies all the time, like I didn't hear them tear me to shreds earlier.

But it's not working.

I can feel the popcorn and Diet Coke working their way up my throat. I pray I don't vomit, though if Carter wasn't here I'd gladly hit all three of them with one toxic spray.

Paris looks at me, then Carter, then back at me again. 'Did you come here, uh, together?'

'Yeah, after KP,' Carter says, winking at me.

Eden looks intrigued. 'KP?'

'Kitchen Patrol,' Carter tells her. 'How good were those muffins?' He turns to me, holding up his hands for a high-five and I oblige.

Talia won't look at me. She picks some fuzz from her creamy knit camisole top that, I hate to admit, looks shit-hot against her olive skin. When her phone buzzes with a message, she taps it slowly, showing off her electric blue gel nails with diamante studs. Meanwhile, Eden and Paris are chatting up Carter.

'You could have been in that movie!' Paris starts off.

Then Eden. 'Have you ever seen any actors in Hollywood?'

Carter laughs and shakes his head.

Talia chimes in. 'Did you start your poem for English yet?'

'Uh, no.' More laughter from Carter. 'Why, did you?'

She squeezes his arm, returning his laughter. 'Didn't you see me writing at rehearsals on Tuesday?'

There's four other people here but Talia's clearly only interested in one of us.

Carter throws his head back and continues the laughfest. 'I thought you were making script notes ... lots of script notes.'

Talia finally looks at me, probably just to gloat, and lets out a little gasp. She probably thought I'd never go through with the haircut. Maybe she didn't think it'd look so good.

'Well, guess we'll see you on Monday,' Carter tells them like we're a couple. The coven lingers.

Whispers follow us up the aisle. They're already talking about us and we're not even a thing ... yet. But the future is loud and clear: Carter taking me to Eden's party, the two of us parading around town. And then the formal, his tie matching my dress. The dress that I can't wait to shop for – after I lose a few more kilos!

When we near the exit, for a moment I think my eyes are playing tricks on me. There, sitting in the back row, is Griff. Alone with his messy curls and a box of chocolate peanut clusters. *Our* chocolate peanut clusters. He cocks his head, munching slowly as he looks right through me.

I stop dead in my tracks as Carter keeps walking. My heart's pounding like it's going to burst out of my chest. I'm desperate to say something but can't find the words.

'Looks like you're feeling better,' he says in a cool voice. He spots Carter waiting near the exit.

'Uh, yeah.' My left eye starts to twitch, broadcasting my lie. I'm praying he'll forgive me.

When he finally looks at me, I can't read his expression.

His eyes seem darker than usual.

Has one lie destroyed my friendship with Griff forever?

CHAPTER 14

Brave New World

To be is to be perceived.
(George Berkeley)

I'm awake before my alarm goes off. Falco's on the foot of my bed, as usual. I reach for my phone, eyes half open, hoping to see Griff's name. I messaged him after the movie and nearly every day since, but he hasn't replied.

It's been nearly two weeks – how long is he going to stay mad? At least he hasn't blocked me.

On the upside, who knew that stress was such a good weight loss tool? I've lost one and half kilos all up but I can't get too excited. That's like a whale losing a fin.

I hold up my phone for a quick glimpse of my morning self. No amount of patting calms down my bed hair and I spot an early pimple right in the centre of my chin. Argh.

Wish Talia a happy birthday, Facebook tells me. I hardly use the app anymore but I've kept my account so Mum feels like we're 'connected'. It's handy for birthday reminders and events too, not that I have any to go to.

I haven't talked to Talia either since the movies. Except for her message later that night, explaining she had to act that way, that it was all part of the plan with Eden, that once she was truly *on the inside*, she'd drag me across. She even joked about her Oscar-worthy performance.

Yeah, she's a great actor. Problem is I don't know what role she's playing. And whether she is acting when she's with Eden, or with me.

I Snap: *Happy 16th birthday to the best friend a girl could hope for!*

That's what I'm meant to say. But my real self is thinking: *Happy birthday to the best fake friend a girl could hope for!* I figure I'll give Talia the benefit of the doubt – for now, at least. I can't afford for her *and* Griff to be ignoring me.

I make a booking for 6 pm at Thai Me Up, her favourite restaurant. We celebrate her birthday there every year.

The floor shifts when I stand, making my room bob up and down like I'm on a rickety boat. Probably my new diet of guilt and stress. I throw my uniform over my head and let the cool cotton fall over my hips where it hangs – *hangs!* – slightly loose. On the first day of school my seams were bursting. Literally. Hard to believe that was only four months ago.

While I'm organising my notes, a photo flies off my pinboard. It's Griff and me, aged seven, according to Mum's scrawl on the back. We're decked out in shorts and singlets, sitting in knee-high scrub at the edge of the clearing on The Mount. Griff, head down, is working flower stems into a daisy chain for my hair.

When I glance around my room, I see reminders of Griff everywhere. The panda poster he gave me after our trip to the zoo. His favourite hoodie that I still haven't returned. I'm a thoughtless bitch. I shouldn't have lied to him about being sick. He didn't deserve that.

When I close my eyes, I can still see him sitting alone in

the last row of the cinema. I don't care what Talia said. Sure, Griff's been acting weird lately, but he's still my friend. A better friend than her lately. I'm not about to cut him off. No way.

I open my journal and scribble a quick message: *Fix things with Griff!!!!!!!!!!!!!!!!* Then underneath I write my new mantra.

Every day, I am thinner and thinner.

<hr>

When I walk into Philosophy first period, I see a new girl chatting with Eden.

Great hair, I think.

Then it hits me like a left hook. It's not a new girl. It's Talia, sporting the same cut as me – and a fringe! I can't believe she not only stole my haircut, but she got highlights, too – copper, the brash sidekick to my caramel. Did she think waiting a couple of weeks would make it less obvious?

I'm trying to find my own style, but everyone's fussing over Talia's new look like *she's* the real deal. Eden runs her hand through Talia's hair, while Paris and Sydney hang off her like she just landed a spot on *Love Island*.

Why doesn't anyone ever notice what I'm wearing, what I'm doing, what I'm saying?

My body's so stiff I can barely make it across the room, but I keep going. I need to get as far away from Talia and the others as possible. I rewind to last year before Talia changed. Before Griff stopped talking to me. Before Mum and Dad started fighting.

Before Nan died.

I collapse into my seat, trying to hold back my tears.

Nan's funeral plays out in fragments, like a movie montage. Her knotted fingers laced peacefully across her chest. Her tiny frame lost in the ruffled satin. The funeral director quietly weaving in and out of the room, the yellow rose on his lapel impossible to miss. The messy queue of mourners snaking its way to the casket in a giant S. And the part I hated most, the empty words from well-meaning friends and neighbours. *She'll always be looking out for you.*

A comforting touch brings me back to reality. 'You okay?' Carter drops his bag on the seat next to mine and smiles. Suddenly, all is right in the world. Maybe Nan *is* looking after me. Somehow. Somewhere. I still can't explain how Nan's old messages have been popping up on my phone, and why there haven't been any in a while. On some weird psychic level, maybe her last one – *Things always work themselves out* – is her way of saying, *You've got this, darling.*

Nan's going to help me win the bake-off, I can feel it. And win Carter!

Then Dr Kanter ruins the moment. 'Okay, everyone. Listen up.' She's far too excited for this early in the morning. 'We've touched briefly on Descartes.'

'I don't think, therefore I am not,' Stu says.

If only.

'Now, we're moving on to the eighteenth-century philosopher George Berkeley. Berkeley is called an idealist because he believed only minds and their ideas were real. In other words, how can we know something exists if we're not there to perceive it?'

Dr Kanter waits for a response that doesn't come, and sighs. '*Esse est percipi*,' Berkeley said. 'That's Latin for, *To be is to be perceived.*' More blank stares.

Dr Kanter spots Griff's hand. 'Yes, Griff?'

He shuffles awkwardly like he hadn't expected her to call on him, and I wonder if he was just stretching.

'Isn't that like the saying, If a tree falls in the forest and no one's around to hear it, did it make a sound?'

Dr Kanter's face lights up. 'Precisely.'

'But what if you perceive something and it's wrong?' Addy asks.

I can't help but think, *Like when your friend says one tiny lie and you blow it way out of proportion.*

'Keep going, Addy. I think you're onto a good point.'

'It's just that when you look at the sun it seems so small, but it's really massive,' she explains. 'Or, you look at the ocean and think it's blue, but at another time of day it's green or black. So, which is real?'

'Well, many philosophers would maintain that all your perceptions are real, but not necessarily true,' Dr Kanter explains.

'Then how do you know what's true?' Sydney calls out.

'Ah, this is where it gets tricky,' Dr Kanter says, her eyes bright. 'Some philosophers believe truth is metaphysical, it's something that just *is*,' she tries to explain, 'while others think truth is epistemological and can be known.'

It's like Dr Kanter is speaking French. I recognise most of the words, but when they're strung into sentences, I'm lost.

'Some heavy concepts, I know,' Dr Kanter continues. 'But that's what philosophers do. They dig deep, challenging the status quo.'

I imagine a T-shirt with the slogan: *Philosophers do it deeper.*

'They're gadflies,' she adds. 'Has anyone ever heard that term?'

'Yeah, about two seconds ago,' Stu jokes.

Dr Kanter continues. 'A gadfly is a person who upsets the status quo.'

'That'd be Griff,' Ty says.

More laughter. Griff's drawing another elaborate design in his notebook, lost in his own world. I want to go over and throw his book out the window and tell him if he'd stop acting so weird, people would actually want to hang out with him. He's kind and funny and smart, not that anyone ever takes the time to find out. He just needs to flick the movie night and move on.

'Philosophers ask big questions about who we are and why we're here,' Dr Kanter goes on. 'Like Socrates who said, "The only thing I know is that I know nothing." He thought the most important thing in life was to know your true self.'

I already know my true self. She's fat and pathetic. Her mum's going through a midlife crisis because her dad is having an affair. Her brother's constantly hassling her. And she's wondering if she'll ever get skinny, get a boyfriend, get a life.

'Ty did it!' Talia brags to everyone between classes. She's beaming like an influencer, lost in a sea of pink '16' balloons and birthday messages crammed into her locker door.

Just as I think I've snuck past, her voice rings out. 'Harls, come here, quick!'

I double back, using all my available energy to lift the corners of my mouth. 'Nice hair,' I call out, wondering if she's fluent in sarcasm.

'Inspired by yooouuu,' she says with a sickeningly sweet smile.

She leans into me, holding up the diamond-encrusted T on her necklace. 'Look what Ty bought me.'

'Do you think it's real?'

'Of course it's real!' She laughs. 'You think he'd buy me a fake diamond?'

It'd go with your fake personality, I so want to say but I smile instead.

Talia pulls me close, holding up her phone so I can read Ty's message, *Happy birthday T! Look forward to celebrating later. Ty x!*

'He wants a pic of me wearing the necklace,' she whispers.

'Okay, well, hand it over.' I grab her phone, but she yanks it back, letting out a giggle then a snort, like I said the funniest thing ever.

'He wants a pic of me wearing *just* the necklace.'

'Oh, okay.' I feel dizzy but I'm not sure if it's that mental image or skipping breakfast. We always said we'd never do that, no matter who the guy was or how much we liked him. Especially after hearing all those stories at the online safety workshop school forced on us last year. But I feel like she needs reminding. 'You're not gonna, are you?'

'Dunno. I might send something tame like a bra shot.' She flashes me a sneaky smile.

'Well, happy birthday!' I say with just enough energy to sound legit. I prepare to walk off when a large bag tumbles out from her locker, nearly landing on my head.

'Shit, I'm meant to drop these to the clothing pool,' she mutters, shoving her uniforms back in the bag. 'They're too tight across here,' she adds, motioning to her miracle boobs.

I grab the bag. 'I'll drop them off tomorrow, I've gotta go anyway.' No sooner are the words out of my mouth than I think, *Why am I doing her a favour when she's been such a bitch?*

'By the way, I made a booking for six o'clock at Thai Me Up,' I suddenly remember, not even sure I want to go. 'Wanna walk over together?'

She fusses with her books, her eyes darting left and right. I know what she's going to say before she even opens her mouth. 'Harls, uh, don't be mad, okay?' She gives me one of her pouty looks. 'But I'm already going there …'

I swallow hard. 'With Ty.'

She nods. 'I'm so sorry, I should have told you but I forgot.' She offers me a large box of birthday chocolates as a consolation. When I push her hand away, her eyes open wide. She looks me up and down. 'Are you on a diet?'

The question hangs in the air like a bad smell. I'm not sure if my food rollercoaster and occasional vomiting count as a diet, but she's staring at me, waiting for an answer.

'Yes. Yes, I am.'

<hr>

Later that night, my phone lights up as I'm about to drift off. It's Talia.

Wish u were my bday date. Ty so annoying

I'm not sure what to say but go for, *Maybe next year.* That's the best I can come up with and I'm over her birthday already.

The '…' is taking forever and I'm expecting a novel any second. If she starts talking about rehearsals, I'm going to pretend my phone's dying. I'm already sick of the damn musical.

She finally replies: *we all good?*

yep, I tell her, because sometimes the truth takes too long.

Then a text from Dad, all questions: *How's school? How's the journal writing? How about a movie when I'm back from Brisbane?*

Great to all, I text back.

I don't have the heart to tell him I've only written a page or two in my journal. First, my room's always such a mess that I can never find it when I'm in the mood to write. Second, well, I'm never in the mood.

An idea pops into my head and I can't believe I didn't think of it before. Instead of wasting my time writing in a book like the olden days, I should just email myself like Dad suggested. I hardly use email anymore so it'd be just like a blog. A private one.

When I close my eyes, the whole awful day plays out. Before I know it, my words are flying across the screen.

Talia the Bitch strikes again! This time she stole my haircut and colour. She doesn't have an original bone in her body. Which is probably why she's turned into an Eden wannabe. Then she ditched me for Ty. And if that's not bad enough, I can hardly get to Carter with everyone still flocking around him like he's Jesus. Griff's still ignoring me all because of that stupid little lie. I only lied so I wouldn't hurt his feelings … does that make me a bitch too?

I hit send, then open my browser to search 'diet hurdles'. One website says:

Dizziness may occur in the early stages, especially in extreme dieting.

I wonder if that's why I've felt a bit woozy lately. Though my diet's hardly extreme. I'm eating really healthy food including heaps of protein – eggs, a few nuts, chicken, some fish. And on a bad day, cake.

Another site explains:

Plateaus are common, but our special herbal supplements, sourced from a rare flower found in the Amazonian rainforest, will kickstart your metabolism in no time.

Problem is, I don't have time. I click *Buy Now* to take advantage of today's special. Two bottles of Rev diet enhancer tablets for the price of one. I plug in the number of the credit card Mum and Dad gave me for emergencies. If this isn't an emergency, I don't know what is.

Less than a minute later, there's a reply to my email: *Yes, ur a bitch. RIP Harley.*

It's Talia. *WTF?*

I scroll down, reading the words I thought were just for me. *Talia the bitch. Eden wannabe.*

Shit! Shit! Shit! How the hell did I click on her name? *Oh, God.*

A wave of nausea washes over me as my brain struggles to process what just happened. I quickly jump on my socials, ready to tackle the haters, the ones who'll rush to defend Talia's honour. I bet she's messaging Eden now, and that means everyone will know. My mind's racing with the most vile and hurtful comments they can hurl at me.

She's such a fat pig.

Can you believe she thinks Carter's into her?

She's why everyone hates fat people.

Her grandma probably died just to get away from her.

I take a deep breath before scrolling through my Instagram. There are countless birthday messages to Talia, heaps of sponsored ads, dumb memes. I flick to Snap – nothing. If people are bitching behind my back and I can't hear them, did it still happen?

I call up Nan's text and read it over and over again.

I believe in you.

Just seeing her words makes me feel better, like she's somehow here with me, giving me strength.

Is that possible?

I wonder what happens when people die. Do they walk towards the light? Or does everything go black? What about their soul, their essence? Last year in physics we learned about energy conservation. How energy isn't created or destroyed. How the amount of energy always remains constant.

Where does a person's energy go when they die?

And where does it go when they're here?

But even these big ideas can't take my mind off Talia. Stupid Dad and his stupid journal idea.

Until an idea lands with a thud, so big, so brilliant, that I can't believe I haven't thought of it earlier. Why am I wasting time writing to myself when I should be writing to the one person who matters?

My brain's telling me I don't know where Nan is, but my thumbs aren't listening and bang out a message.

Where are you?

I hit send then stare at my screen for ages. If only she'd reply.

CHAPTER 15

Revved Up

Let mourning stop when one's grief is fully expressed.
(Confucius)

On the last day of the term, I strut into Food Tech, muffin ingredients safely housed in my cute new insulated tote bag. Talia's not the only one with style. A quick scan confirms she's not even here. She's probably home sick, feeling guilty for bitching about me to everyone. I just know she did.

But I have more important things on my mind. In approximately one hour and twenty minutes, Carter and I will be announced as the winners of the bake-off! My eyes dart around the classroom, a study in organised chaos. There's no real competition.

Carter holds up his hand at the back of the class, as though I need directions, and I can't help but smile. I slow down at Griff's workbench, willing him to make eye contact, but he doesn't look up. It's like I'm invisible. And he still hasn't replied to any of my messages. What is wrong with him? One little lie and he's acting like I burned down his house.

I plop my bag on our workstation.

'Here, let me help,' Carter offers.

He studies each item like there's going to be a memory

test, displaying them within reach. Flour, sugar and nuts first, then the berries. I grab the milk, butter and eggs from the fridge.

'Now what?' he asks.

I point to the laminated recipe that I blu-tacked to our workbench. It's clear he has no idea what to do next so I give him an easy job.

'How about putting the muffin papers in the tins?'

'Got it.' He opens the pack, popping the cases into the trays while I start mixing the ingredients.

Talia finally rocks up, playing it cool. I remember I never dropped off her uniforms to the clothing pool. Then I remember we're no longer speaking so it doesn't really matter.

Addy takes her spot next to Griff. Instead of her usual unimpressed look, she's smiling. What's *that* about? Griff smiles back, juggling some apples while she looks on in amazement like she's watching a Cirque du Soleil performance. I try to ignore them but my eyes keep darting back to Griff. He looks ... happy!

The air's stuffy and warm even though the windows are cracked open. Probably all the ovens preheating. My legs feel wobbly.

Out of the corner of my eye, I see Addy leaning into Griff, nudging him with her hip. There she goes again. Giggling. *What the hell?*

Addy's pathetic. Griff would never fall for someone like her. Someone so ... *obvious*.

My head feels like it's burning up.

'Are you hot?' I ask Carter.

'Most people just say incredibly good looking.'

'I'm serious,' I nudge him, trying not to laugh. Within

seconds, sweat's dripping off me like I'm trekking across the desert. A familiar sensation takes over. The clenching and rumbling in my stomach, the taste of bile in my throat. I race out of the classroom and crouch on the cold lino floor, my head between my knees, praying the rush of blood will revive me.

'Everything all right?' Miss Zhang pokes her head into the hallway.

'Yeah, I'm fine, it's probably just some bug,' I tell her. Maybe it's the Rev. I just took my first tablet this morning. My body probably just needs time to adjust.

When I return to class, Carter's working the room like a politician on the campaign trail, tasting ingredients, cracking jokes, hi-fiving everyone.

He follows me to our workbench. 'You okay?'

'Yeah, I guess so.' I quickly inspect the trays before popping them in the oven. 'Maybe it's something I ate.' *Or didn't eat.*

***

Half an hour later, our muffins look too good to eat. Perfectly round golden cakes with glimpses of raspberries and just the right amount of white chocolate and macadamia nuts peeking through the top.

Stu and Ty have nearly eaten their chocolate chip cookie, the size of the baking tray. Across the aisle, Sydney is staring at her burnt cheesecake while Paris fights back tears.

I plate up like a Masterchef contestant – a few raspberries around the edges and a dusting of icing sugar. First prize is in the bag. And what better way to end the term?

'I think we should taste everyone's dishes and vote,'

Sydney suggests. 'You know, like a real democracy.'

'Democracy sounds good in principle, but often doesn't work in practice,' Miss Zhang replies, and I wonder if she's quoting anyone famous.

A taste test suits me. These muffins could grace the cover of a food magazine. Carter pats me on the back. Even he knows we've won.

Our turn.

'These look and smell great,' Miss Zhang says, bringing one of our muffins to her lips. I exhale, ready to bask in the glory, but her mouth tightens. Seconds later, she spits the food out with such force that it lands in Sydney's hair. The class roars. Stu's laughing so hard he nearly falls backwards.

'I'm so sorry. That was friendly fire,' Miss Zhang explains, her face still contorted. 'I'm tasting cream of tartar. A *lot* of cream of tartar.'

'That's impossible! There's none in the recipe!' My words escape in a confused slur. 'We don't even have any here, see?' I line up our ingredients as proof.

She doesn't look convinced. 'Be my guest,' she says, passing me a muffin.

A bitter, powdery taste explodes in my first bite and I nearly gag. *Definitely cream of tartar.*

I scan the class, searching for the culprit, thinking it could be anyone. Then I hear Talia's snort. She and Eden can't stop laughing.

'How long were you gone?' I ask Carter.

'Gone?'

'Yeah, when I was outside and you were, you know, chatting to everyone.'

'Dunno, maybe a minute or two. Why?'

I hesitate.

He catches me staring at Talia and Eden. 'You don't really think they could have ...?'

I shrug. 'I don't know what I think.'

But I do know. Talia and Eden are behind this. There's no point protesting to Miss Zhang when I can't prove it's true. It just is. Guess that's a metaphysical truth.

Paris's eyes tear up as Sydney hides their deflated cheesecake disc under a tea towel.

'Okay, class, listen up.' Miss Zhang clears her throat. 'It's obvious many of you found this task, uh, challenging.' She rubs the front of her neck in one long, fluid motion and I wonder whether she's coaxing down a bite of cheesecake or muffin. 'But there are a few tasty desserts here, which makes my job difficult.'

She clears her throat before continuing. 'The recipe I have chosen for the Teenline Fundraiser and as the winner of the class bake-off is ... drumroll please ...'

A deafening rhythm echoes around the classroom as everyone bangs out a beat, except me, and Paris, who's on the verge of hyperventilating.

'Eden and Talia, for their baked arancini. A recipe from Talia's nonna that goes back generations, isn't that right?'

Talia catches my eye and smiles. 'Sure does.'

If someone reached into my chest and ripped out my heart it couldn't hurt as much as this. I want to cry but refuse to give her the satisfaction.

I didn't even rate Talia in the kitchen. Worse, I've eaten her nonna's arancini – her mother makes it all the time – and it's seriously delicious. I also underestimated her capacity for revenge. Just like with her haircut, she took her time, waiting for the right opportunity for maximum impact. A delayed strike when my guard was down.

I want to crawl under my workbench and never come out. I know this is just a stupid cooking contest, but we should have won. *I'm* the foodie! I'm the only one who can cook, not that I've had much practice lately. It's too hard to cook when I can't eat. Why torment myself with tantalising sights and smells with no payoff?

Why does everything in my life suck?

'Well, I think we're winners,' Carter says. His shoulder squeeze is so reassuring I actually believe him for a moment.

The message Talia never should have seen is embedded in the back of my brain, right next to my lie to Griff. I need to talk to her, to explain that it's all a big mistake.

The problem is I don't trust her. And I have a feeling she doesn't trust me either.

CHAPTER 16

Sweet Dreams

In order to understand the world,
one has to turn away from it on occasion.
(Albert Camus)

I ditch the bus after school to walk home. There's a sign outside the fish and chip shop: *Hiring now! No experience needed!* I seriously consider it for a moment then imagine what all the hot, greasy oil would do to my skin, and the calories to my thigh-bulge. No thanks.

I may as well add 'Climb Mount Everest' to my wish list because that's more likely than me getting a job, a boyfriend or a life. I need to face the truth: I'm a loser. And Carter's a winner (with an overseas girlfriend!) who wants nothing to do with me. If he wasn't so polite, he'd probably tell me point-blank.

When I get to my street I turn left rather than my usual right, knowing exactly where I need to go. I'm amazed it's taken me so long to realise it.

Four blocks later I'm standing in front of Nan's house. One week, Mum says she's selling it, the next week, renting. But she's doing nothing to make either happen. The house looks different, lifeless – just a stack of grey bricks, a black roof and iron railings. It's been over five months since Nan died and whoever Mum's organised to look after the lawn should be sacked. There's nothing but tufts of dry grass, overtaken by weeds. Hanging baskets with tangles of dead blooms line the verandah. Mum's been hinting at a family day here, calling it a 'working bee' so it sounds light and fun, but she's been too busy with her new job. Good thing too, because I have a feeling we'd be here for ages. I grab the spare keys from under the pot plant and let myself in.

The first thing that hits me is the heat and a musty smell. I nudge open a few windows to let in some air. Nothing inside has changed. It's as though Nan just ducked out to the shops. Her umbrella with the oversized wooden-duck handle is still resting in the chipped pot near the front door. Hanging on the hook is her straw hat, the one with the black-and-white polka dot ribbon that she bought at the markets last summer.

Two tall frames dominate the centre hallway. They display every single school photo of Luke and me. At the bottom of the first frame is my kindergarten photo broadcasting my pudgy face and freckles. I glance upward, taking in the unsightly progression. In Year 3 my eyes were too far apart; in Year 7, my mouth widened, thanks to braces. I never really noticed until now what an ugly child I was. Am. Even my eyebrows darkening into a nice arc and my freckles finally fading don't hide that fact.

Luke's frame is a different story. He can't take a bad photo, looking cute even in the worst one – Year 5, when Mum cut his hair, leaving a jagged fringe. Each year he became more handsome, like he took slow-release good looks tablets. By high school, his face had matured in perfect symmetry, thanks to Dad's strong jawline.

The kitchen is pleasantly cool, as though the heat is so dense that it lacks the energy to move through the house. I rinse and refill the kettle then choose the Blue Willow teapot, proudly displayed on the antique sideboard that belonged to Nan's grandparents. Rummaging through the cupboard, I settle on jasmine, Nan's favourite, tossing a handful of leaves in the pot. The African violet on the windowsill has seen better days so I water it, then give the Irish Blessing plaque alongside it a quick wipe.

There's nothing in the fridge, but the freezer's overflowing with food – and good thing, because I could live off this stash for weeks. I wonder if Mum forgot to turn off the power or kept it on for cleaning. All of Nan's specialty dishes are here: spaghetti carbonara, beef casserole, some sort of soup and stacks of desserts, each in labelled containers as though she was planning for my arrival. I seriously consider the tub of chocolate chip cookie dough ice cream for an entrée but grab the carbonara instead. I microwave the container until the creamy sauce is thick and warm. I'm not sure how long food lasts in the freezer but this smells and looks great, like Nan made it yesterday.

I take my seat on the far side of the oak table, my usual spot for Nan's Sunday dinners. I get lost in the first bite, taking my time to make the taste last longer. My brain's screaming, *Don't do it*! but my hand's not listening and I take another bite ... and another. When I'm done, I microwave the other dishes, piling a bit of each on my plate. I feel better with each mouthful, like Nan's nourishing me through the day's defeat.

When I'm finally done eating, four chimes ring out from the grandfather clock in the lounge room, or *parlour*, as she always called it. It's Nan, telling me she's here.

I head upstairs, skipping the steps that creak out of habit. Nan's bedroom looks just like it did when I helped Mum choose her funeral dress. The green slippers that I gave her for Christmas rest near the bedside table, like all she needs to do is get up and step into them. Nan's tattered basket is bursting with purple yarn on the trunk at the foot of her bed. I follow the wool trail and pull out the jumper that she was knitting for me. When I caress the sleeve, memories flood back: Nan teaching me to knit and purl when I was ten, picking up my dropped stitches with a smile, telling me mistakes can always be fixed. Who'll teach me now?

A wave of nausea washes over me while the tea, casserole and carbonara announce themselves in a loud burp. My belly is hard and bloated.

You're repulsive, the voice chimes in.

I wrestle off my uniform and rummage through Nan's dresser, quickly settling on her lilac nightgown with lace trim. I let the buttery-soft material fall over me then climb into bed, snuggling under the summer blanket that smells like her favourite Joy perfume.

Sweet dreams, I type before my phone dies, hoping my message finds Nan.

It's nearly dinnertime when I stumble out of Nan's house, feeling stuffed like a piñata in danger of breaking at the slightest contact. A police car screeches around the corner. That'd be just like Mum to panic and call the cops. But the car zooms straight past me.

By the time I get home, our house is etched in charcoal, nearly swallowed by the dark sky, and looks like an old photograph, everything a shade of grey. Of course, everyone's out looking for me. And thank God, because there's no way I can get in trouble if they don't know when I got home.

When I'm nearly through the front entry, the lights flick on, startling me. I stumble backwards, grabbing the umbrella stand for balance.

'How's my girl?'

'You scared the crap out of me,' I tell Dad, but he's too busy hugging me to reply. There's no point telling him I forgot he was coming home today.

Falco jumps up to play, licking my ankles when that doesn't work.

'New haircut?' Dad asks.

I follow Dad into the kitchen. 'Yeah, you like it?'

He stares for a moment but a subtle smile breaks through. 'I do. But the important question is, do *you* like it?'

Dad should've been a politician. 'Yep, not sure about Mum though.'

His expression turns serious. 'Oh, speaking of your mother, she's in bed with a headache.'

'And Luke?'

'Out with his mates.'

I can't believe this. I don't come home from school until after dinner and no one even cares. I could be bleeding to death on The Mount and everyone's going about their business. I really *am* invisible.

Falco follows me into the kitchen. Sometimes I think he's the only one who truly cares about me.

'Did you have something on at school?' Dad asks, scanning the noticeboard, like he's trying to catch up on family life episodes after missing half the season. How's that musical going?'

'I never tried out,' I tell him. I don't try to explain why. Because I have no idea.

If I tell him I was at Nan's, he'll have me cleaning the whole house from top to bottom next week. I don't mind helping in my own time. Other than The Mount, Nan's is the one place I can relax, at least judging by my nap today.

Dad unpacks half the fridge onto the bench. Cheese first, followed by a tub of salad then some leftover stir-fry that he pops in the microwave, his finger hovering over the controls. He's been gone so much he's probably forgotten how to use a simple appliance. If I didn't feel so gross, I'd offer to cook him something.

The microwave dings and he tests the stir-fry temperature with his finger, then takes a bite. 'By the way, try cutting Mum a break,' Dad tells me. 'She's going through a lot of stress at her new job and said she's copping a fair bit of attitude from you.'

I'm home less than five minutes and he's already laying into me.

'So you're just gonna take her side?' My voice is so loud, so angry, that I nearly don't recognise it. But it feels good. I wonder if this is why Mum's always yelling.

'Harley, I am *not* taking anyone's side,' he says, taking another bite. 'I'm just reminding you that your mother's under a lot of pressure at the moment so go easy on her, okay?'

Dad's unbelievable. He's roaming all over the world, cheating on Mum, and when he finally makes a cameo appearance at home, he acts like he's the boss.

'Well, I'm under a lot of pressure too!' I snap. 'Not that you'd know because you're always away!'

I want to ask him what her name is, what she looks like, and how he could do this to Mum. To us.

The colour in Dad's face drains. 'Harley, I don't like being gone one bit, but I have no choice. At least for the time being.'

'You'd rather spend time with, with …' my voice wavers but I keep going, 'lab rats.' *Don't cry, don't cry*, I tell myself, afraid I won't be able to stop.

He squeezes my shoulder. 'Pumpkin, things should calm down when this study's over. Promise.'

'And when's that?'

He takes off his glasses and rubs his eyes. 'A month, two max.'

'Two months?' My tears don't listen, streaming down my cheeks.

He lifts my chin so I'm forced to look him in the eye. 'You sure everything's okay?'

I nod.

'Is there anything you want to talk about?'

I shake my head, trying not to watch him spread a generous wad of creamy blue vein cheese on a cracker. It makes me want to throw up.

'Here, have something to eat,' he says, passing it to me. 'You'll feel better.'

I jerk up my hand to refuse. The spaghetti carbonara is congealing in my stomach. Or maybe the ice cream was the problem. I had no control at Nan's – my stomach and head were at war. Now it's payback time. The fatty sludge in my gut is churning.

Dad pops the loaded cracker in his mouth. 'Harley, you're as white as a ghost!'

I bolt down the hallway with seconds to spare, propelling

a kaleidoscope of semi-digested food into the toilet. When the aftershocks come, I hold my head over the bowl, waiting for the repeat performance. With every heave, I hate myself more.

'You okay?' Dad shouts down the hallway.

'I'm fine,' I croak, praying he doesn't come in to check on me. I vomit until there's no more food to come up.

When I finally find my feet, I nearly don't recognise myself in the mirror. The face staring back at me looks tired, defeated. Blood vessels have taken over the whites of my eyes, blue-black circles cast a shadow beneath.

There's a gentle knock, followed by Dad's head in the doorway. 'You sure you're alright?'

'Yeah, it's probably just some bug going around,' I lie. That's my excuse for everything lately. I let him help me up, gripping his arm as he leads me to my room.

'What have you eaten today?'

You wouldn't want to know.

'Please, Dad,' I beg, kicking off my shoes, 'can we not talk about food right now?'

'Harley, I'm sure you don't want a lecture, but you need to be careful. I know you've been talking about dieting for a while and I can see you've already lost some weight ...'

I nod half-heartedly.

'Just remember what's important is your health, not your dress size.'

I try to summon a smile. Dad wouldn't have a clue about what's important in my life, but I don't have the energy to bring him up to date. He wouldn't understand how much work it takes to be a fifteen-year-old girl. He wouldn't understand how much work it takes to be *me*. All the thinking, worrying. For nothing. Griff's written me off, Talia hates me and, as much as I don't want to admit it, Carter has friend-zoned me.

'Do you want me to bring you a glass of water?'

'I'm fine, Dad, thanks. I just want to sleep.'

'Okay but call out if you need something,' he says, leaving my door open a crack.

I toss my uniform on the floor. Then I throw on my oversized Mickey Mouse shirt and collapse on my bed, relieved the carbonara's finally out of my system. The more I ate, the hungrier I became. Each bite brought Nan closer.

I'd give anything for one of her hugs right now. One of those big embraces that would squeeze the air out of me in a single breath.

'There, there,' she'd say, stroking my hair. Her words were like fairy dust, banishing all the bad feelings.

I know Nan's gone but some days it feels like she's still here, looking after me. I think about all the movies I've seen, where people die but their spirits linger with their loved ones. I so want to believe this.

I take out my phone and type a message, *Send me a sign!*

This time Nan replies.

I'm here.

WINTER

CHAPTER 17

Soul Mates

Poetry is nearer to vital truth than history.
(Plato)

On the first day back at school, I drag myself into English, barely functioning. Mr Perera looks tan, and I wonder if he went to Queensland over the break, maybe Fiji. I wish I could've escaped to some tropical retreat.

School holidays are meant to be fun – a time for rest and relaxation. But how could I sleep when the texts were getting stranger and stranger?

When the first one came through a few months ago, I figured it was just my phone glitching. Then more of Nan's old texts started coming up, like *I believe in you.*

But the last message was different. I asked Nan to send me a sign and she replied.

I'm here.

That was a *new* text! I read every message she had ever sent me, and she never, ever uttered those words. Who's pretending to be Nan? Why would someone mess with me like that?

Griff catches my eye and maybe I'm overtired, but I swear there's the trace of a grin on his face. Finally! While

I'm trying to think of something meaningful to say, Addy brushes past with a 'Hey.'

'Hey,' I reply, suddenly realising the greeting wasn't for me.

She tosses her bag next to Griff then whispers something in his ear. What the hell? Are they a thing now? Talia was trying to get me to steer clear of Griff but it looks like he's doing the driving.

If this was a movie, the camera would track my long journey to the back of the classroom, zooming in on my face as I slump in my chair. My glassy eyes are saying I have no idea where I want to be, but I know it's not here. Why bother reinventing myself when no one's even paying attention?

Except maybe Carter. We haven't been talking much lately. It's like we lost the bake-off and something changed. So with nothing to do over the holidays except try to not think of food, I dissected the issue from every angle. It didn't take me long to work out the problem: I need to activate my wish list! It's way too passive – just some random words in my journal. I'm not game to email myself again after the Talia fiasco.

So, hello, *manifesting*! I dedicated the whole break to learning the ins and outs of thinking my dreams into reality. All the sites said journaling is key – *tick*! So are positive affirmations. I ditched some of the suggestions I found online – *I am worthy, I believe in myself* – in favour of specifics, setting my intention as clear as possible to give my thoughts and words extra power:

Carter is into me.

Carter is thinking of me.

Carter wants me.

The affirmations greeted me each morning when I woke, and lulled me to sleep each night. Just for fun, and figuring the extra work wouldn't hurt any, I wrote pages and pages of them in my journal too.

And sure enough, who messaged me on the weekend to see if I wanted to hang out (*uh, yaaas!*). At first, I was convinced Stu had swiped his phone. But the more I read, the more I knew it was Carter.

CARTER: *wanna go ice skating this arvo?*

ME: *you said arvo ha, yeah sure.*

CARTER: *yeah I'm bilingual now haha. Session's at 3 so meet 2.45?*

ME: *yep. hey can you skate?*

CARTER: *I was state champion for my age group.*

WTF? I can barely get to the rink without falling. How's that going to work?

ME: *impressive*

CARTER: *I'm joking*

ME: *ahahahahaha.*

'Okay, who's going to lead the way?' Mr Perera calls out. 'Who's going to share their poetic prowess?'

No takers.

'Come on, folks. Poetry is the language of love.'

His face softens when he spots a hand in the air. 'Yes, Sydney. Go right ahead and remember, read with *audacity*!'

'Okay, here goes.' Sydney stands in front of me slowly, hiding behind her notebook. She launches into her poem, called 'Alone', something about stars sighing and no mercy in the distant blackness. I have no idea what it means but it sounds great. Even Mr Perera looks pleasantly surprised.

When she sits down, I lean forward to whisper. 'That was so good.'

'I pinched part of it from Mum's journal,' she confides, but not before flashing me a sneaky smile. Her eyes linger. 'You look amazing, by the way.'

'Thanks!'

Introducing New Harley.

'Did you change your hair?' Sydney whispers.

'Just the cut and foils, but that was ages ago.'

She eyes me again. 'Your face looks different, maybe ...'

I know she wants to say thinner. I didn't think I'd fit into Talia's uniform so soon.

'... new make-up?'

I shake my head and lean forward again. 'Just trying to slim down a bit.' My voice is so soft I can barely hear it.

Over the break I went full throttle on my diet, shaving off 300 calories a day. I even started weighing my food to be spot on. I don't know why it's taken me so long to realise that weight loss is simple maths – more energy out than in. No wonder I'm tired.

Sydney's brows shoot up. 'Don't know about that. You look amazing already.'

If she thinks this is amazing, wait till she sees the real deal.

Mr Perera interrupts our girl talk. 'Let's hear a male perspective.'

Carter's eyes are on his laptop. Most of his words are mine so I doubt he'll volunteer.

It was nearly midnight when he messaged me last night, like I was his saviour.

HELP! My poem sucks. Send inspiration!

I spat out enough lines for him and half the class if they wanted them. They were good ones too, like someone had injected creativity serum into my veins. No doubt inspired by our ice skating afternoon together.

Legend! he replied.

Ty's busy looking for something in his bag, probably the poem he never wrote. Stu bolts out the door, insisting he left something in his locker. Across the classroom, Griff's notebook is open, a river of ink spilling out of the margins. Addy looks on approvingly at his sketches, pointing to the top of the page. I can't make out the title.

'How about you, Griff? You strike me as the poetic type.'

Griff puts down his pen and takes a deep breath. 'Uh, yeah, I suppose.'

I figure he'll read from the page, but he stands without any prompts, clears his throat and announces, 'It's called 'Before You'.'

Before I knew you,
I didn't realise Oreos tasted better
when you ate
the inside first.
Before I met you,
I didn't know there were
one hundred and thirty-three Crayola colours
and we had the same favourite: cerulean.
Before we talked
I didn't realise that words, awkward,
like a first dance,
could mean so much.
Before you smiled at me
I improvised my life,
making no plans,
waiting for destiny to unfold.
Before I saw you with him,
I never knew

there could be anyone
but me and you.

He sits awkwardly, his eyes fixed on the poetry prompts on the board. Mr Perera takes a few moments before rendering his verdict: 'Powerful stuff.'

I close my eyes. The memory is so clear it could be yesterday. The two of us sitting at the little table and chairs that Mum painted in a rainbow pattern, me trying to cheer up Griff with a cerulean crayon when I accidentally broke his Pacific blue.

'It's the best one,' I insisted, and he'd liked it straightaway.

When I open my eyes, Griff's staring at me but quickly looks away. Now I know for sure. The poem is his way of telling me, sorry I've been ignoring you the past few months. I know it started at the movies, when I lied about being sick. I tried to apologise in all those messages that he never replied to, and his silent treatment has taken it to a whole other level. I always think of Griff as being super logical, stubborn even. Maybe he just doesn't know how to say sorry.

When the bell rings I race up to him, relieved to finally be able to cut all the weird tension between us.

Addy stands by his side, ignoring my *Get lost* look.

'I loved your poem,' I gush to Griff.

He shrugs *whatever*. I've missed talking to him for so long, but I haven't realised how much until now, when he's standing right in front of me. How much I miss hanging out with him. Laughing with him. How much I miss *him*. When he opens his mouth to say something I can nearly hear the breath rushing in and out of my lungs. But no words come out.

'Can I have a copy?' I finally work up the nerve to ask,

holding out my hand.

His eyes meet mine and there's a glint of something. Is he trying to pull me in or push me away? When he disappears down the corridor with Addy, I have my answer. He doesn't want me as a friend anymore. Addy has taken my place.

The lightness I woke up with this morning suddenly feels like emptiness – a hole I wish I could fill with a focaccia, maybe a ham and cheese toastie, preferably with haloumi. Or a gourmet veggie pizza with artichoke hearts, sundried tomatoes and roast capsicum. Maybe a pavlova. I think about eating each and every one, but what's the point? There's no food that can fill the ache inside of me.

Of all the people in my life, I never thought I'd lose Griff.

At lunch I sit under the jacaranda tree, propping my feet on the roots that curl and snake under its thin crown. Clusters of yellow leaves dangle from the branches, just managing to hold on when all they want to do is fall. I scroll through my feed, laughing occasionally, then pretend-messaging, so I don't look like a no-hoper sitting under a tree with no one to talk to. But mainly so I'll stop thinking of Griff.

I'm here.

I always find my way back to Nan's words. Maybe the messages are from a hacker. That's what Luke said a few weeks ago, when I finally showed them all to him. Then he quickly changed his mind, telling me Nan's number had been reassigned.

'Think about it,' he said. '*I'm here* means *I've arrived.* Someone's probably just meeting up for a coffee or something.'

Makes sense, I guess.

I managed to forget about the messages. Until Dad returned from his latest trip and launched into a lecture on grief – how it unfolds in stages over time, how each person experiences it differently.

Across the quad I spot Carter – no entourage, for once. Strange. I close my eyes and manifest silently, but this time I kick it up a notch.

Carter will break up with his girlfriend.

Carter is into me.

Carter wants me.

Carter will ask me to the formal.

When I open my eyes, he's sitting next to me. I breathe in the salty, greasy aroma of his steaming chips. 'Here, have some,' he insists.

'No thanks,' I tell him, 'I just ate.' An entrée of carrot and egg, followed by a main course of guilt, confusion and sadness.

'Do you miss your friends at home?' Random, but anything to avoid the food issue.

'Yeah, sometimes.' He pauses for a moment. 'But this is home now. I've made some great friends here.' He smiles. I'm not sure who he's talking about but I'm hoping it includes me. 'But it sucks that Australia's so far away from everything.'

It's hard to concentrate when the chips are calling my name. 'Yeah, but it's not far from New Zealand. Or Fiji. Or Vanuatu. Or ...'

He laughs. 'You know what I mean.'

I nudge him in the shoulder. It feels good. 'Yeah, I know.'

'Guess I'm just bummed that my girlfriend and I broke up, not that it was a surprise or anything.'

I'm so lost in his perfect lips that it takes a minute for what he said to register. HE BROKE UP WITH HIS GIRLFRIEND!

I use every available muscle not to jump up and do a happy dance in the middle of the quad. This time, when he offers me chips, I allow myself two.

'Hey, I know this is kind of last minute but are you free this weekend?' he blurts, and I nearly drop one of my precious chips.

This manifesting thing really works!

I'm thinking, *For you, I'm free every minute of every day.* But instead, I say, 'Uh, yeah, I think so. Why?'

Carter sighs, leaning back as though he's one with the tree, and I wonder if he's this relaxed around other girls.

'Well, I was hoping you could go over lines for the musical with me.'

He holds up his hands in prayer like he's begging. Begging *me*! I'm concentrating so hard on staying cool that I forget to answer.

'So ...' he hints.

'Oh sure,' I tell him.

'You look good, by the way,' he says.

Now he's complementing me! But I'm not used to praise so I laugh and give him half an eyeroll.

'I'm serious,' he says. 'You look ... happy.'

I'm not really sure what happiness feels like, but with his breakup news flash, I think I'm getting close.

I smile. 'I am happy.' *I think.*

He shakes the chips, urging me to have the last handful but refusing is easy. Because in this moment I realise my true happiness is a direct result of eating less, not more.

After the final bell I head to my locker, plotting evasive tactics for home. Mum gets home from work around three, plenty of time to arm herself with carbs and sugar, ready to pounce when I step through the door. I keep telling her I'm trying to lay off the junk food, but she keeps telling me there's nothing wrong with my weight. Anything less would be unhealthy, she tried to convince me this morning.

What planet is she on?

Worse, now Dad's getting worked up about my weight. The other night he told me I was looking a bit 'drawn' and wanted to know how many kilos I'd lost. I shrugged and mumbled, 'Not enough'. Then he got angry, launching into a ten-minute lecture about the importance of nutrition and its effect on growth development and brain function. I can still grab chunks of flab on my hips, I wanted to shout at him, I'm hardly malnourished.

As I near the Drama room, every nerve cell in my body tells me to keep walking, but I sneak a peek instead. Mrs Stevens is flicking through the script, looking even more stressed than usual. Eden's showing off her cartwheels and splits while Talia practises her dance routine. I haven't spoken to Talia in over a month. Except for her being offline over the summer, the longest we haven't talked is three days.

The glass panel on the door is fogged with my breath. I wipe it with my sleeve and watch the cast. Carter's sitting on the stage, eating an apple. Paris and Sydney are hunched over their phones, giggling. Stu and Ty are locked in a wrestling move, calling out to Carter, who cheers them on, but I can't hear what anyone's saying. That's when I realise two things: Nearly everyone from my year group is there.

Except me. And they've been rehearsing for this dumb musical F.O.R.E.V.E.R.

Carter tosses his apple core in the bin and starts spinning Talia around the room. She's throwing her head back, dancing with my crush, laughing so hard that the sound echoes throughout the hallway.

I didn't manifest *this*.

I walk away, a small part of me dying inside. When I get to the end of the hall, I can still hear Talia laughing.

It's after midnight but sleep is out of reach, thanks to Falco's snoring and a second dose of Rev after dinner. One tablet a day isn't going to make a dent in my thighs. Mum and Dad yelling at each other isn't helping any.

They've been going at it for over an hour, words flying like bullets, punctuated by name-calling. Maybe that's why Dad's never here. Or is that why they're always fighting? I toss and turn, thinking about Carter, trying to stay positive. He tells me he breaks up with his girlfriend (how convenient). Then he asks me to run lines with him (probably just an excuse to hang out with me). It's so obvious we're soulmates.

The term 'falling in love' is wrong. I feel light, ethereal even, like love is making me airborne.

I'm *ascending* in love.

When I see Talia online I realise how much I miss our chats. But it's not like I can get her take on the Carter situation when we're not even speaking to each other. I can't think straight with Mum and Dad wrecking the mood.

I almost wish Talia and I would shout and call each other names then get over it. The wall of silence is getting tired. I have no idea what she's thinking or saying behind my back.

It's time to clear the air. I type whatever comes into my head.

Hey, dunno why it's taken so long to say this but I hope you know the bitch comment was just a rant, me feeling sorry for myself, maybe jealous too cos we don't hang out that much anymore and everything's changing and it's just confusing.

The message is way too long but I don't care. It's how I feel and I've nothing to lose. I hit send.

Before I can put my phone down I see the '...' then, seconds later, her reply.

TALIA: *forgive and forget?*

I don't know if she means for my bitch message, the haircut, the bake-off or all three. But it doesn't matter. Best friends go off each other from time to time but always find their way back. I miss the old Talia.

Done, I reply.

When I roll over, Falco nestles into the back of my thighs, growling softly. I wonder if he's dreaming or if all the commotion is bothering him, too. I'm used to Mum and Dad arguing behind closed doors, but tonight it's open warfare.

I roll over again but can't get comfortable. I try another pillow, then no pillows. Face down. Foetal position. I turn on the bedside lamp and reach for my journal. My revised wish list looms large on the page:

Get skinny.

Get a boyfriend.

Get a life.

Underneath I write so big that it takes up the rest of the page: 0/3.

Other than Carter breaking up with his girlfriend, the

only good thing in my life is Talia and I are talking. I think. I have a feeling the ceasefire won't hold for long.

Below my wish list is the quote from Nan.

You reap what you sow.

I've sowed and sowed but the soil is toxic. Maybe I'm the one who's toxic.

I call up Nan's thread on my phone. Within seconds, my words are flying onto the screen. Talia and I making up but something still not being right. Griff writing a beautiful poem while continuing to ignore me. Mum and Dad tearing each other down. Carter flirting but never following up.

Nothing in my life is as it seems. Perception versus reality. The words come easily.

What should I do?

I don't care if a hacker or some random replies. I'll take anyone's help.

My pillow muffles the noise from down the hallway but it can't block out the sound of my breathing, quick and shallow, then slow and deep, like my heart's beating for two people.

The front door slams, then a car door. Seconds after the engine starts up, a bright light streaks across my mirror. The last sound I hear is tyres screeching.

When I peek out the window, Dad's car is gone.

CHAPTER 18

Selfless

The soul is dyed with the colour of its thoughts.
(Heraclitus)

Two weeks later, my stride is so easy, so efficient, that I make it to the shops before the bus pulls up. Talia's the first to exit.

'You're walking now?' The look on her face says she can't believe I got there first on foot.

Every day, I'm getting faster and faster.

'I've been walking since I was a toddler,' I try to joke.

I don't recognise her new smile. It's a cross between *We're mates* and *I don't trust you.*

'I just mean, it looks like your diet or fitness craze or whatever is getting serious,' she adds.

'Yeah, I guess.' Something's telling me. *Proceed with caution!*

'Let's hit the bakery!' she says so convincingly that I forget I'm not eating and follow her.

When we step inside, Talia crouches to peer in the display case. Her long fringe flops forward and she tucks it behind her ears. Not only is she growing out the cut, she's also toned down the copper highlights. I wonder if that's her way of saying sorry for stealing my style. I bend down alongside her, eying the colourful cupcakes, glazed donuts and other goodies that are strictly off limits. It feels strange, but nice, being close to her like this.

'Split a custard tart?' she asks.

She knows my backup when there's no lemon meringue.

My brain says no but my mouth says, 'Sure.'

When we sit down, it's the old Talia who smiles at me, the one who stuck up for me in Year 5 when Stu called me a 'giant turd', the one who always makes me laugh. But even though we're acting like we're friends, something's different.

We stare at the tart in the middle of the table, saying nothing. At first, I think it's because something that looks this good deserves a moment of silence.

'Rehearsals going okay?' I finally ask, keen to jumpstart the conversation. I figure things can't be going that well if Carter wants me to rehearse with him.

Talia rolls her eyes, leaning in like she's about to let me in on a big secret. 'Eden's prancing around like a diva even though she has this much talent,' she says, holding up her pinky finger. 'I'm waiting for her to ask for a trailer, so she can rest when she's not needed, which is virtually *all* the time.'

I laugh. Talia always finds a way to crack me up.

She takes a bite, moaning softly as she chews. 'The more I get to know Eden, the more I see how many minds she's infected ...'

'Like a virus.'

'Yeah, a highly contagious one.' She brings another mouthful to her lips. 'I know it's taken ages but I'm definitely on the inside now and soon you will be, too.'

I may have seemed keen at the start of the year but I've

learned a lot since then. My idea of hell is obsessing over fashion, brows and thigh gaps with Eden and her minions. But I'm not sure how to tell Talia that. I just want two things: Carter being into me, and Griff and me being friends again. Maybe three: Talia being normal. But I'm smart enough to know life doesn't always serve up what you want. If it did, then Nan wouldn't have died last summer, Dad would be home and Griff would still be talking to me.

She pushes the plate towards me. 'Here, have some.'

There's a misshapen half left, a pale imitation of its earlier promise, but I don't want to undo all my hard work. I lost another kilo – 1.2 kilos actually, according to my new scale. My stomach's always growling like a wounded animal. On the upside, my body fat percentage is creeping down. But I can't get ahead of myself. For every kilo gone, there are heaps more that haven't budged … and probably never will.

I stare at the tart, feeling confident and powerful.

I don't need it.

When Talia and I shared the sundae at Scoop way back when, I was doing most of the eating. Now the tables have turned. Hot chips, pizza and all the yummy baked goods – even the custard tart – no longer have a hold over me.

This morning, when we were getting changed for PE, Paris said, 'Harls, it's like you're shrinking.' It's a massive exaggeration, but also a good motivational tool.

I coax a piece onto my fork to get Talia off my back.

'I mean, you look good, Harls,' Talia says, 'but it's not like you were ever *fat*.'

Her words seem sincere, but the tone's not right, and my bullshit meter's running hot in the red zone.

'You don't want to lose *too* much weight,' she adds.

'I had a sandwich before,' I lie, wondering whether she

believes me. Then I turn my head and cough the mouthful into a napkin. If there were professional qualifications for food trickery, I'd have a PhD.

'Oh, I nearly forgot,' Talia says, passing me her phone. 'Look at this.'

It's an event page on Facebook for Eden's party at the end of term. At the top it reads, *112 invited. 83 going.* All the beautiful people from Mount Pleasant High have said yes, along with heaps from St Ant's. Talia's name is halfway down the list – I wonder if Eden's trying to tell her she's in, but only just.

'What the hell, this can't be right,' I blurt, scrolling through names of people I'd hardly call popular. I don't even want to go but it doesn't look like she's tried that hard to get me an invite. So much for her Oscar-winning performance.

Another eyeroll. 'Oh, them? That's because Eden's event has now been mashed together with a lame cast party. You can thanks Mrs Stevens for that.'

I stare at Talia blankly, unable to process her words. Then I take another bite of the tart.

'Don't stress, Harls,' she reassures me. 'I plus one'd you, see?'

My eyes follow her manicured finger to my name, the last one on the list.

She strokes my back, like she's patting a puppy. 'But there's a catch.'

<hr>

That night, Mum tells Luke and me that we need to talk so we gather in the family room: Mum on the sofa, Luke in the recliner and me on the floor because I have no idea what's about to unfold and already feel like I need space.

Choking back tears, she tells us she and Dad have separated, as if she needed a few weeks to be sure. She's quick to add, *for the time being*, as if he could just walk through the door at any moment like it was all some big misunderstanding. She clutches a velvet pillow close to her chest, probably to keep her heart from shattering.

Luke joins her on the sofa. 'Meika are I are having a break too,' he offers, though I doubt that little news flash is going to make Mum feel better. He puts his arm around her and she squeezes his hand.

'Are you okay, Mum?' I ask, taking her other hand. What a stupid question – of course she's not okay – but I have no idea what to say.

She nods, dabbing her eyes with a tissue.

'Dad will be back,' I reassure her.

Luke is glaring at me. Maybe she doesn't want Dad back. At least not yet.

Her voice sounds far away. 'We'll see.'

Somehow, I don't think it was her plan to split up. Was it Dad's?

She starts to say something but stops herself. I want to tell her, you don't have to explain, I already know. Dad cheated on you. On us.

'Sometimes people love each other,' she mumbles, shifting her gaze between Luke and me, 'but don't like each other very much.' She exhales loudly. 'Sometimes they just need some time apart.'

How much time? I wonder.

I can't sleep, thanks to Mum's talk and a hunger so intense, I'm convinced my stomach is eating itself.

I grab my phone from the bedside table. TikTok's For You launches into a series of pygmy goat videos. The little hoppy animals are super cute but I've never searched any, so I'd love to know how their algorithm works. Food videos follow, which aren't helping me get my mind off eating. I try to trick the algorithm, punching in a few random searches – nature, beaches, Selena Gomez, flowers – anything to break up my pathetic feed. Instead, it just makes me wide awake.

The custard tart is still taking up space in my head. How the crumbs gathered to my fork magically. How I caved and had two bites too many. All because of Eden's stupid event list. I can still see Talia, full of energy, feeding her face, probably metabolising the calories on contact. Her words ringing loud and clear. *But there's a catch.*

<hr>

By recess the next day, I feel slightly more comfortable about Talia's idea.

After forty minutes of rehashing what she's been telling me all year, she finally convinced me. Griff *is* strange. Maybe my oddball radar didn't pick it up because I've known him since forever. He talks strange, thinks strange, acts strange. When he's not lecturing, he's overreacting – he can be so intense at times. I'm his closest friend, his only *real* friend, unlike Addy. They have nothing in common. I can't even imagine what they'd talk about.

Eden and Talia wave me over from the quad, quickly escorting me to the stairs at the back of the science labs.

'Time to make it official,' Eden instructs. She places her phone on the landing along with her canteen lunch, which smells amazing. Chicken burger, I think.

'Just repeat after me,' Talia says with a smile I don't recognise, 'I, Harley Rae Mercedes Hastings.'

'I, Harley Rae Mercedes Hastings.'

'Do solemnly swear.'

I roll my eyes. 'Do solemnly swear.'

'That I will no longer hang out with losers ...'

This is sounding like a bad movie, and I don't know the ending. I'm hovering above, screaming at myself, *Run!* But I've lost control of my legs. And mouth.

'That I will no longer hang out with losers ...'

'Like Griff,' she says, stressing the double f.

I close my eyes and the year runs on playback – how weird Griff's been, how he's written me off over some dumb lie at the movies ages ago. How he's been paying so much attention to Addy lately. It's obvious he doesn't really care about me. Why am I trying to protect him?

I can feel Eden's eyes on me, Talia's too. They're casting a spell, making me do the unthinkable. I fill my lungs with air and repeat the words as fast as I can, hoping if they slur together, maybe I wouldn't have said it.

'Like Griff.'

'And will join my new sisters in the Alliance.'

The Alliance? WTF?

Do they think if they come up with some bullshit name it makes their group legit? I don't know what's more upsetting: the fact that I'm ditching Griff or repeating their idiotic lingo. My brain's working in overdrive, trying to drown out my heart. And it works.

'And will join ...' I can't say it.

'Come on, Harls. You're gonna feel worse before you feel better,' Eden says.

Talia locks eyes with me. She nods gently and smiles ever so subtly, as if to say, *Trust me.*

I think back to her comment at the start of the year about Eden opening doors for us. I'm standing at the door now but don't know if I want to step through. If I don't like it on the other side, can I come back?

I clear my throat. 'And will join my new sisters in the Alliance.'

Door shut.

'There,' Eden picks up her phone and burger, which I want to snatch and inhale. I can't think of the last time I ate something that tasted good. 'Now, that wasn't so bad, was it?'

My hands are shaking and I can feel the sweat dripping down my back. Before I can reply, Eden's gone.

Talia winks at me then comes in for a double air kiss, the scent of her coconut shampoo lingering long after she catches up with Eden. I want to go home, crawl into bed and not wake up for a month or two.

Before I even get to the quad, Griff appears. He's less than a metre away, looking right through me, saying nothing. There's no doubt in my mind now. He's definitely strange.

'May I help you?' I ask, trying to fill the awkward silence.

He practically shoves his phone in my face. 'What's this?'

I push his arm away. 'Oh, so *now* you're talking to me?'

'Seriously, Harls?' His voice sounds different. Strained, maybe. I can't tell if he's pissed off or confused. 'This is how you're going to play it?'

Out of the corner of my eye, I spy Eden and Talia leaning against the wall, giggling.

'I'm not playing anything,' I insist, staring Griff down with newfound attitude.

But when he turns to walk away, shaking his head, I'm not so sure.

Within minutes, Ty's in my face. His eyes are wide open and his mouth is pulled tight like I ran over his dog. This day is getting worse by the minute.

'Look, Griff's not really a bro, but I think what you're doing is a bit, I dunno, basic.'

Addy storms up to Ty, fuming, and I'm wondering what idiotic thing he's done now. Then I realise she's glaring at me.

'What the hell are you talking about?' I ask him, trying to ignore Addy.

'Your pledge,' he says, spraying me with his P.

All the colour fades from view. 'Pledge?'

Please God, no!

He pulls out his phone to play the video. 'It's been Snapped all over,' Ty adds, 'as if you didn't know Eden was recording it.'

Shit, no, no, no. What have I done?

When I get to the quad, Griff's eating his lunch. Alone. He's bent forward, eyes locked on his phone. I want to go up to him, to explain that it was all a mistake, some sort of sick joke. I want to run over and hug him and make him smile again, because I can't remember the last time we laughed together.

When he sees me coming, he turns around, facing the wall. Addy runs up and sits beside him, and whispers something in his ear.

It's too late.

It doesn't take me long to find Eden and Talia at the

canteen.

'You set me up!' I shout. I don't care if everyone's looking at me. 'How could you do that to me. And to Griff? He's never hurt you.'

I want to call Dad. He's only been gone a few days and I already miss him. More than all those times he's been away for work. Who's going to help me now? Not Mum! Dad's the calm one. The one who listens and never judges. The one who gives good advice. But I don't want to give him the satisfaction of helping me. Not after wrecking our family.

'You did the right thing,' Eden reassures me.

'Yeah, we're actually helping him,' Talia chimes in. 'He just doesn't realise it yet.'

CHAPTER 19

Be Yourself

Be kind, for everyone you meet is fighting a hard battle.
(Philo)

My three days of being sick with guilt about Griff are a distant memory by Sunday. If I added together all the best moments of my life – the day we brought Falco home, my first trip to Movie World, getting Selena Gomez's autograph – it still wouldn't describe my excitement level.

Please, please, please let this be the best day of my life.

Time for a quick mirror check. I study my body from all angles, but can only see the work that's still needed, instead of results. I wish I could outline my shape on the glass, like when Mum would mark my height on the kitchen doorframe, so I could measure my progress. I may be smaller than when I split my uniform on the first day of school, but I'm still far too big. I know Carter likes me. But if I'm thin, I think he'll love me.

When the doorbell rings at precisely two o'clock, I practically fly down the hallway before coming to my senses. I don't want to fling open the door and have Carter see some hyperventilating desperado. I take a deep breath and turn the knob slowly, smiling ear to ear, like when the postie has a surprise delivery. My heart's beating double-time though I'm not sure if it's Carter or all the Rev I've been taking lately.

Of course, Carter looks like he just stepped off the runway at Fashion Week. He's wearing black jeans and a T-shirt with a massive star that's somewhere between teal and turquoise, the perfect shade to offset his eyes. A cream-coloured jumper is draped around his shoulders, the ensemble finished with Vans featuring a cool California map design that I'm guessing he customised.

He hands me a box of chocolates and steps inside. 'You're a lifesaver, Harls.'

A lifesaver.

'Yum, thanks.' I study the assortment of dark, milk and white Belgian chocolates like it's a work of art hanging in a museum. Something to be admired from a distance, never touched. 'And I doubt you need saving,' I add, leading him down the hall before Mum arrives home to bore him to death with small talk. 'Everyone's saying what a great Link you are.'

When we get to the games room, Carter turns to me, his face suddenly serious. 'If only you had tried out.'

If only, what?

I wish I could turn back the clock. Whenever I bring up the musical, and how I should have put myself out there, Mum tries to make me feel better with some stupid inspirational quote she swiped from Pinterest. Like yesterday when she took her mud cake out of the oven, turned to me and said totally out of the blue, 'You know, honey, out of adversity comes strength,' and I seriously thought of showing her mine by flinging the cake pan across the room.

'Yeah, probably should've,' I offer Carter with a shrug.

'But at least I'm going to Eden's party,' I add, in case he thinks it's just for the cast. Eden's still whinging about the two events being combined, but I'm on the list and that's all I care about.

'You are? Great, it'll be a night to remember.'

Whoa, what? It will be a night to remember, or *he and I* will have a night to remember? I pray it's the second one. I'm not sure if it's because I love drama and this musical, or I'm looking less fat than usual, or I'm just having a good hair day, but standing opposite him right now, I feel strong and confident. Carter is at my house, in my games room, wanting to rehearse the musical with *me*!

I so want to bring up the formal – to plant a seed and finally get the damn ball rolling. But what if he laughs? Or leaves? And how would I even slip it into the conversation?

'So, where do you want to start?' I ask instead, taking charge while he digs around his backpack for the script.

'I was thinking maybe at the end of the party scene.'

He leans into me so I can read the lines, letting me breathe in his scent. I should tell him I already know the scene by heart, but I keep my mouth shut and enjoy the ride, thinking about the musical so I can get into the right headspace. It's the scene where Link tells Tracy he can't accompany her on the march. He says that her plans are too big and she thinks he's talking about her being fat.

Who needs to get into character? I'm already living this role.

'Hey, wait a sec.' He flips through the script. 'I think we're doing that scene at rehearsals tomorrow.' Then he flicks to the end. 'Do you mind if we skip ahead to the finale?'

To the scene with a big kiss? No, I don't mind!

'Yeah sure,' I reply, trying to sound casual.

'Let's do it!' He leaves his phone and script on the table

and stands in front of me.

I sneak in a quick prayer. *Dear God, sorry I was doubting you, but if you could just help seal this deal, I'll go to Mass every Sunday for the rest of my life!*

From the moment Carter utters his first line, I'm having an out-of-body experience. We say the dialogue and dance around the room like we're taking the show to Broadway. He sings even better than I imagined, and our voices blend in perfect harmony. I feel graceful, dainty even, with lightness in my steps.

We're having so much fun that I lose all sense of time and place. I want this to be my life, just like the old movies Nan and I used to watch. I want to live, sleep and breathe romance with a dash of adventure and a pinch of heartache – only a pinch. I want a life filled with light moments where I can spontaneously burst into song. And of course I want the happy ending.

I want Carter. I want this.

Carter seems more interested in the songs than the dialogue and when he launches into 'Without Love', I wonder if he's using the lyrics to tell me something. That he may look good on the outside, but I've made him what he is today. That he's in love with me no matter how much I weigh – just like the song says.

By the time we hit the chorus, Carter's standing behind me, our bodies pressed together. His hands move to mine as he rocks me from side to side, gently singing in my ear. A zillion goosebumps explode all over my body. Then he spins me around and pulls me close, our foreheads nearly touching. He smells like lemons, for some reason, and musk. His lips are so close that his breath tickles my eyelashes when he sings. Adrenaline's rushing through my body, and

I'm afraid to move, afraid I'm going to mess things up. The moment I've dreamt about every day since he walked into Food Tech is finally here.

'Harley!' The door flies open and thuds against the wall. Mum is standing there, her mouth wide open. She blinks a few times then a smile takes over her face. 'Well, hello, Carter.'

It's official: Mum can add vibe killer to her cv.

'Hey, Gina,' he says, like he's known her forever. When his phone buzzes, he quickly reads the message like he's been waiting for it.

Mum keeps staring at Carter until I break the spell. '*What*, Mum?'

'Sorry, I didn't mean to barge in but I called out for ages, honey, and you didn't answer.' Her eyes plead for forgiveness, but her feeble excuse can't undo the un-doable.

'Because I was busy,' I hiss through gritted teeth, hoping she gets the message. 'Can you close the door on your way out, please?'

'Oh, yeah, sure,' she says, quickly retreating.

When Dad left, I think he took Mum's brain with him. I let out an almighty groan. 'God, she's so embarrassing.'

When I turn around, Carter's already packing his things. Then checks his phone again. 'Sorry, I've gotta go!'

'Already?' I hope he didn't hear my voice crack. 'But we didn't do much.'

'You helped heaps!' he tries to convince me but even his shoulder squeeze doesn't cut it. When he heads down the hallway, I have no choice but to follow. He gives me a quick hug before opening the front door.

'Thanks again, Harls. You're the best.'

My words are tangled and can't find their way out.

When I close the door behind him, I hear the window of opportunity shut too, followed by Mum's dog-like panting over my left shoulder.

'How'd your afternoon with Carter go?' she asks, in a slightly breathy voice. Not only does she burst into the games room like a crazy woman, now she has amnesia.

'It didn't go anywhere, thanks to you.'

She raises her eyebrows. 'Pardon me?'

'I said, thanks for ruining my life!'

Mum puts her hand on my shoulder, the same old mother-daughter bonding crap she always tries when she knows something's amiss. 'Harley, what's going on?'

A tsunami of tears rolls in. Now that I don't feel like talking, my words spill out.

'Every time something good's about to happen in my life, it turns to shit,' I tell her, 'and there's nothing I can do about it.'

I think about my wish list, all those empty words taking up space in my journal.

Looks like the Year of Harley is coming to an abrupt end. Or maybe it never even started. New Harley is just as pathetic as Old Harley.

The tears in Mum's eyes tell me she feels my pain. 'Oh, honey, I wish I could wave a magic wand and make everything better.' She draws me in for a hug. 'But all this ... stuff, it's all part of growing up.'

I muster the little energy I have left into a weak smile, so she'll think her words matter and I can end this conversation. Mum's always trying to be useful, giving me advice I didn't ask for, advice that most of the time doesn't even make sense. Why did I open my mouth? I have enough to cope with, and this mother-daughter moment is the last thing I need. If I have kids, I'm not going to be selfish like her. I'm not going to ruin their lives.

As I trudge back to my room, Nan's name pops up on my phone. Finally! When I asked *What should I do?* I didn't think it would take so long to get a reply.

Be yourself.

I would. If only I knew how.

CHAPTER 20

Plus One

No virtue can be conceived as prior to this virtue
of endeavouring to preserve oneself.
(Benedict Spinoza)

Two weeks pass in a heartbeat and nothing good has happened except losing another kilo.

I haven't heard from Talia since I confronted her and Eden about Griff. When she messages me, I figure it's to finally explain what's going on, how we're somehow *helping* Griff, as she put it. But instead, Talia's reminding me to meet at Room 112 after Philosophy for some boring planning meeting for the formal. I don't remember signing up to waste my lunch period, and I wouldn't put it past Talia to have put my name down. But part of me is happy that we're still speaking. Just.

A list is sticky-taped to the door.

'There she is, first as always,' Talia says. She etches an X through Eden's name, then gives me a wink.

Her mood seems light, like everything's normal between us. But it's not. How can I forgive her for the pledge? How can I forgive myself?

I poke my head into the classroom. It's empty. 'Looks like

we're early,' I tell her, stating the obvious. I'm not sure what else to say.

She practically pushes me through the doorway. 'That's okay, we can eat lunch while we wait.'

Lunch?

I've already lost my appetite, thinking about working with Eden's squad for the rest of the year. Besides, I'm too wired to be hungry. I didn't understand Newton's Second Law in Physics last year, but now I do.

Acceleration is definitely inversely proportional to mass.

The fog has lifted too, thanks to the Rev. It's a game changer. I'm not obsessing about food ... well, at least not as much as before. In fact, I've lost enough weight that even Talia's uniform is slightly big. A far cry from *Get skinny* but it's a start.

With all the time I'm saving by not eating, it's been easy to get to school most mornings with half an hour to spare. Plenty of time to parade in front of my growing band of admirers.

Like Carter. The other day in Food Tech, he stopped whisking the eggs for our frittata, his face suddenly serious. 'You look different.' His eyes pierced straight through me till they found my soul. 'It's like you're glowing.'

I laughed, telling him it must be all the water I was drinking. About two litres a day and endless cups of green tea. Of course, I didn't explain why. All the water's taking the edge off an appetite still raging inside me. Even the Rev can't kill that off.

And my glow? That's simple.

I'm in love.

Talia and I quickly rearrange the desks, transforming the useless U-shape into a large rectangle in the centre of the room. She claims a seat at the head in an early power play, though I'm not sure whether it's for her sake or Eden's.

I toss my notebook into the centre, grabbing the seat alongside Talia. I so want to tell her about Nan's messages, how I can't work out who's sending them, how I don't know whether they're a mistake or someone's messing with me.

But when I play the conversation forward in my head, I don't see the point. Knowing Talia, she'd call Mum, oozing fake concern about online predators.

If only it really was Nan.

Talia snaps off a lid and digs into her salad: rocket, tomato, heaps of shaved parmesan and a drizzle of balsamic. It looks good, though I reckon the cheese would add 50 calories easily. I pull out my carrot sticks, polishing one off in two bites.

'I know it's just for Year 10,' I tell Talia, 'but we should go all out for this formal, you know, like they do in America. We just need a good name, maybe a theme.' There's too much saliva in my mouth, making my words run together. 'Hey, Carter would know.'

'Whoa, slow down,' Talia insists, 'it's like you're speaking Spanish. All I got was 'America' and 'Carter'.'

My legs are tingling and my heart's racing. I take a deep breath, vowing to lay off the Rev for a few days, and exhale slowly. 'I was just saying Carter would probably have some good ideas.'

She shrugs. 'Maybe.'

I see he's online so I send a message, reading my words to Talia as I type: *Any ideas for formal names? Brainstorming with Talia.*

My phone vibrates.

Talia's mouth twitches. 'That was quick.'

I read her Carter's suggestions. '*Come what may, Time of my life, I'll always remember you.*'

Her eyebrows are so high they're lost under her hair.

'*Once upon a time,*' I continue. 'Oh, and a kiss.'

Her eyes open wide. 'Seriously?'

'Not for a name,' I explain, showing her my phone. 'Just a little *x* at the end of his message, see?'

She raises her eyebrows again. 'Gay.'

'Gay or *gay*?'

'Gaaaay.'

I don't believe it. 'No way.'

'Yes, way.'

'You think if he likes me he must be gay?'

Talia laughs so hard that she practically bounces off the table. 'Who said he likes you?'

'Isn't it obvious, you know, in the way we get along?'

Most nights I lay in bed, convinced that Carter's not into me, then I spend the next day trying to find proof that he is. Like now. I wave my phone in front of Talia, like it's Exhibit A in *Law & Order*. Then I swipe through the rest of my messages with Carter, mostly late night convos. We've got such good banter.

'They're getting flirty. Look.' I show her the message he sent last night.

Describe your ideal guy.

I rattled off *kind, funny, supportive.* I steered clear of physical traits so he didn't know I was describing him.

I know a few guys like that, he replied with a winky face.

Message received.

'Carter gets along with *everyone.*' Talia waves away my phone and picks through her salad. 'Besides, he has a girlfriend.'

'An ex-girlfriend,' I say, energised by the fact that I knew first.

She cocks her head to one side. 'Really? Are you sure?' Then she hunches over her phone to message someone. Probably Eden, something like, *Harley thinks that Carter likes her. As if.* Or worse, *News flash: Carter available!* She offers me one of her biscuits, a cute little marshmallow dome with a layer of raspberry jam, but I wave her away with a smile. When she bites down, her teeth leave a jagged mark on the white mound, like footprints in the snow.

Then it hits me, an idea for the formal so spectacular that I practically shout it for the whole school to hear, 'I've got it! Winter Wonderland!'

'Ooh, like fake snow and stuff?' she asks, suddenly interested. 'Does it matter that it'll be summer?'

I shrug. 'Expect the unexpected.'

She nods vigorously. 'All the more reason to wear a skimpy dress.'

I crunch the numbers. Four months is nearly eighteen weeks, a quarter kilo a week, give or take, is another four and a bit kilos. Seems do-able, though six or seven would be so much better.

'Think ice sculptures, pearls draped everywhere, crystals.' I'm making this up as I go. 'And hundreds of silver balloons.'

'Filled with helium?'

'Yeah! Then at the end of the night we cut the strings and they float up to the ceiling, forming a giant mirror.' The more I talk, the more I impress myself. I have so many ideas I feel like my head's going to explode. 'I bet Ty would go for the winter theme,' I add when I'm finally done. 'He's into snowboarding, right?'

She makes a face. 'Who cares about Ty? I'm probably not

even going to the formal with him anyway.'

'What? Why?'

She shrugs. 'I think he's still hung up on Addy,' she tells me, rolling her eyes so big that I automatically roll mine back in a show of support. 'She's messaging him all the time, and he always replies straight away, like his mission in life is to make her happy.'

Addy? I thought she was into Griff. But now that I think about it, I haven't seen them together in a while. For a second I feel bad for Talia, but then I think she kind of deserves it. Addy and Ty make a better couple anyway.

Talia lowers her voice. 'Then last night, when his phone kept going off, I thought, *screw this*, so I finally asked him point blank, "Are you still into Addy?" and he denied it, but I know he's lying.' When she comes in close, I know the story's about to get even better. 'So, when he was at rugby training, I did what anyone would do.'

'What's that?'

'I checked his phone.'

'You know his password?'

She looks at me like it's a no-brainer. 'I've only seen him punch it in a hundred times.'

This would make a good Netflix series. I'm already sucked in. 'So, what happened?'

'Well, I had to be quick, but he's definitely into her. Lots of begging.'

'Begging?'

She rolls her eyes again. 'For *nuuudes*,' she whispers, drawing out the word so I can follow. 'Seems I'm not the only one he's pressuring.'

'And, uh, did you find any?'

'Nah, but I bet I would if I could hack into his laptop. But who cares? I'm gonna dump him anyway. Getting bad vibes all around.'

She snaps the lid on her lunch container and pops it in her bag. 'Harls, you gotta stay on the committee. Don't leave me with those Barbies.'

'Dunno.' All my great ideas for the formal have vanished, and Talia and Addy are dancing around my head, naked. I can't think of anything meaningful to say.

'Seriously, it's dangerous,' she says. 'Every time they point, their fake nails flick off, like BB guns firing all over the place.'

I cough and laugh in the same breath, nearly spitting out some chewed carrot. 'Okay, okay, I'll stay.' How can I not, with Talia providing the entertainment?

'Look on the bright side,' she tells me. 'With Eden working on the formal, all the choice guys will get roped in.'

'Like Carter.'

She nods.

Visions of Carter in a midnight blue suit pop into my head. 'I wonder who he's gonna take?'

She grins. 'Maybe Stu.'

I give her my best death stare. Talia doesn't know it, but he's going to take *me*.

The next day after school I head to Nan's instead of home, feeling guilty that I haven't been back since I ate my way through her freezer. There haven't been any new texts this week. Maybe Luke was right. Maybe it was just some random who's been reassigned Nan's number.

I dump my bag and head straight to the backyard.

'Everything you need to know can be found in the garden,' Nan often said.

I hate to think how she'd feel if she saw her garden now. It looks abandoned, like it belongs to a haunted house. Weeds have overtaken the beds and some of the plants are sagging so much they're nearly touching the ground. The whole yard is depressing. When Nan was alive, her garden was always in bloom, dazzling colours taking turns to debut, as though extending thanks for her devotion. But there's no colour today, only woody plants, dead branches and slimy, smelly leaves on the ground.

I thought Luke was meant to tidy up around here with Dad. At least that's what Mum's been saying for ages. Everything here will be dead by the time they get their act together. I make a promise to myself and to Nan. The garden will look beautiful again.

And now's as good a time as any to start.

I find most of the supplies I need in Nan's shed. I put on the long-sleeve gardening gloves I gave her for her birthday and I'm instantly energised. I work harder and faster than ever, pruning two tiers of native plants, cutting back all the dead growth. I even tidy up the mulch and do my best landscape design, moving a few pots around to create splashes of colour. The bonus? I'm torching kilojoules!

The sprinklers pop on at dusk, splashing my ankles before I can dart out of their path. Thank goodness for irrigation because it hasn't rained in forever – stupid el Niño – and there's no way I'm standing here with a hose every other day.

I relax on the back deck with a cup of lemongrass tea. There's still heaps of work to be done, but I know I can do it.

I can feel Nan by my side, helping me.

When I finally get home, I grab the mail from our letterbox, mostly junk, a few bills and the freebie newspaper that no one ever reads. Dad hasn't forwarded his mail, so I figure he and Mum aren't getting divorced. At least not yet. When I glimpse the date on the paper, I'm hit with a news flash: Eden's party is less than a month away!

I started planning my outfit as soon as Talia plus one'd me. I went straight to the op shop and found the coolest pair of high-top jeans – straight cut and super-soft, with rips in all the right places – and the cutest tangerine, off-the-shoulder crop-top. Skinny jeans aren't my friend … yet. But when I tried everything on, I actually looked good. Well, good-ish. New Harley needs to get out more, and soon. No point looking good in my room.

I flick through the mail. Most of it is promo trash despite the No Junk Mail sign on our letterbox: two-for-one kebabs at the local takeaway; a supermarket special on ham, cereal and soft drinks; and an appeal to Get in Shape NOW! from a new fitness centre. I head to my room, bypassing temptation in the kitchen, nearly tripping over Falco, who's tearing down the hallway with Dad's slipper clenched between his jaws.

'Dad doesn't live here anymore,' I tell him when he drops the slipper at my feet.

He cocks his head, like *WTF?*

In a weird coincidence my phone buzzes with a message.

DAD: *Haven't heard from you in ages.*

I feel guilty for a second or two then get over it.

ME: *sorry, been busy. school and stuff.*

I still haven't visited Dad at his apartment. Why would I

want to see the bachelor pad where he sips his fancy pinot noir, savouring the taste of freedom? When I bumped into him at the shops the other day, he just stared at me.

'Hello, I'm your daughter,' I finally said. It was a dumb joke, I know, but I figured it'd break the ice.

'You're so ... thin,' was all he could come up with.

So, I've lost another kilo and a bit since I saw him last, big deal. The way he was carrying on, you'd think I was about to disappear.

If only he had heard the girls at school lately. Sydney's always telling me how good I look. Paris too. And yesterday, she was convinced I'd had a makeover.

The compliments seem legit but it wasn't too long ago that they were ignoring me. Or worse. No matter how hard I try, I can't forget the pledge. Those girls are like hissing snakes, known to strike without warning.

Well, I'm a snake too. Shedding my skin.

DAD: *We need to talk.*

ME: *it's alright, I know.*

DAD: *???*

ME: *mum already told us*

DAD: *Told you what?*

ME: *about why you left.*

DAD: *?*

ME: *gotta go.*

DAD: *Text me when you're free. Love, Dad*

I always laugh when Dad signs his texts. As though I don't know they're from him.

ME: *k*

Talia Facetimes me after dinner to resurrect her theory about Ty cheating. I can't stop thinking about Mum and Dad.

'Maybe you and Ty just need some time apart,' I tell her. I use every muscle in my face and throat to mirror her fake sympathy. 'Maybe he needs to go back to Addy to work out it's you that he wants.'

Maybe Dad needs to go back to whomever he's been messing around with to realise how much he loves Mum.

Not bad, I think. Two pairs split for the price of one: Ty and Talia, and Addy and Griff.

Her eyes seem small, like black pebbles. 'Maybe he does,' she says, 'but I'm not about to wait to find out.'

CHAPTER 21

Doublespeak

Nothing is so difficult as not deceiving oneself.
(Ludwig Wittgenstein)

Friday after school, Talia begs me to come for a sleepover and I so want to say, 'Oh, I suppose Eden's not free?' I lasted three meetings before I dropped off the formal planning committee, tired of the superiority vibe given off by Eden and her group. I still don't trust Talia but I'm hanging out for some one-on-one time, and I can't keep waiting around for Nan or Carter to message me, so I think sure, why not?

Talia and I used to have sleepovers at least once a month – our record was four in a row a few summers ago – but I can't even remember the last time I was at her house. I sprint the six blocks there, energised by the winter chill and glad I packed my warm pyjamas. I started wearing them the other day when the temps dropped. I tried cranking up the heat, but Mum kept turning it down because she's living in Menopause Central.

The moment my knuckles rap the door, a nagging thought pops into my head, one I've tried to ignore all afternoon: *What if Talia's become one of* them *and doesn't even realise it, like a zombie bitch?*

Then more thoughts. *What if Eden's hiding in there, eavesdropping on our conversation? What if I'm being set up?*

Talia flings open the door, wearing black bootcut jeans with a ribbed top the colour of mustard, which only she could pull off. Her make-up's perfect, just a hint of smudged olive kohl around her eyes, plump lips in a matte taupe, and flawlessly applied BB Cream – not a pore visible.

'You look fantastic,' she gushes, with far too much enthusiasm for my baggy pants and hoodie.

'You too,' I gush back on autopilot.

When I step into the kitchen, the floor moves like the earthquake ride at the science museum. I grab a seat at the table. I should have nibbled something before I got here, maybe a few nuts or a piece of fruit.

'Mum and Dad are out so I made us mac and cheese for dinner, your favourite!' Talia announces proudly, bringing over the pot for me to inspect. 'How are your parents by the way? I haven't seen them in ages.'

'Yeah, they're good. Same old.'

There's no way I'm going to tell anyone Dad has moved out. Then I remember I never texted Dad. But he hasn't been chasing me either. Probably too busy chasing what's her name.

The noodles are swimming in a creamy orange sauce that looks like congealed fat and makes me want to vomit. I imagine it coursing through my veins, grinding to a halt on my hips and thighs, hardening into more lumps that nothing but a jackhammer could break up. Maybe that's why it took so long for the weight to start coming off. Fifteen years of mac and cheese.

'You must be hungry,' Talia says, whacking a spoonful in a bowl for me. '

I can't even remember what I ate today. *Did I even eat today?*

When I started taking Rev, I felt like I had superpowers. Even though I've cut back to one a day, I'm still amped-up most of the time.

'Oh, sorry. I already had dinner,' I tell her, pushing the bowl away. Lying's becoming a habit.

Talia gives me her best eye roll, and it's been so long since we've hung out that I can't tell whether she's joking.

When I step into Talia's bedroom I can't believe how different it looks. Her walls are now a soft yellow and there's a double bed under the window, instead of her usual single.

'Love it!' I flop down on the bed and she sprawls out at my feet. 'Cool light too,' I add, admiring the new stained-glass fitting overhead.

The late afternoon sun sneaks in under the blind, casting our shadows against the wall. I spy a familiar photo on her pinboard and pull it off for a closer look. Griff's carrying me on his shoulders in the Mount Pleasant pool, I think the summer before last. We're both grinning, waiting for another round of Marco Polo. Talia's opposite him, her hair slicked back, skin bronzed like an Italian movie star from the sixties. She's looking up at us, eyes closed, spitting a stream of water into the air like a fountain. We all look so ... happy. I've spun the issue every way I can in my head, but there's no denying it. I did the wrong thing by Griff.

'You know, I haven't had a proper convo with Griff in months,' I tell Talia, still finding it hard to believe. When I turn around, she's Snapping someone. I wonder who. And whether it's about me.

'I wish you hadn't made me take that stupid pledge,' I add, opening the door for her to admit it went too far.

Instead, she answers without looking up, emojis flying across her screen. 'We didn't *make* you.'

'You know what I mean.'

'The pledge was Eden's idea,' Talia explains as an afterthought, checking her messages. 'And sometimes it's easier to go along with her and her dumb rules. At least this way we're guaranteed to go to her party, now that you're part of the Al-li-ance.'

She drags out the word in a mocking tone, her way of saying we're in this together. But that's the least of my worries. The only thought in my head is how Eden's party is the best chance – probably the only chance – for Carter and me to get together. Eden is plastered all over Talia's pinboard. It used to be jam-packed with our memories. Goofy photos, movie tickets and café napkins with random words scribbled in fits of laughter.

I pull off the pic of Talia sitting on Eden's lap, basking in her beauty aura. Underneath, there's an old photo of Talia and me in our reindeer pyjamas next to the Christmas tree, the pushpin stabbing me in the eye like a voodoo doll. Dotted around the edges are photos from *Hairspray* rehearsals. If she's only pretending to like Eden then why has her wall been taken over by The Talia and Eden Show?

'How's the show going?' Not that I need to ask. It's obvious from the photos that everyone's having a blast.

She finally looks up from her phone. 'It's gonna be amazing. You're coming, right?'

I try to muster enthusiasm, knowing I'd rather have an organ transplant than watch everyone have fun on stage without me.

'You bet!' I tell her, even though I have no intention of turning up.

A photo in the bottom left corner of her pinboard catches my eye. It's Talia and Carter, gazing at each other, mouths open in song. I crumple the pic, quickly shoving it in my pocket. I can't wait for this stupid musical to be over. Just a few more weeks.

'Oh, my God!' Talia shrieks and I jump.

How could she have seen me?

Then she holds her phone over her head with two hands like a Wimbledon trophy, parading around the room. 'I cracked a thousand!'

'A thousand what?'

'Insta followers.'

No freaking way!

I pretend that I'm not interested. 'That's good.'

'I'm telling you, it's the Eden factor. Popularity by association.'

She shoves her phone in front of my face, scrolling through the names. 'See all the guys from St Ant's? And there's heaps of Year 11s and 12s too. Look, even guys who graduated last year like Declan and Raj.'

'Why do you want them to follow you?'

She springs to her feet. I haven't seen her this excited since the new season of *Stranger Things* dropped. 'Because if they're following me, then their followers are going to follow me. Obviously, Harls! Remember last year in Maths when we did exponential graphing?'

'Kind of.'

'Well, my popularity line's heading upwards.' Talia's standing less than two metres from me, but I can't even see her. She's a hologram.

A magpie pecks on the window like it's trying to tell me something. When I close my eyes, Dad and I are at the

Mount, being swooped by a maggie. I'm screaming, running in circles, like any five-year-old would do, while Dad calmly explains the magpie's just protecting its babies.

I wonder what Dad's doing, and whether he's happy on his own or misses us. Misses me. I should have texted him back.

'Hey, you want a cup of tea?' Talia asks, shifting her attention from her phone to her laptop. Looks like she's loading some sort of software. Obviously, I'm boring her.

'Mum bought this really delicious blend,' she adds. 'Pineapple, ginger and lime.'

I'm sad our conversation is so forced. The old Talia and I would be rolling on the floor, laughing at something – anything – by now. 'Just a glass of water, thanks.'

'God, Harls, you're gonna disappear,' she sings out from the hallway.

I return to the pinboard, staring at the pool photo. Griff looks relaxed, content, like he has a sense of peace in himself.

'Tap or bubble?' Talia calls out from the kitchen.

I poke my head into the hallway. 'Bubble!'

Her laptop keeps beeping, so I hit the spacebar, bringing up her desktop. The school webmail is open on the Philosophy tab, which reminds me we have another assessment due soon.

'Do you want any help?' I call down the hallway.

'No, just fixing us a snack.'

She's as bad as Mum – always trying to get me to eat.

My eyes drift back to her screen. My brain's telling me, *Walk away,* but I lean in for a closer look. I click on the Assessments folder, but there are only a few files from last semester and nothing worth reading in Notes, so I click on

Posts instead. The website's so slow I want to scream. I hit the spacebar and the wheel starts spinning and spinning. Shit! I've frozen her laptop. I select 'Force quit' and a message pops up.

Load Anonymous?

When I click OK, a new window launches with a post from the start of this year.

I eat, therefore I am. (Harley)

I can't breathe. I feel sick. My head, hands, everything starts to sweat.

The room spins around me while I stand motionless, unable to move. Tears prick at my eyes. I blink them away, erasing my friendship with Talia in the same moment. The bake-off may have been retaliation but her post was a pre-emptive strike. Have I been battling her the whole time without knowing it?

My hands are shaking so much that it takes four clicks to close the post. The second I do, a photo slowly loads. Soon it's taking up nearly the whole screen.

I've seen Talia's body before, but not like this. She's sitting on her bed, her shoulder angled so her left breast is visible, while only a hint of her right can be seen. Her long, toned legs extend from one end of the photo to the other and where they meet, her red undies are barely visible. She's smiling slyly, like the photographer caught her off guard, walking in when she just happened to be sitting on her bed, topless. Except it's a selfie, according to the file name, and she's the photographer ... with a thousand followers.

There's a pulsing, throbbing sound in my ears. I have a feeling that's not the only photo of her but I'm not sticking around to find out.

I bolt down the hallway, nearly toppling the tray Talia's

carrying with our drinks and a plate of veggies and dip.

'What's wrong?' she cries out.

My heart has hardened like granite. 'There's a problem at home.'

The tears come as soon as I'm out the front door.

CHAPTER 22

Core Business

*Reserve your right to think, for even to think wrongly
is better than to not think at all.*
(Hypatia)

In my bedroom, my bag is buzzing. I take out my phone and watch the notifications fill the screen.

Talia's the last person I want to talk to. I finally see her for what she is. A deceitful, two-faced bitch who'd do anything to claw her way to the top of the popularity ladder. She's been lying to me all year. And she's betrayed me.

How could she have made that Philosophy post? What else has she been putting out there to humiliate me?

My phone's still buzzing.

'Honey, is everything okay?' Mum sings out, knocking when she's already in my room.

'Stay out, I'm getting changed!' I grab my robe and practically close the door on her hand.

'I thought you were staying at Talia's.'

'Change of plans.' I glare at her with a look that screams, *GET OUT!*

'But honey, I thought …'

'Leave me alone!' The door slams like it has a mind of its

own, abruptly ending the conversation. I listen for backlash. Silence.

My phone buzzes again. I read Talia's latest message:

Harls, it's not what you think!!! Yes, I did make that post but that was to get Eden off my back. It was just some dumb initiation to get in her stupid group. Yours was the pledge with Griff. I've explained the plan to you heaps so it's not like you should be surprised.

The popularity plan? I want to believe her, but then another thought hits me like a sledgehammer. *If the pledge was my initiation then why am I still on the outside?*

Some truths are hard to accept. The people I was close to are no longer my friends, and the ones I thought were becoming my friends aren't – and I'm not even sure I'd want them as friends anyway.

I guess Carter's a friend but I want him to be more. *Why doesn't he just make a move?*

Oh God, maybe he *is* gay.

And Griff. I miss his quirks, his weird sense of humour, our chats up The Mount. I miss the Griff from last year before he retreated even further into his own world. He and Nan kept me grounded, and Talia too, before she turned into Eden Wannabe No. 1.

I read the rest of Talia's message.

Don't take this the wrong way, Harls, but you've been acting weird lately like totally paranoid. I'm only saying this cos I luv u. I'd tell u that myself if you'd answer your phone.

I scan her words again and again, unable to absorb them. She has nude selfies on her laptop and she thinks I'm acting weird? I ask: *And the pic?*

Part of me shouldn't care – it's her body – but something's not adding up in her reply.

Ok, not that you've got any right to judge but I sent it to Ty just to get him off my back and it was just for him, ya know, not for all his stupid mates. but guys are dickheads, they gotta boast and they don't care who they hurt. now it's all over the place so don't rip into me, Harls. I've got enough shit in my life with all the haters. you wouldn't believe how bitchy those St Ant's girls are, some are actually scary.

I don't know what to believe anymore. It's times like this that I miss Nan the most. She always wanted to know what was going on in my world. I remember how her eyes would light up whenever I told her about my day. The hand-painted box she gave me, stuffed with her favourite recipes. How she would hum songs without realising it.

It's been over seven months since she died, but some days I wake up and forget she's gone. It's strange, but I savour those moments most – when I open my eyes, thinking she'll be in our kitchen making French toast, like she often did. I'm happiest in that slice of morning when I can linger in my dreams with Nan.

I waste nearly two hours being miserable before I finally declare to the universe, 'I give up!'

My door opens. No doubt it's Mum, back to torment me.

'I said leave me ALONE!' I fling a pillow across the room to make my point.

But there's no sign of her – just Falco, farting his arrival as he jumps on my bed.

'Stop yelling!' Luke shouts down the hallway.

My phone's buzzing. If I have to switch it off to get rid of Talia, so be it. But the message isn't from her. I read the words over and over again.

Keep faith.

With those two words, I feel lighter. Safer. A flame's

building inside me, deep within my soul. There's no more doubt and worry. I stare at the number and for the first time I see what I've known all along.

It *is* Nan.

Half an hour later, I spy Mum sitting at the kitchen table, sipping a white wine as she's flipping through the junk mail. My life's crumbling to pieces and she's already started Happy Hour. I sneak past the kitchen to the front hall where I rummage through the mail on the table, hoping she doesn't hear me because, other than Talia, she's the last person I feel like seeing right now.

'You want to talk about it?' she calls out.

I forgot about her supersonic hearing. 'It's all good,' I assure her. I can feel her eyes on me as I step into the kitchen.

She's holding a flyer at arm's length, squinting to read the headline, 'Get in Shape NOW!'

'I've been looking for that!' I tell her, snatching the flyer to refresh my memory. 'It's for a new place called Core Business.'

'Hmmm, I wonder if they're behind all those annoying texts. Everyone at work's been getting them. *Lose weight fast* or something like that.'

I point to the *We Want You!* At the top of the page. 'See? They want customers *and* staff.'

'Are you trying to get me to join?' Mum asks.

I laugh because the thought of her going to the gym is the funniest thing I've heard in a while. Then I imagine Dad messing around with whatever her name is. Maybe I should try to get Mum to join the gym to get in shape. I quickly come to my senses, banishing the idea, along with the thought of catching up with Dad anytime soon.

'I was hoping I could get a job there,' I tell her instead. 'Not only would I get paid, but I'd get a free membership.'

I need to make things happen. When TikTok isn't sending me workout videos or salad recipes, it's weirding me out with Tarot readings like, *The boy who likes you doesn't know how to show it.* I need to take matters into my own hands. My formula is foolproof.

Get skinny + Get a job = Get a boyfriend.

And the bonus? Getting a boyfriend just in time for the formal.

'You do *not* need to work out,' Mum says, eyeing me up and down. 'You've lost enough weight.' Her eyes narrow into slits as she zeroes in on my arm. 'What's that?' she demands, pulling me towards her.

'What? Where?' I flail about, trying to escape but her grip is firm.

'Ouch, Mum.' I manage to break free, rubbing the spot she was pressing.

She frowns. 'It's a big bruise.'

'Yeah, that you just gave to me.'

'It's not the only one. Look.' She inspects my other arm. 'Did you bump into something? Maybe you need glasses.'

My eyes are fine, I want to tell her. It's my heart that hurts.

I jump up to escape her clutches and lose my footing. My legs feel like jelly and my head's spinning.

'Harley, what's the matter? Are you okay?' Mum places her palm on my forehead, checking my neck and arms. 'Do you feel like you're coming down with something? Let me see your throat.'

'It's fine,' I tell her, sticking out my tongue as proof. *'I'm fine.'*

She doesn't seem convinced. 'I think we should make an appointment for you to see the doctor.'

I try to brush her off. 'Mum, it's nothing, I just stood up too quickly.'

But she's already flicking through websites on her phone. 'No more dieting, Harley. Enough is enough.'

If I wanted a lecture, I would've messaged Dad.

'Mum, it's all good. Seriously.' I pinch my thigh. There's nothing to see with pants on but I know the fat is still there. It feels like a lumpy mattress. 'Look, it's not like I can't afford to lose a bit of weight,' I tell her, squeezing my thigh as proof.

More than a bit, actually. Some days I look in the mirror and see a new shape emerging, like a sculptor chiselling marble. But today, my thighs still look like tree trunks. I should have more to show for all my hard work. If this is as good as it gets, I may as well give up now and order a pizza or something.

'Honey, every woman's thighs feel chunky when they're squeezed like that.'

Chunky?

She pinches her own as proof, though I hardly think she's a good comparison. 'You need to focus on your health, not what the scales say.'

'I'm just trying to feel good about myself,' I tell her, holding her gaze. 'I bet you were the same at my age. If you can remember back to last century.' I wink.

Mum manages a weak smile in return. 'That may be, but I'm going to buy you a good multivitamin and some protein powder. And iron.'

She's eyeing me from head to toe. 'You need supplements. You're not eating enough.'

You have no idea.

'That's why you're bruising so easily.'

The bruises on my skin will go away soon enough, I want to tell her. But what do I do about the bruises in my heart?

CHAPTER 23

Thinspiration

Everything in excess is opposed to nature.
(Hippocrates)

I jog to Core Business, keen to arrive at least fifteen minutes early for my first day as a Fitness Assistant.

The upside about Talia and Griff not talking to me: I have plenty of time to work – and work out. The best part? Free use of all the equipment – when I'm not working, that is. And working out will help me seal the deal with Carter. It has to. I'm running out of options.

I'm still blown away that I could score a job so easily. The manager, Bree, called me right after I submitted my online application a few weeks ago and I met her for an interview the next day. She said she liked my energy. Thank you, Rev.

The moment I step into the gym I notice two important things. The first: Carter and Talia ... on the poster for the musical. *Opens Friday! Limited seats left!* Please don't tell me I have to sell tickets for this waste of an evening. The second: All the other girls in the gym, and even some of the guys, are thinner than me.

'You can store your bag here,' Bree says, showing me the change-room lockers. 'Put this on and I'll see you at the front desk.'

She hands me a T-shirt, black with Core Business in big white letters across the back and a small logo on the front. Her arms are sculpted – *everything* about her is so ... defined. I'm tempted to ask her how long it'll take for me to look like that.

On the other side of the change room, a girl with black hair streaked with electric blue is working leggings over her toned thighs. She looks my age and about half my size, with perky, well-proportioned breasts, a slim waist, and a small, gravity-defying bum free of dimples. I'd do anything to look like that!

Meanwhile, my tights showcase every bulge.

So much for *miracle microfibre*.

I can't help staring at the girl's thigh gap. I could stick my whole hand through it; her legs don't touch till her knees! I want to ask: *How do you do it? Do you ever eat carbs? Is there an exercise you can show me?* She sees me looking at her and smiles. She knows she looks good.

When I look in the mirror, I want to see the body of the girl next to me, but instead there's a slightly smaller version of me, an eighty-per-cent-reduction photocopy of my usual disgusting self. I switch to trackies to hide my flab, and head out to the floor. My legs are anchors, weighing me down. All the women are prancing around in skimpy leotards and sports bras, like they're in Bali, even though it's freezing.

My two-hour orientation flies by. Bree shows me everything, from the gym equipment and class schedules to phone bookings and the computer system, mentioning at least three times that I'm a quick learner. I feel good, but exhausted.

'Great job, Harley, see you tomorrow,' Bree sings out

when we're done. I make a mental note to smile all the time like she does.

As I head out the door, Ms Perfect Body's breaking a sweat on the treadmill, music blaring through her headphones. I can't believe anyone works out for two hours. And she doesn't look like quitting any time soon.

I know what I need to do.

I dump my gear in the corner of the studio and hop on the treadmill alongside her. I tap Beginner then hit 10:00 and start a slow jog, plugging in my headphones to pass the time. A hissing noise cuts in, like bad reverb, and I know what's coming next.

You're fat!

For the first time, I realise the voice is actually helping me. Motivating me. I hit the up arrow.

I'm freezing, but sweat's pouring off me in sheets. My body is a blob of wax. Not an elegant candle, but one of those thick ones in a holiday centrepiece. Exercise is my flame, making me melt. I trudge through the hills, my heart maxed out, unknown muscles oozing acid as I try to find a comfortable rhythm. When the machine finally powers off, I imagine Carter, arms open to embrace a skinny me. He's wearing a tuxedo with a purple flower in his lapel. The formal lights are low – just the glitter ball bouncing light around the hall.

I tap the incline to fifteen per cent then hit Start for another ten minutes. I'm in the zone, as elite athletes say. It's only a matter of time before the fat disappears.

When I make it home, I'm so sore that I spend the entire afternoon lying on my bed, music cranked, trying to shut out the outside world. But the questions keep circling in my head.

How can Nan be gone but still be here?

If I tried explaining it to anyone they'd think I was nuts, but on some level – call it energy transfer, unexplained psychic phenomena, whatever – a part of Nan has stayed behind. There's no other way to explain her messages. I clutch my phone close to my chest.

It has to be Nan! I hadn't even texted her when *Keep faith* came through. All I did was call out, 'I give up.'

What the hell is going on?

I think back to what I said in Philosophy at the start of the year: that the mind was like the soul, and when people died, some part of it continued to exist. Nan once showed me an old family photo, where her grandmother was smiling in the back row ... taken years after she had died. Strange things happen. Like Nan staying behind to look after us.

After me.

I *know* it.

As Dr Kanter said, sometimes truth can't always be shown. Maybe Nan being here just *is*.

Falco scurries into my room and drops his lead near my bed. Subtle. My legs are aching from this morning's workout, but I clip it on his collar anyway, remembering Bree telling me gentle movement can help with muscle recovery. I grab my hoodie and head out the door.

I start off slowly, trying to keep my breath low and controlled, Falco matching my pace. When I turn the corner, I break into a light jog, thinking how far I've come from the start of the year when I couldn't even walk to the bus without breaking a sweat. Maintaining focus is the key and that's easy. I hold a picture of Carter in my head. He's at Eden's party, waiting for me.

'Keep going, you've nearly made it,' he urges, and I run towards him.

The image flickers to Griff in the back row at the movie theatre.

I see you're feeling better.

Then my words. *That I will no longer hang out with losers … like Griff.*

I shake my head as I run, trying to flick Griff out of my thoughts, but he won't budge.

A strange feeling comes over me, like someone, or something, is controlling my movements. Is it Nan?

Before I know it, I'm climbing The Mount, Falco leading the way.

Griff's favourite tree dominates the clearing, gnarled branches shooting skywards like the tendrils of some mythical creature. I half expect to find him sitting there. A dark halo of leaf matter is strewn around the base. Griff's tree talk comes back to me, how the nutrients are sent to the trunk to conserve strength before the figs bud in spring, though it's been so dry and dusty lately, I'll believe it when I see it.

I snatch a faded leaf in flight, driving a sliver of tanbark under my fingernail. Maybe it's a sign. We've hardly come here all year, our escape from the world. It's fractured. Like us.

The wind picks up, blowing enough leaves in my direction

for a makeshift seat, which I gladly claim. Within seconds, Falco's on my lap.

A flash of fluoro bobs in the distance and I'm convinced my eyes are playing tricks on me. Until I hear his voice.

'Hey.' There's a hint of orange ribbing under Griff's blue jumper, probably his favourite Hurley. His camera dangles around his neck, the yellow strap brighter than usual and I wonder whether he washed it. He looks good.

'Hey,' I mumble, my nerves kicking in the moment he sits beside me.

Words are floating in my head, colliding with emotions that I can't put a name to. Should I apologise for the lie about being sick all those months ago, for the pledge? Should he say sorry for ignoring me for ages? We sit in silence for so long I want to jump up and do a cartwheel just to burst the tension. It's hard to believe a lifetime of conversation needs a jumpstart.

'Come here, boy,' he says to Falco. 'Come to Uncle Griff.' The voice is his, but it's different. Detached. Falco dutifully obeys, scrambling off my lap to lick his hand.

'I'm sorry.' I turn to Griff, holding up my arm to shield the winter sun.

He stares at me, expressionless. The filtered light bathes him in a sunburst, straight out of those sci-fi movies where the person's about to be abducted by aliens. The thought of it makes me laugh.

'What's so funny?'

'It's just the way the sunlight's hitting you,' I tell him. 'Makes you look extra-terrestrial.'

'You saying I look like ET?' He looks like he wants to smile but has forgotten how to.

'No, no, you're just illuminated.'

'I'm Illuminati?'

'No, *illuminated*.'

Shit, it's like we've lost our mojo. Our timing's off. Everything's off.

I'm not sure we'll ever get our banter back so I jump right in, figuring I might as well start at the beginning. 'I'm sorry I bailed on you at the movies and went with Carter instead. I don't blame you for being mad.'

Griff's eyes are a dark, velvety black. I haven't seen his face close up in a long time. He still has the messy rock star look working for him, but he seems older somehow.

'I was pissed off because we've known each other forever,' he starts to explain, 'but for some reason you felt you had to lie.'

When Griff says it that way, it sounds worse than I remember.

He discards a few twigs in favour of some dried leaves, which he quickly arranges for a photo. 'Actually, I was probably more disappointed than mad,' he adds, snapping from multiple angles. 'Then you threw in that loser stuff.'

There's a highway of thoughts in my head, blocked by roadworks. How can I explain the pledge to Griff?

He wipes his hands on his jeans – the faded black ones with the two rips across the left knee. 'What's the big deal about Carter anyway?'

How can I even explain Carter to Griff – stunning looks, great body, movie-star smile, easygoing personality? I'm so glad Griff's not invited to Eden's party. He'd just bring me down.

In some ways Carter's the opposite of Griff. Carter lives in the physical. He's so *present*. Griff takes refuge in his head. And all the layers of meaning, the mixed signals, the lies people tell each other – that's all lost on Griff.

Why can't people just say what they mean? he's always asking. I'll give Griff credit – I always know where I stand with him. At least I used to.

'It's hard to explain,' I say, hearing how lame that sounds. 'Carter and I seem to click for some reason.'

'*We* used to click.' He drags a stick through the dirt in a straight line.

'We still click,' I say.

He turns to look straight through me. 'You've *changed*.'

Something in his tone is off.

'You can't see it,' he continues. 'No one can really know themselves, that's the problem.' He ditches the stick to gather some stones, separating them by colour and size. 'Remember Dr Kanter talking about perception?'

'I'd need to borrow your notes,' I joke.

There's no trace of a smile on his face. I wonder whether he's developed immunity to my sarcasm.

'Maybe you just need a new filter,' he tells me, snapping one on his camera then passing it to me.

I aim skyward, capturing the rosella landing on a nearby branch. 'Wow, I'd love these for sunnies,' I gush. 'The colours are unbelievable, they look so real!'

'They are real.'

'Yeah, maybe in *The Wizard of Oz*.'

'I'm serious. You think the colours aren't real because you're using a filter, right? But what if I told you the filter was correcting the colours, not distorting them? What if it's actually restoring reality?'

'Then I'd tell you to lay off the weed.'

He smiles, even though I'm sure he's never touched the stuff. When I look in his eyes I see traces of the Griff I've known all my life. How long will I have to wait to get the whole Griff back? I want to throw my arms around him. I want to tell him everything that's happened, and hasn't happened, this year. I want to cry on his shoulder. But I can't. And I don't even know why.

I lean back against the tree, angling my face towards the weak sun. The crows caw and rattle overhead, reminding me of the nature song we played in Drama last year *to free our minds and bodies* before our performance.

'Harls, seriously, what if someone drugged you when you slept and inserted some undetectable contact lenses in your eyes so you saw these colours all the time? You'd be sure what you were seeing was real.'

My brain's shouting, *Don't reply!* but the signal gets lost on the way to my mouth. 'And your point is?'

'My point is you have a filter inside your head that influences how you see yourself and the world. And I think yours is a bit off.'

'So, why did Socrates say, "Know thyself" if it's impossible?' I ask, amazed I remember anything Dr Kanter has said.

'I think he was just trying to say that we shouldn't be led astray by others.'

'You mean, *Be true to yourself*?'

He turns to me, bowing. 'Yes, Grasshopper.' His lip curls, like he's trying to stifle a smirk.

A giggle ripples in my throat. We try to hold in our laughter but there's no use.

'The riches you search for are within your heart.' Griff jumps up to bow in front of me. 'Listen to your heart and you will find your goals.'

I join in, thinking it's been ages since we recited *Kung Fu* dialogue, well not actually dialogue but our version.

'What we seek cannot be gazed upon,' I reply, returning the gesture.

'It is said that the moth that lives close to the flame leads a short life,' he counters.

'Okay, okay, no more!' I shout, covering my ears. My laughter comes freely for the first time in ages.

It feels good to catch up on all the laughs we could have shared this year – if only we'd been speaking to each other. I want to tell him about Dad moving out but I don't want to feel sad again.

When he smiles, all the awkward stuff between us doesn't matter anymore.

'Don't move,' he says, picking a crumpled leaf off my hoodie. He switches to a new lens then fires off a few shots.

'That's enough!' I shout, palm in front of his camera like a crazed star trying to protect her family.

'Last one,' he says, before shooting another six.

'Seriously, I look like crap.'

He laughs. 'As if.'

A dragonfly comes out of nowhere, landing on my shoulder, buzzing loudly. When I yank off my hoodie, his eyes widen.

'Wow!'

'What?' Has he never seen a crop top before?

'How much weight have you lost?'

I laugh. Griff's acting like I'm scrawny. 'Maybe *you* need a new filter. Or an optometrist.' I pinch the skin around my waist as proof and put my jumper back on.

His gaze is intense. 'I'm serious.'

'Now you sound like Mum.'

All the lightness I've been feeling is crushed by the weight of Griff's judgment.

I should have known. The real Griff's never coming back.

He grabs my arm but I refuse to look at him. 'Harls, I'm just saying I think you need to ...'

I yank my arm free. 'I'm sick of everyone telling me what I need to do!'

Then I run off so fast that Falco struggles to keep up.

'Just make sure it's weight you're losing,' I hear Griff call out, 'and not your soul.'

CHAPTER 24

Technically Speaking

Do not spoil what you have by desiring what you have not;
remember that what you now have was once
among the things you only hoped for.
(Epicurus)

I've laid low all week, trying to avoid the musical hype. *Best show ever!* all the teachers are saying. And the parents. And the students. The last show is tonight and not a moment too soon.

I don't need to be on stage to feel like I belong. The gym's my home now. When I'm not working, I'm working out. My upgrade still has a few bugs but is nearly complete. New Harley: Improved features, greater compatibility and optimised performance. Launching next term at the Year 10 formal!

SOS Harley! Tech off sick. Can you do lighting tonight?
Desperately yours, Mrs S

Aargh! I've told Mrs Stevens at least ten times that I don't want to do tech but she won't let up. This is the fourth message in forty minutes.

The only thing I have space for in my head is Eden's party tonight. Carter and I have talked enough. It's time for action. I've been working hard, sowing the right seeds. It's time to start reaping.

Pleeeaaase.

I'm tempted to tell Mrs Stevens that I'm working. But for some reason, Dad pops into my head, something about turning a negative into a positive. On the plus side, I could go to Eden's party as a member of the production team, not as Talia's plus one.

My thumbs hover and twitch.

OK, see u at 6, I finally reply, thinking she's lucky I even checked my email in time.

Seconds later, Mrs Stevens sends a row of prayer and thumbs up emojis. A sick feeling erupts in the pit of my stomach.

What have I done?

***

Mount Pleasant High isn't known for its drama productions. So rather than be tucked away in a tech suite where I can work the controls like a true professional, I'm seated out in the open, two-thirds of the way back in the school hall – the uninspired setting for *Hairspray*, starring Not Me. The heavy maroon stage curtains are drawn and the MPHS crest in the centre is starting to fray. I take ten minutes to review the cues.

I test the controls, watching the crowd filter in. Mothers air kiss, pretending they're delighted to bump into one another. *You look fabulous! Your skin's incredible, what are you using? Love your hair!*

Note to self: *Please never act like this.*

The air is warm and stuffy with laughter and bullshit.

Mrs Stevens works the crowd, grinning from ear to ear, accepting praise as though she composed the damn musical herself. She finally makes her way over to me, I assume to thank me for helping out, but she sits down instead.

Shit! Why didn't she tell me I'd be working alongside her? *Probably because she knew I wouldn't turn up.*

'Harley, you're a saviour,' she leans over to whisper. 'Thank you.'

'Happy to help,' I assure her through gritted teeth.

So much for not hiding in a tech role. I'm still low-key cut that Mrs Stevens never sent anyone out to get me at auditions.

With a red pen, she makes a series of dashes near the highlighted cues, as if she needs the double reminder, hmm-ing and harrumph-ing as she flicks through the pages. Finally, she places the script on the console between us. 'Ready?'

I nod.

'Okay, in ten, nine, eight,' she starts off, counting us in as I dim the lights. I've already finessed the first three cues, adding a few creative touches. All the directions are so basic – Drop house lights, General wash, Spot up, Centre. It's so *Intro to Theatre Production.* Doesn't anyone know how to layer the cues to establish mood and atmosphere?

Mrs Stevens manages to not stuff up the opening sounds – traffic, cat, bike bell, alarm clock, easing in the backing track to 'Good Morning Baltimore'. I bring up the centre light on a chubby Talia, bolting upright in bed to greet the day. When Talia described the fat suit, it sounded silly, like one of those sumo wrestler costumes, but she looks believable. If only it formed a second skin. Then she'd have to live her life as a *big-boned girl.* That's what everyone says when they don't want to use the f-word.

I'd pay to see that.

Talia finds her stride halfway through the second song and I can't believe how much her singing has improved. Carter's a natural, shining in his solo a few scenes later, sounding even better than when we rehearsed. Eden *is* Amber. In fact, the whole cast is better than I ever imagined. I don't want to admit it, but the show's hanging together really well. Judging from the laughter and applause, the audience is loving it.

I nail the cues, my gaze shifting seamlessly between the page and the stage. I know intuitively what lighting's needed and when. In fact, this page-turning is becoming a bit boring and I'm not sure how I'm going to survive three more scenes until the interval.

My mind drifts to the KitKats I spied in the lobby earlier with the other refreshments, imagining how they'd taste – four rows of smooth chocolate covering a crisp wafer. *Mmmmm.* I turn the page for a cross-fade on Corny Collins, followed by a wash of light on the ensemble.

Shit! Did I take my tangerine top out of the dryer? I don't want to iron it, the fabric seems too delicate, but I can't wear it to Eden's party all creased.

I turn the page, bringing up a warm light on Carter, who looks better than Timothée Chalamet, if that's even possible. When he sings 'It Takes Two', he looks past the audience to the back of the hall … to me! I want to jump up and sing, or wave, or something. Anything. In fact, the lyrics seem like they're written about Carter and me. He's my king and I'm his queen and no one can come between us.

So many thoughts cram into my head that I don't notice Talia worming her way next to him. When she opens her mouth to sing, I fumble the switch, bringing up the central spotlight, practically blinding them in the middle of the duet. I can feel Mrs Stevens's eyes on me as I quickly recover.

During the interval, I try to go backstage to tell everyone what a great job they're doing but the door's locked and there's a sign that says 'Strictly Off Limits'.

This isn't Broadway, people.

I can't wait for this dumb show to be over and everyone to go back to their cliques when the drama glow has worn off. I give it three days.

Mrs Stevens returns fifteen minutes later, chocolate on her breath. 'The show's going really well, don't you think?'

'Yeah,' I reply with a fake smile, even though I'm sure it was a rhetorical question. I can act too.

I plough through the script, barely pausing to take a breath. I'm so in the zone that thirty minutes pass like three. Before I know it, the final number's upon us – the big dance emporium scene. The whole cast is decked out in retro gear. Talia's hair is straightened and stiff, nicely capped off with a fuchsia headband that matches her dress. Everyone looks good, I think, even Stu and ... wait a sec, where's Ty? I suddenly realise that he wasn't in the first half. I know he didn't have a big part, but how can he just not turn up? If Mrs Stevens wasn't breathing so heavily, I'd ask her what happened.

Carter has changed into a shiny tux that looks metallic, his hair slicked back to perfection, like he just stepped out of the sixties. When he slinks over to Talia, every muscle in my body tenses.

Mrs Stevens flashes me a smile, knowing we're nearly there and she can put this headache behind her. *It was the highlight of my teaching career,* I can picture her saying afterwards, despite yelling at every rehearsal, according to Talia. She brings up the backing track for 'You Can't Stop the Beat'.

'I'm heading backstage for the curtain call,' she whispers. 'It's just lighting from here on, except for the reprisal.'

'Okay,' I tell her, my eyes following the script.

I cut the red and blue cues, bringing up the warm backlight then a spotlight on Talia and Carter. They're standing so close they look like they're stitched together. That should be me up there, centre stage. But instead, Carter leans in to kiss Talia, and when they're finally done, her eyes find me and her smile says it all.

The stage sways gently through my tears as the hall goes black. The backing track keeps playing even though no one's singing and the buzz of the audience soon builds to a crescendo. My hand is moulded around the master switch, somehow locked into the off position. My palms are sweaty and my ears are ringing. The fish Mum made me eat for dinner is on its way back up. I can't catch my breath. Or think. My mind is a black hole.

Harley, Harley! The slow chant builds, my name echoing through the hall, but I can't tell whether it's coming from the audience or the stage.

I race out into the cold winter air and run all the way home.

Other than Falco's endless growling when he spots his chewy toy under the sofa, the house is strangely quiet. I figure Luke is at Meika's until I remember they're still 'on a break', then wonder if he was at the show tonight. Mum's probably working late again. I don't really feel like talking but I need the distraction. Something to take my thoughts away from the fact that I just humiliated myself in front of my whole year group … and, most of all, Carter.

Even if Carter did like me, there's no hope now. He'll never ask me to the formal. I feel something hard in my chest, like someone poured concrete over my heart.

I head to my bedroom and open my journal. My eyes lock on the second line of my wish list.

Get a boyfriend.

The words taunt me. If only the journal could talk back. If only it could tell me what to do.

Then I remember, there's someone who can.

I go into overdrive, telling Nan how the evening went off the rails all because of a little technical malfunction. How I tried to switch the spotlight back on, but my hand was paralysed. How everyone chanted my name, knowing I was the one who stuffed up. My text is way too long, but I keep going, explaining how I've waited so long to go to Eden's party, but I don't want to humiliate myself, how everything I do turns to shit.

I collapse on my bed, unleashing the sobs I've pent up all night, all term. All year.

I HATE TALIA!

How can she steal Carter from me?

I never told her to stay away from Carter, but surely she knows how much I like him?

How can Carter even talk to her? Can't he see how fake she is?

That's what made my hand twitch – the look in her eyes, the 'you're a loser and I'm not' smile she swiped from Eden, the sense of satisfaction on her face, like Year 10 is a competition and she's won.

I'm not going to Eden's party tonight. I can't. There's no way I'm going to front up so everyone can fling shit at me.

My eyes lock on the tangerine top I've laid out. It's the perfect colour. And it looks unbelievable with the skinny jeans that I've practically tortured myself to fit into, the ones I was going to wear tonight. And I've waited soooo long.

I think about Carter. Tonight's my last chance to make something happen.

My phone says it's just after ten. Everyone would be on the way to Eden's by now.

There's a sick, sinking feeling in the pit of my stomach and I'm not sure if it's hunger, nerves or the reality that my friendship with Talia is one big lie and that lusting after Carter is pointless. I wander down the hall to the kitchen, feeling my willpower crumble, but it's not food I want.

I bet Selena Gomez could help, if only I could sit down with her – two girls chatting about life, love and everything in between. She'd lean forward, her hand on my knee, reminding me that times like this define us, that we need to embrace the pain, to rise above the haters so we can emerge on the other side fully formed, ready to face the next challenge.

Selena's not here. I open the fridge door.

But Mum's Chardonnay is.

CHAPTER 25

7ᵗʰ Heaven

Patience is bitter but its fruit is sweet.
(Jean-Jacques Rousseau)

Eden stupid bitch with all her rich neighbours and their fancy houses hiding behind these insane hedges. I gotta take off these stupid strappy heels they're killing me and how could her house look so close on the map? Screw her for having a mansion, it's so big I can't even find my way inside. And screw Talia too for wanting to be like her and dumping me and trying to steal Carter when she knows he's mine.

Haha I spewed in her bush, thanks Mum for leaving the grog in the fridge and if she wonders where it went I'll say geez Mum, maybe you need help if you can't even remember polishing off a wine bottle on your own.

Finally, there it is 44, but it's so hard to find you'd think they don't want visitors. Ouch, this gravel is bullshit, my feet are getting all cut up, gotta put these damn shoes back on. Hahahaha I can't even do up the strap, I knew I should have worn my slip-on wedges but damn I look shit hot in my tangerine top, I do have good shoulders and I can't believe my jeans actually fit but they're feeling tight now 'cos I'm bloated from the wine. And all the cheese I found at the back of the fridge. It tasted sooooooo good.

Shit Eden's house is massive, like three times the size of ours and how long is this driveway? My phone's squawking and that's funny 'cos I don't remember going into settings then my screen lights up like magic and tells me to *Be brave* so I think okay and take another swig of Chardonnay, and then I see it's Nan messaging me and I feel bad 'cos there's no way she'd want me chugging white wine or any wine really.

Eden's driveway is so bright a plane could land any second then I think that'd actually be kinda cool and *Woooooooo! Here I am, everyone*, brave Harley, yes, *thank you, thank you*, I sing out when I see everyone in the backyard. I know I did a superb job at the show tonight with my expert lighting and all … except that minor stuff-up at the end but we'll just say that was an equipment malfunction and why did I run out, well, I was sick, see, I've been really sick but out of the goodness of my heart I went in to save the day when Mrs Stevens *begged* me to do lighting and I can't help it if I got worse.

Everyone's staring at me and I can't remember if those thoughts are in my head or if the words escaped. *Your flick's way too thick*, I tell Paris and she puts her hand near her eye like she can feel her eyeliner, God she's so dumb. *Oh, that's a nice shirt*, I tell Sydney but her mouth's all straight like someone sewed it shut, such an uptight bitch. I keep walking and walking, does this place go forever, shit Eden's yard's on fire and then I realise it's a bonfire and who are all these people huddled around trying to stay warm, and *WHERE'S CARTER?* There's heaps of guys from St Ant's and a few older kids who graduated last year, geez who'd wanna go to a Year 10 party when they're eighteen. Losers.

Oh no, Eden says when she sees me and I can't take my eyes off her lips they're so plump and lush and when did she get a piercing? There's two studs, one in the middle of her bottom lip and the other just under and I wonder if it bled much and will she have to take it out for school and does it hurt to kiss someone? *What've you been doing,* she says and I say I'm here for the party silly, my name's on the list you can check if you don't believe me. She just shakes her head then she opens her mouth and starts singing and I think, shit her voice is even better than mine till I realise someone's playing Sia's 'California Dreaming'. I bet it was Carter 'cos he's from California and maybe I should request The Beach Boys, they were one of Nan's favourites then I think of Nan and start crying.

Harley, what the hell's wrong with you, Eden asks hanging her arm around my shoulder pulling me down to sit. I don't even remember telling my hand to move but it snatches my phone out of my pocket just before my bum hits the step and thank God the screen's not cracked. I can't tell if she's pissed off or feels sorry for me but who cares what she thinks? *Ya know Talia hates your guts,* I tell her, *and she's just using you to get popular but tears shreds off you all the time.*

I don't give a rat's what that little slut thinks, Eden says and I think oooooooooooh, this is getting good and there it happened again, I don't know if I said it or if the thought's stuck in my head, banging on my skull trying to get out.

But you two look so tight, I tell her, *so WTF?*

Then she shakes her head so hard it makes me dizzy.

All she does is copy me, Eden says, *she doesn't have an original bone in her body, hell she even stole your haircut remember?*

Yeah you're right, I remember then I tell her *Talia said I should be flattered* and Eden laughs her big throaty tilt her head back laugh and I'm not sure if she's laughing at Talia or me.

Talia got Ty expelled, Eden tells me and I think *Oh, poor Ty, no wonder he wasn't in the play* then I remember what he did.

Stiff shit, he's scum, I tell her, *he sent Talia's pics to everyone, you can ask her.*

TALIA! TALIA! I scream but she doesn't answer.

Shhhh! I took her off the list, Eden says and she's looking me straight in the eye and she's so pretty I wish we could swap faces. Then she leans over and whispers, *Ty didn't forward the nudes to his mates, Talia did.*

Whooooaaahhh no way, I shout and Eden shushes me and says she just found out then I think yep that makes sense 'cos Talia told me she knew his password. *Okay it's kinda obvious I'm shitfaced but it's like I don't even know who Talia is anymore.*

Me neither, Eden says then I realise the words in my head escaped again. *You can stay here,* she tells me, *but no more drinking,* then she tosses my empty wine bottle in the bush saying her parents are away and all the neighbours are watching.

But they can't see over your stupid hedge, I shout then she laughs and walks away.

I jump up suddenly remembering why I'm here. *Where the hell is CARTER?* Everyone's staring at me and I think shit, I hope I didn't just yell his name then my freaking heel snaps off and I nearly do my ankle. I lean on the nearest tree trying to fix it 'cos I don't want to hobble around all night and it's good to stand still when everything's spinning like I'm on a merry-go-round.

Carter walks out of the darkness just like in the movies. I can hardly see, these stupid Japanese lanterns are useless, it's like holding up a match but he looks good I can see that. Finally, he says he's been watching me all night and I think that's cool, that's very cool.

Sydney fronts up with two drinks and Carter shakes his head but I grab one anyway and just when I'm about to scull it he takes it from me, saying *You don't need that* and I think damn, he has an Aussie accent now I never noticed before. And he's right, Mum's wine is working its magic, calming my nerves, telling me this is it and no more waiting so I stand on my tiptoes and throw my arms around his neck pulling him close and within seconds I can feel his breath then his soft lips on mine.

His mouth makes a funny noise like he's surprised and excited at the same time then he pulls back and whispers, *No*, and I'm thinking ah, he's such a gentleman, he thinks I'm wasted so I tell him, *it's all good, I've only had a sip* then I kiss him again and he guides me back against the tree, our lips still touching. His hands are running up and down my sides like he's not sure where to put them and even in the dim light I can see he's into me. My whole body's tingling and burning like I'm on fire and I think, *Please God don't let me be on fire 'cos that'd wreck this moment and I've been waiting all year for this all my life actually*. And his perfect lips are full and firm but soft and lovely and I thank God my nose isn't blocked 'cos I wouldn't be able to breathe but I can't think of a better way to die so either way I'm cool with that. I feel light like the skinniest girl in the world floating above all the skanky girls and my whole life, my whole future plays in my head like a movie. There's my wedding dress and all our kids, four I think, no maybe five, boy-girl-boy-girl-boy so there's no gender wars like we learned about in humanities last year and everyone gets along just like *7th Heaven* damn that was such a good show why is that never on anymore, I guess we'll just have to make our own heaven.

He pulls away and my breath escapes in one super long sigh and when he smiles his teeth are so white they nearly glow in the dark.

You sure your girlfriend won't mind, I ask, and he laughs and shakes his head then he leans into me and before I get nervous we're kissing again and it's even sweeter and better than the first time and there's no sense of time only me and Carter and I can feel his heart's beating even louder than mine. When we finally take a breath I don't feel so good, the pool looks all wobbly and everyone's faces are stretched like they're made of rubber.

Griff what are you up to, Stu calls out and in that moment Carter's hair is darker than before with messy curls and his eyes are brown not blue and suddenly he doesn't look like Carter anymore.

There's a fire in my throat but I can't swallow it and my body feels inside out then I make a strange noise like a dying animal, oh please God make it stop. I don't even know if the sound's coming from my stomach or head or heart but I lurch forward and before I know it, I've spewed all over Griff, big lumpy smelly bits of slop all over his shirt and even some in his hair. And then I hear *sorry* and think I said it the second before I spew all over him again, even worse than before.

And that's all I remember.

SPRING

CHAPTER 26

Faith No More

To one who has faith, no explanation is necessary.
To one without faith, no explanation is possible.
(St Thomas Aquinas)

I'm startled awake from a terrible dream. I'm standing in a glass cage at the zoo, wearing a string bikini, flab hanging out everywhere like stacks of fleshy shelving. Children are throwing unshelled peanuts at me.

'Look at the elephant! She's so big!' a boy shouts.

Then a pre-schooler yells, 'I like the monkeys. They're cuter!'

I eat the nuts, shells and all, crouching to make myself smaller but I'm inflating like a giant hot air balloon. Suddenly, I'm in Food Tech.

'That elephant ate all the food!' Carter shouts, pointing at me. Then Griff pushes past. He has no eyes or nose, just a mouth. When I kiss him, his lips part ever so slightly then in a low, gravelly voice he says, *'Cogito ergo sum'*. Eyes and a nose appear but it's not Griff. And it's not Carter. It's an eerie mix of both, their features fading in and out. I scream but no one hears me.

I'm starring in a new horror movie: *Nightmare in Mount*

Pleasant. I roll over, trying to escape the sliver of sunlight where the blind doesn't quite meet the windowsill. I didn't open my eyes for nearly two days after Eden's party and it took another two to sit upright. My headache lingers, reminding me loud and clear of my night of humiliation. I can't believe I got drunk so easily. The bottle was nearly half full when I swiped it.

Ever since I can remember, I've wondered what it's like to kiss a boy, to lose myself in that magical moment where there's no me or him, just *us*. But Griff? I don't remember much except the moments our lips touched. I was tingling all over, feeling like anything was possible.

Oh, God. I think I liked kissing Griff! Surely that's only because I thought he was Carter?

My phone lights up, snapping me back to the present. TikTok is throwing up another *Signs he likes you*, this time telling me to look out for daisies and stars. Random. I'm not sure what's worse – no action with Carter even though I'm manifesting the shit out of everything, Eden's party or all of Griff's messages. When Griff's not saying *Hey* (I lost count at seven) he's being way too direct. His latest: *Can we talk?* Most people would take a hint when there's no reply. Not Griff. Mum said he stopped by a few times, but she explained I needed to rest. How am I going to tell him this isn't going anywhere? That we're friends, that we used to be such good friends that the idea of anything more seems ... kind of weird. Weird, but maybe not terrible. God, I'm so confused.

If I didn't know Griff and saw his face on a magazine or caught a glimpse of him in a crowd, I'd think, *Hmmm, not bad.* But I *do* know him. Griff's like a cosy blanket that makes me feel safe and warm. Which isn't a bad thing in a boyfriend, I guess, but he's just not ... Carter. When I think of Carter, I'm in a different universe.

I read my hangover message to Eden, amazed by all the typos and the fact that I don't even remember sending it. Maybe Mum read it and that's why she took my phone away for nearly a week.

ME: *wtf happened*

ME: *???*

EDEN: *you tell me. everyone's still talking about the musical*

Does she mean me messing up? I had hoped everyone had forgotten.

EDEN: *and my party*

ME: *??>. can't rmember.*

EDEN: *no surprise there*

ME: *howd I get home?*

EDEN: *you passed out and ur mum came*

ME: *shit mum was there?*

EDEN: *mmm hmm*

ME: *?!!!???!!!*

EDEN: *yep Griff called her*

ME: *he did?*

EDEN: *don't even know why he was there, guess Addy plus one'd him*

That'd be right. They may not be hanging out anymore but I see how he looks at her.

EDEN: *but thank God he was cos you were legit wasted*

I try to flick Addy and Griff from my head.

ME: *and what happned befor that?*

EDEN: *you figure it out*

Mum pokes her frizzy head into my room. 'Good morning, or should I say afternoon,' she jokes, checking her watch. 'We're going to Mass so please get up and eat something.'

'Whoa, what?' I sit up too quickly, which makes me dizzy. I knew it was only a matter of time before her inner dictator took over. 'You said I could go back to church when I was ready, remember?'

Mum gives me one of her you've-got-to-be-kidding looks. 'We're leaving in twenty minutes so get cracking.'

I can't believe Mum wants me to waste time on the last day of school holidays listening to a boring church sermon when I could be doing something useful, like dreaming about formal dresses – not that Carter's asked me. He's had plenty of opportunities. I haven't seen him all holidays but we've been Snapping – mostly boring stuff about what shows we're binging or random pics. What's taking him so long?

Seconds after I fall back into bed, my doona's whipped off me. Mum is standing over me on the verge of hyperventilating.

'I mean it. Get up.'

I find the strength to sit up and yawn.

'What's that on your pillow?' Mum asks.

It's a clump of my hair. When I run my hand through my hair, more falls out. 'Oh my God, look!'

She studies the hairball on my pillowcase then picks at my scalp like she's fossicking for gold. 'You're fine,' she insists. 'It's what would've come out if you'd brushed your hair lately.'

I haven't done much of anything these past few weeks. I seriously need to get motivated. I scribble desperately in my journal. An updated wish list.

My top five things to do:

1. Apologise to Talia and Carter for ruining the musical.

2. Find out whether Carter saw me kiss Griff.

3. Get Carter to ask me to the formal.

4. Tell Griff the kiss was a mistake.

5. Lose another two kilos by the end of the month.

Make that six things.

6. Finish fixing up Nan's garden.

Thanks to being horizontal over the holidays, I've been thinking a lot about Nan's garden. How she and I spent so much time there together planting, pruning, weeding. How after school we'd sit in her favourite spot under the Japanese maple, chatting over cups of peppermint tea. I bet she's wondering where I've been and whether I've forgotten her. It's not like I have to go every week – thank you, in-ground sprinklers – but I actually want to go. Nan's house is where I feel like I can be myself.

'Make sure you keep pumping those vitamins I bought you,' Mum insists, bringing me back to the present. 'You're obviously run down.'

The vitamins I haven't opened yet. I can't even remember where I put them.

'Sure,' I tell her. 'Is Luke coming to Mass too?'

She shakes her head.

'He's at work.'

'Luke works?'

She gives me a look like she can't believe she gave birth to me. 'He's been working nearly every day at that new restaurant in town.'

I raise my eyebrows. Luke and hospitality don't seem like a good match.

Mum sighs. 'Oh, that's right, you've been in bed forever. Well, Sunshine, time to get up and join the land of the living.'

My phone buzzes. It's Griff.

GRIFF: *feeling better?*

ME: *yep*

Seems a bit abrupt so I keep going.

ME: *thx for checking on me over the hols*

His […] is taking forever. Finally!

GRIFF: *no prob. btw did you hear about Talia?*

ME: *no, what?*

GRIFF: *suspended for term. Ty back tmw*

Wow, Talia got off easy. But I can't even process the news with Mum glaring at me.

'Harley, would you put down your phone and get ready?'

If that's a legit question, the answer's no.

Mum's standing in my doorway with her hands on hips, eyes scrunched, lips tight – a power play move that comes naturally. 'Today's your grandmother's seventy-third birthday, in case you've forgotten, so get dressed and grab a muesli bar or something because we're leaving in TEN MINUTES!'

'Well, Nan's not here, is she?' I shout back, jumping out of bed. My Ocean Alley T-shirt creeps up and I stretch it down over my big bum.

Mum's eyes pop open, and I immediately regret my words. 'Sorry, Mum.'

'Look at you, Harley!'

'What?'

Her eyes fill with tears. 'Enough with the dieting! You need to start …'

Not this again. 'I'm NOT too thin, I'm NOT going to Mass, and I'm SICK of you telling me what to do!'

She grabs my wrists, hard. 'Harley, what's going on?'

'Fuck off!' I scream, trying to wrangle free.

The sound of the slap comes first, like thunder, then the lightning sting of her hand.

'I'm sorry, honey. I'm sorry,' Mum babbles quickly, running all her words together in one feeble apology.

I nurse my cheek, raw and hot with tears. She's not going to break me. I hate her.

And I want to scream it loud and clear until she realises she needs to fix her own problems and stop worrying about mine. But in this moment, I don't say anything. Because silence is more powerful than words.

***

The moment I step into church the musky aroma of frankincense takes me back to Nan's funeral. Mum nods across the aisle to the very back, and I sneak across and into the pew. Father Janik is decked out in gold like he's auditioning for Eurovision. When he walks to the lectern for his sermon, I nearly punch the air, realising our late arrival has shaved fifteen minutes or so off Mass.

'Before I start,' Father Janik begins, 'I'd like you to turn to the person next to you and tell them, *God loves you.*'

I use every available muscle to hold back an eye roll. 'God loves you,' I lean over to whisper to Mum.

'God loves you,' she replies, though her monotone delivery tells me she's not so sure.

I like the idea of a supreme being, someone who can protect me, like a divine safety belt. If God really does exist, maybe he, or she, can talk some sense into Talia and make Griff forget about Eden's party ... oh, and put in a good word for me with Carter.

'It's not easy telling such a personal truth to a stranger,'

Father Janik continues. 'But it's even more difficult to tell the person in the mirror.'

I don't really see what this has to do with me so I daydream about formal dresses instead – short cocktail style; full skirt, ankle length; slinky ball gown; dressy pantsuit – anything to zone out on the Father Janik soundtrack. When the collection basket comes my way, I scrounge around in my handbag for a few coins and sneak a peek at my messages. There's a link with more pics from the party. I've been holding my breath every time someone posts but, thank God, there have been none of me yet. In fact, you'd think I wasn't even there.

I click. There's Sydney teaching Stu some dumb dance steps; Addy on the tyre swing in the back corner of Eden's massive yard; Paris dancing under strobe lights. Someone I don't know trying to get Eden's cocker spaniel to swim. Then I see it. The photo I've dreaded for the past few weeks.

It's Griff and me under the tree, eyes closed, our lips locked. Judging by my body language, I look totally into him.

A second later, Paris's message pops up in Instagram. *Cute couple*. Followed by two lines of laughing emojis.

I click on the next image.

Me passed out near Eden's rubbish bins, food scraps all over my tangerine top. This cannot be happening! Oh God, did Carter see me like that? Well, he will now. Is that when Griff made the call? The voice kicks in on cue.

You're disgusting.

This time it goes for two rounds.

You're still fat.

I wish Nan was here. Sometimes I miss her so much, my whole body aches. *Happy birthday, Nan. I'll never stop missing you.*

I'm not a huge believer in prayers but I pray Griff and I can get past that stupid kiss. The more I try to forget it, the more the idea lingers and the sensations flood back – every nerve cell tingling when our lips touched, my heart soaring.

That kiss belonged to Carter!

***

After dinner, I'm sitting in the lounge room sketching formal dresses when Dad's name flashes on my phone. I give myself five seconds to find some enthusiasm. 'Hi Dad!'

'How's it going, Pumpkin? Haven't heard from you in a while.'

'I'm uh ... okay,' I tell him, trying to keep up the pretence but my tone's all wrong, like I'm borrowing someone else's voice.

'Have you recovered from the Chardonnay episode?'

My heart stops. It never occurred to me that Mum would tell Dad. I didn't even know they were speaking to each other.

'It sounds worse than it was.'

'That's what they all say.'

I assume he's joking but I don't laugh, just in case. 'It was all a mistake,' I'm quick to explain. 'I did lighting for the musical and stuffed up big-time so I wanted to redeem myself.' And pash Carter. 'And I saw Mum's Chardonnay in the fridge and thought it'd give me a bit of courage, I guess.'

'Harley, there's a big difference between being brave and being foolish.'

I think of Nan's message, *Be Brave*, and bet she'd agree.

'Yeah, I figured that out,' I tell Dad.

'It's hard being young.'

As if he'd remember. 'Yep.'

'How's that young fella your mother told me about? Connor?'

'Carter?'

'That's the one.'

'He's fine,' I say, wishing he'd worry more about his own love life than mine. 'I don't think it's a mutual thing,' I add, wondering why I'm even telling him this.

'Oh,' he says. Then a deep exhale. 'I see.'

Do you Dad? Do you really see?

Before Dad and Mum split up, he was hardly ever home. And when he was, he was like a guest in the house, trying to catch up on our lives. Now that he's moved out, it doesn't seem much different. So why am I opening up to him? He's hardly a role model for good relationships.

He's been phone stalking me for ages, wanting to talk about their 'situation' and I've been doing everything I can to avoid the subject. I finally blurt out what I've been holding inside for months. 'I know about your affair.'

There's a long pause. 'Harley, what on earth are you talking about?'

I let out an exasperated sigh. I've started a conversation that I'm not in the mood to finish. 'The woman you left Mum for.'

His breathing is fast and loud. 'Harley, I'm not sure where this is coming from.' Another long pause. 'Is that why you think I moved out?'

I have to concentrate hard to not cry. 'Yep.'

My screen says we've been on the phone over four minutes and I pray one of our batteries dies in the next thirty seconds.

'Sometimes, people just grow apart and need to ...'

'Stop trying to justify it.'

I hear his sharp intake of air, then another, like he's struggling to catch his breath, or maybe he has the hiccups.

'I've been doing a lot of thinking lately,' he continues, his voice wavering. 'My career means nothing if I'm losing my family in the process.'

I have no idea what I'm meant to be doing with this reveal.

'Maybe you should tell Mum that.'

CHAPTER 27

Wearing Thin

Men often act knowingly against their interest.
(David Hume)

For the past month, Dr Kanter's been talking about the laws of nature – these *immutable* rules, as she calls them – that the universe must obey. But she's forgotten the most important one.

Avoid shopping with your mother at all costs.
Especially for formal dresses!

Carter not asking me to the formal wouldn't be so bad if Talia and I were still friends. We always said we'd go together if we couldn't get dates. But even if we were on speaking terms, Talia's suspension means she can't go to the formal anyway. Who am I going to go with now? Griff? I don't think so.

The formal is meant to be the official debut of New Harley. Time to bask in glory after all my hard work this year. And nothing's going to stop me, even if I'm basking all by myself.

So, I figure date or no date, I need a dress. A special dress. And that means goodbye Mount Pleasant dress shop, hello, three-level mall. The ninety-minute car ride felt more like three hours with Mum's non-stop questions and old people music. I'm hoping the trip is worth it.

Within seconds of stepping off the escalator, Mum's scanning the window displays, zeroing in on the sales signs. In fact, Mum's so excited about shopping for my formal dress it wouldn't surprise me if she bought one for herself, thinking she's going to tag along. She points in mock horror to a beaded red dress featuring a pink flamingo in a shop window.

'Oh, my goodness. Do you see that, honey?' she shouts, even though I'm standing right beside her.

'Mum, shhh.'

'That's an example of what *not* to wear to your formal.'

The word *formal* jumps out like those 'Which word doesn't belong' puzzles. It's just a stupid dance. But it's a dance that could change my life.

The mall is Mum's mecca, her home ground – surprising for someone whose idea of high fashion is to pair her best tracksuit pants with a sparkly tee. She makes the journey regularly for a dose of *civilisation*, as she calls it, or to be 'alone with her thoughts', which probably means to get away from Luke and me. She means well, but she's out of touch and her excitement over a simple window display is scaring me. Maybe she's throwing herself into shopping to take her mind off Dad.

My phone buzzes. I wish Talia would give up.

Mall today?

School's been back for four weeks and I'm kind of getting used to not having Talia there. She's been so caught up with Eden and her squad all year that she may as well not have been there anyway. Lately, she's been bombarding me with messages, each one more urgent.

Wanna catch a movie sometime? Sleepover?

We need to talk!

CALL ME!

Everyone's written her off, which I'm sure is the only reason she's trying to message her way back into my life. But I can't deal with Talia right now. Mum's enough to handle. She reminded me on the way over that I'm lucky to get a dress at all after the 'stunt' I pulled at Eden's party.

Stunt? She makes it sound like I got drunk on purpose and made an idiot of myself purely for entertainment. If only I had a stunt double, someone to stand in for me for all the crappy parts of my life, leaving me with star billing for the highlights.

I toss my phone in my handbag.

'Mum, I know you don't like *Sassy*,' I say, nearing the shop.

Her eye roll is hardly subtle.

'Harley, is that the image you're trying to convey – *sassy*?'

'What's wrong with sassy?'

'Well, they may as well just call it *Slutty*.'

Here we go. 'I thought *sassy* meant *cheeky*.'

'I don't know what dictionary you're using, honey, but in my book *sassy* means rude or disrespectful.'

'You do know it's *my* formal, don't you, Mum?'

Silence.

'Besides, have an open mind. Isn't that what you're always telling me?'

The dress of my dreams is sophisticated, elegant – not a slinky, shiny, skimpy frock like all the girls will be wearing. I've had my eye on one for a while. One that I'm sure doesn't fit. But I need a goal. My gym work's starting to pay off but I'm nowhere near the finish line.

I steer Mum towards the shop, where I quickly find the

dress. I grab a few different sizes, then spend the next few minutes explaining to Mum why she's not needed in the change room.

The lighting in there is hideous. My skin looks yellow and rough like I need a 24-hour exfoliation. My cheeks are still fat and there are dark hollows under my eyes. I'm not wearing make-up, but still.

I strip off my clothes and see only one thing.

Fat.

I don't care if the number on the scales keeps going down. The mirror doesn't lie. No matter how I tilt my head, the extra chin follows, like Mona Lisa's eyes. My hips and thighs are dimpled with cellulite.

After five minutes of jiggling, I get the dress on and want to spew big time. The cut is too low – it just hangs in front over my puny boobs. Worse, the spaghetti straps are carving into my shoulders, forcing me to hunch forward like an old lady. Staring back at me from the mirror is a fat girl, with an okay face, suffocating in a mountain of midnight blue tulle and chiffon.

'Come out for the big reveal,' Mum chirps and I want to slap her. She's so annoying.

When I peek through the narrow slit in the curtain, she's tapping her foot impatiently. Time to stomp on that idea.

'Don't even bother,' I tell her. 'It doesn't fit.'

'Let me have a look.'

'It's a no from me!' I call out, thinking maybe she'll understand *Australian Idol*. I don't think she's ever missed an episode.

Mum sighs so heavily I swear the curtain flutters.

We spend the next hour zigzagging through the mall checking out a few boutiques, a department store and a new shop that Mum forces me into, even though the cringey clothes are obviously for tweens.

'How about a snack?' she suggests. 'I need to recharge my batteries.'

The shops close in ninety minutes and all Mum wants to do is eat. 'I'm not hungry,' I insist.

'Nonsense. You didn't have lunch and I bet you didn't eat much breakfast, either.'

'So now you're keeping an inventory of what I eat?'

Her glare is intense. 'Keep your voice down. I'm just saying you look drawn, like your body needs something.'

It does. Carter.

Mum links arms with me on our way into the food court and I pray no one from school is here. 'Don't worry, honey, you'll find a beautiful dress,' she assures me with a warm smile. This from the woman who slapped me not so long ago.

'Finding a beautiful dress isn't the problem, Mum. It's finding a beautiful dress that looks beautiful on me.' I suck in my belly but it still jiggles.

'Harley, listen. I don't know any female, young or old, who loves her body. Trust me.'

'Mum, just because I'm not hungry doesn't mean I have a problem with food.'

She stops mid-stride. 'I'm serious.'

The food court is crowded. I grab a table and Mum returns minutes later with enough plates for a family of four.

'Here, look what I got you,' she exclaims.

I opt for the Thai beef salad but the more I pick through,

the more I can see it's loaded with calories. *Pass.* She offers pizza instead, dangling the steaming slice in front of me.

'I already told you, I'm not hungry!'

I ignore her glare, thinking if I speak loudly enough, maybe my stomach will believe it. The formal's just over a month away so there's no time to waste. Lately, I've watched every calorie, taken my Rev and upped my exercise but the scales have hardly budged in weeks. Time to turbocharge.

'Poor Talia,' Mum says, 'to have glandular fever and have to take the whole term off and miss the formal.'

So that's the story? It's amazing how quickly bullshit can spread in a small town. 'Yeah, poor Talia,' I agree.

'So, what's your plan? Are you going with Griff?'

What the hell? Does Mum know about the kiss? I stare at her hard but her eyes aren't giving anything away. There's no way she could know. It's not like Griff would've said anything when he visited over the holidays. Would he?

'Uh, these kinds of dances aren't really Griff's scene,' I start to explain, wondering why his name popped into her head first rather than her mum-crush, Carter. 'And it's not like I *have* to go with someone,' I add, trying to convince myself.

She chomps down on her pizza, Mediterranean veggies cushioned by gooey mozzarella. My stomach rumbles and I wish I could snatch it off her and swallow it whole.

'Besides, Griff's not a fan of the music DJs play,' I add. 'If it's one of Spotify's 100 most-streamed songs, he automatically hates it.' My phone buzzes with a message. 'Speak of the devil.'

We should talk about Eden's party.

I'm assuming he means the kiss, not me vomiting all over him. I let his words sink in while I try to come up with the right reply, figuring it's time to clear the air.

ME: *chardonnay's not my friend haha*

God, that sounds lame. It's hard to think with Mum breathing pizza all over me.

ME: *so no worries, already forgotten.*

As soon as I hit send I feel guilty, like I'm brushing him off. But what else can I tell him? I mean, I don't want to think about Griff being into me. I can't deal with that right now. But friend-zoning him after what happened … it feels, I don't know, rude, and I don't want to hurt his feelings.

He's typing forever and I'm thinking, *Great, prepare for some totally over the top analysis of the kiss that never should have happened.* It's not like I can tell him, *Sorry, I thought you were Carter.*

Finally, his reply comes through.

Ok.

I don't feel as relieved as I thought I'd be.

'Harley, you're nearly sixteen and this formal is a big thing, I get it,' Mum says. 'Believe it or not, I remember battling Nan on the same issue when I was about your age.'

'And what did she say?'

She leans back in her chair with a smile. 'Well, for my school dance, I wanted to wear this really bright mini dress with lots of netting, you know, just like Cyndi Lauper.

'Who?'

'Nevermind. The point is Nan hated the dress. Not only the length, but the colour.'

'What was it?'

'Canary yellow.'

'Yuck, Mum. What were you thinking?'

'Remember, this was the eighties. I thought I looked fabulous and nothing Nan said could convince me otherwise.' She puts down her pizza and looks me in the eye. 'Honey, it doesn't matter whether I like your dress, as long as you do. It's your night, after all.'

'Is that what Nan said to you?'

She sips her coffee. 'Are you kidding? There was no way she was going to let me wear any dress she didn't approve of.'

Mum's exaggerating, as usual. Nan was always so nice, so easygoing. 'So, what did you end up wearing?'

'Well, she made me a simple, but so elegant, black organza cocktail dress with a low back. But not too low.'

I laugh, remembering how old-fashioned Nan could be at times.

'You take after her in so many ways,' Mum tells me, as though she's reading my mind. 'But back to the dress,' she adds, wiping an early tear. 'It was so classy – and tiny! Hard to believe I was so skinny back then.'

Yes, that is hard to believe.

Her body language, her whole being, changes before my eyes. 'It fanned out just above my knee,' she starts to explain, waving her arms about, 'and had a lovely bow to accentuate the waist ...'

Mum's eyes drift to the giant skylight overhead. The sun streams onto her face and she closes her eyes briefly. 'Everyone should have a little black dress like that,' she adds dreamily.

'Sounds like a dress Audrey Hepburn would wear,' I say.

She nods vigorously, wiping a few pizza crumbs off her jumper, the same ugly grey as the roots she should have had touched up weeks ago. I can't believe she ever had good taste.

I sigh. 'I wish Nan were here and could make me a classy

dress.'

It doesn't take long for Mum's eyes to tear up. She smiles, gently squeezing my hand. 'I'm sure she would've loved that.'

I want to make a grand entrance at the formal like the big reveals in *Extreme Makeover*. Everyone already knows what they're wearing and I'm still at the starting line. Eden's dress is from some fancy UK label, hot pink with white feathers. I heard she's dying her hair to match. Rumour is Addy, who has the fashion sense of an antelope, found a beautiful retro gown with a beaded bodice on some American site.

'Do you still have your dress, Mum?'

'Hmmm, I'm not sure,' she says, staring off into the distance again. 'It's probably around somewhere. Why?'

Thoughts are spinning in my head at warp speed. 'Just wondered.'

She shoves her crumpled tissue into her empty coffee cup and not a moment too soon. 'Ready?'

A change of mood creeps up on me like a bad memory. 'Maybe we should just go home.'

'Nonsense,' she insists, loud enough for other shoppers to turn around.

I follow her out of the food court. When we turn the corner near a homewares shop, she stops suddenly like she's hit an invisible roadblock.

'Come on, I feel good about this,' she says, ushering me into some new shop called *After Dark*.

The moment I enter the shop my five per cent confidence level soars off the charts. In the corner, draped on a tall, faceless mannequin, is the most stunning dress I have ever seen.

'Wait here!' I call out to Mum, snatching a few sizes from the rack. I grab a wrap that I'd never wear, figuring it'll keep her off my back. I'm sick of all the weight talk.

Flying into the change room, I practically rip off my clothes. I raise my arms overhead and, for once, a dress actually fits me, the silky smooth fabric hugging me in the right places. I spin around then step back for a full view. It's as though the dress is reining in pockets of flesh, making me look less revolting than usual. Can a frock have magic properties?

I toss the wrap around my shoulders and open the curtain.

'OMG!' she exclaims.

I'm so happy I don't even mind how embarrassing she is. She scans me from head to toe as I twirl left, then right. The dress is so classy: deep violet silk, midi, off-the-shoulder. I don't know what I love more – the asymmetric gathered bust, the elegant rosettes along the back, or the way it shimmers. It's the type of dress Nan would adore.

'Harley,' she says with a deep exhale, clutching her hands to her chest, like she's just witnessed a minor miracle. 'This dress is so flattering on you. It's a real showstopper.'

'I know, right?' I agree, studying myself in the angled mirrors.

'The skirt is so lovely and full,' she adds, reaching out to tug it for no reason, 'but here, take off the wrap and let me see the bodice.'

I practically slap her hand away. There's no way this wrap is coming off.

She dabs her eyes with a mangled tissue, marked with her lipstick. For a second, I think she's tearing up because I pushed her away. Then I realise she's simply caught up in the moment.

She squeezes my hand. 'I wish Nan could see you.'

If only I could tell Mum I've been talking to Nan, that I've been texting her and she's been texting back. But she'd never believe me. In fact, she'd probably call an ambulance.

'She can, Mum, she can.' My hug is so big that it startles her.

She stands back for a final look, smiling. I haven't seen her like this in ages. Happy.

'Here, take this and pay, honey,' she urges, handing me her card when she spots our neighbour in the mall. 'I'll be right out front.'

She returns to tell me her pin. I don't have the heart to tell her I've known it since Year 7.

In the dressing room I spend the next five minutes staring at myself in the mirror, wishing I could slice a few centimetres off my hips and bum and paste them on my boobs. I guess that's what push-up bras are for.

I look good. But I want to look great. And I'm running out of time. I carefully step out of the dress, standing back to admire it on the hanger.

On the way to the front counter, an idea strikes. I backtrack, swapping the dress I tried on for a smaller size, and hand it to the cashier.

Good things come in small packages, Nan always said.

It's nearly midnight when my head sinks into the feathery lightness of my pillow, waiting for a profound sleep to embrace me. The street lamp outside my window casts a sliver of light on my bedroom door, forcing my eyes to adjust to a new shape hanging from the hook. Inside the garment bag bearing the *After Dark* logo is my one-of-a-kind gown.

Hello, future happiness!

When I tried the dress on after dinner, I didn't expect it to fit but thought I'd at least be able to get it on. Stepping into the dress was easy but no amount of twisting and turning could get it past my flabby bum. I can't think of a better incentive to hit the gym even harder.

I'm going to fit into this dress if it's the last thing I do.

CHAPTER 28

If the Dress Fits

Always recognise that human individuals are ends,
and do not use them as a means to your end.
(Immanuel Kant)

I get to the gym early. I've really amped up my cardio the past few weeks, jogging here nearly every day. New Harley does everything at hyper-speed. It's like a storm cloud has parted and the sun has come out, melting the fat and fuelling my brain. Even meals are quick. An apple and two espressos, some protein like egg or chicken, maybe a few nuts. If I'm in a hurry, I'll pop a Rev instead to tide me over.

I reckon another kilo, two max, and I'll fit in my dress.

Carter may not have asked me to the formal, but at least he hasn't asked someone else. But the more I think about it, the stranger this seems – the hottest guy, who gets along with everyone, is showing no interest in the biggest night on the school calendar. Maybe Carter has some weird social phobia. Maybe he can't dance.

I've been manifesting my truth for ages – how long am I meant to wait for the universe to deliver? I just pray I'm not the only one turning up to the formal on my own.

On the way home from the gym I stop in town at Mount

Pleasant Plaza, a totally hyped name for the cluster of run-down shops. It's eerily quiet except for the clanking of doors, a few screeching toddlers and someone shouting 'Shannon!'

A massive sale sign plastered across the shoe store window grabs my eye. I've been so focused on my dress that I haven't even thought about shoes. What colour goes with violet? Silver or black? Maybe even taupe? And what style? Strappy heels? Slingbacks? Open toe? I scan the window, feeling slightly overwhelmed by choice ... and price. Maybe I should get a cheap pair of white heels and paint them purple. Mum painted hers for an emerald green dress she wore to a wedding last year and they looked fantastic ... until it rained and the dye rubbed off on her feet, making it look like she had gangrene.

When I turn the corner I spot a tall guy with a much shorter woman, waiting for the tailor's shop to open. It's Carter! He's carrying a garment bag over his shoulder. The woman is an older, feminine version of him: soft curls of chestnut-brown hair, ideally proportioned face and piercing blue eyes. Exactly how I imagined his mother.

He whispers something to her as I approach, and she breaks into the same wide smile. 'At last, I get to meet the girl that Colt has told me so much about.'

He's talked about me? I hope he didn't mention the bake-off fiasco, or my tech disaster at the musical. Or how I made a complete fool of myself at Eden's party.

'I'm Judy.' She pulls me in for a big, familiar hug – the type you'd save for a long-lost relative.

'Hi,' I squeak. *Keep it together, Harley.*

'It's good to see you looking so well,' she adds. 'Colt told me you were terribly ill at that girl's party.'

'*Mum,*' Carter pleads. It's the first time I've seen him

blush. He's so adorable.

'I think it was some weird reaction to my new hayfever meds,' I say. That'd make sense if I actually had hayfever. I've graduated from stretching the truth to outright lies.

Soon others join them. 'I'm Evan,' Carter's father tells me, extending his hand. 'But you can call me Buddy.'

'Hi, I'm Harley,' I tell him, shaking his hand, 'but my friends call me ... Harley.' God, that's pathetic.

Carter laughs.

'And this is Colt's brother, Mikey,' Judy adds. 'He'll be at your school next year. Won't you, honey?' She pulls to her side a blushing boy with gorgeous blond curls. 'And here's Caroline.'

'Wow, your whole family's here,' I tell Carter.

'Yeah, family shopping day,' he replies.

I laugh, thinking my family wouldn't last ten minutes. Then I realise he's serious. Maybe it's an American thing.

My eyes wander back to the garment bag. Through its plastic window I can see a dark suit and my heart stops. Why would he be getting a suit tailored unless he's going to the formal? And if he's going to the formal, does that mean he's already asked someone? It can't be Talia – she's banned. If it's Eden, I'll scream.

My saliva evaporates in one hard swallow. 'You wearing that to the formal?' I ask, nodding at his bag with a frozen smile.

He shifts nervously. 'Nah, this is just for a wedding. My cousin's marrying an *Aussie*.'

All the air leaves my body in a giant laugh-sigh. His *Ow-zee* sounds like something you'd say when you fall.

'Have fun.' My voice is squeaky again, like I've been inhaling helium.

Judy wanders off and I swear she flashes Carter a look, like *Go on*! I wonder if she's trying to give us some alone time.

Carter leans in to whisper, 'This wedding's going to be so boring. Too bad you can't come.'

I smile. I'm picking up a vibe. 'Yeah, maybe next time.'

What the hell am I even saying? How about: Ask me to the damn formal!

We stand less than a metre apart, smiling and blinking. Blinking and smiling. Out of the corner of my eye, I see Judy smiling too.

'Wanna catch up tomorrow after school?' Carter suggests.

My pulse quickens. *Definitely a vibe.*

I will my face to cooperate but it's no use. My smile is so wide I could eat a banana sideways. 'Sure thing.'

'It's a date,' he confirms, walking off when Judy waves him over.

'Lovely to meet you, Harley,' she calls out, a cue for his perfect family to wave goodbye. I'm half expecting them to break into 'So Long, Farewell' from *The Sound of Music.*

Now he just needs to ask me to the formal. It's only a week and a half away.

Then it will be The Year of Harley after all.

Maybe he's just a last minute kind of guy?

As I watch his family wander into a shoe store, it hits me like a ton of bricks. Carter's going to ask me to the formal tomorrow! Why else would he want to do something after school? That wedding story is probably an excuse to throw me off track. He's already bought his suit!

I practically sprint to the gym. Time's running out so I better start doubling up on my workouts. The invitation I've been waiting for all year is less than 24 hours away.

I manifest the express route to my future happiness. If Carter doesn't ask me to the formal tomorrow, I'm going to ask him.

On the way home I stop at Nan's for my weekly gardening session, clocking in at just under twenty minutes, like a champion race-walker in an Olympic qualifying heat. I have to keep upping the ante to trick my system into overdrive. Nearly 250 calories vaporised into oblivion, according to my phone app, and a minute off my fastest time – a new personal best!

Nan's house smells fresher, not musty anymore, thanks to the airing-out I gave it last week. There's a layer of dust on the furniture as though the molecules are in a state of flux, flying around when I'm here, resettling the second I leave.

While I'm waiting for the kettle to boil, I wander through the house to make sure everything's in order, pleased with my efforts though I haven't come nearly as much as I had hoped to. I've cleaned out wardrobes, organised cupboards, wiped skirting boards and scrubbed grout. That's more than I've ever done at home. An added bonus: it keeps my body moving and the calories burning.

Mum and Dad's wedding photo is on the table in the front entry. That's odd. I'm sure I put it on the mantel last week. Even stranger, Nan's seventieth birthday book is on the sideboard, not the coffee table where I left it last week.

Who else has been here? Who's been moving things around?

I check the back door, relieved to find it locked. Maybe Mum's been here but I would've thought she'd try to drag me along.

The sun's already behind the trees. There're only a few hours left of sunlight and I need to hit the garden.

I've made such good progress lately – aerating the soil, digging in the fertiliser, planting bulbs. I even found the perfect bowl in Nan's garden shed for a birdbath and some old glazed pots for a mosaic.

I snatch the gardening gloves from the basket near the back door and step outside. Everyone's saying how unseasonably warm it is lately but I can still feel a chill in the air. The main bed looks fabulous. Bright pink buds are sprouting on the azalea bushes and clusters of daffodils are popping up everywhere.

I break up some sticks and debris near the base for mulch. Nan's gardening stool makes the work much easier. It's only when I move to a new spot that I notice the mass of daisies at my feet – bright purple petals with a buttery yellow. I clear out the leafy debris from the daisies, along with a large stick that's wedged firmly like a root. When I finally yank it free, I realise it's a piece of timber, like a broken fence paling. *Nan's garden* is painted on it in black.

I know every inch of Nan's garden and have never seen this sign before.

Who put it here?

～～～～～～～～～

When I get home, I retreat to my room to check out the group page for the formal. All the girls have posted photos of their dresses, a polite way of saying *Don't even think about buying this.* Over thirty images have already been uploaded. Not bad out of fifty or so girls in our year group.

I'm tempted to upload my dress but I prefer the element of surprise. I can't wait to burst through the doors in my red-carpet-worthy gown, watching everyone's mouths drop open. Besides, I don't think I need to worry about anyone buying my dress. Judging from the photos, it's way too classy for them.

Out of the corner of my eye I spy Luke standing in my doorway. 'What's your problem?' I snap, getting in first.

When he's done staring, he finally speaks. 'You need to eat more.'

Great, another passenger on the *Save Harley* bandwagon. Dad probably figures if he can't be here to hassle me, Luke can be his deputy.

'Thanks for your concern,' I tell him but he ignores my sarcasm and plops down on the foot of my bed.

'I've been doing a lot of thinking lately,' he starts off.

This can't be good.

'And I wanted to say sorry.'

'Sorry?'

'Yeah, for all the weight jokes.'

His stare is so intense that I look away.

'Girls are always obsessing over their looks,' he adds, nodding, like I have no choice but to agree.

But I won't give him the satisfaction.

'I was just trying to get in your head,' he says, 'because you're always going on about food and stuff.'

He turns away and wipes his sleeve across his eyes. If I thought Luke was actually capable of emotion, I'd think he was crying.

'But you've taken it too far.'

This time I'm the one who turns away.

'I'm worried about you, Harley.'

I'm not sure if this is a sermon or an apology but I'm not buying either. 'Why the sudden concern?'

He avoids my gaze, taking his time to speak. 'Let's just say Meika has some issues. And that's opened my eyes a bit.'

When he closes the door, I jump out of bed, throw off my T-shirt and step into my formal dress, taking care around the rosettes. This time, the dress finds its way to my waist, though I can hardly breathe. I waddle towards the bedside table for my phone then lean back against the wall, holding up the top that I can't quite get on. I look good … ish.

I smile for me, for the dress, for Nan as I take a selfie. She would be so proud if she could only see me. Then I remember she can.

I hit send.

CHAPTER 29

Reality Bites

A wise man is content with his lot, whatever it may be,
without wishing for what he has not.
(Seneca)

Carter finds me at my locker after school. 'Ice cream or pizza?'

'Why not both?' I joke, knowing I can't have either. I'm running out of excuses. *I just ate. My stomach hurts. I can't do lactose.* I'm making it up as I go.

When I remind Mum that I'm meeting up with Carter after school, I see my selfie to Nan didn't go through last night. Strange. I hit send again.

'See you tomorrow,' Carter calls out to Eden and Sydney, who are waiting to board the bus with all the others.

Eden's jaw practically drops to the ground like an anime character. Sydney's too. There are hushed whispers from girls I don't even know as we walk past the line.

They're just jealous.

'How's your job going?' Carter starts off, slowing down his stride to match my leisurely pace. I want this afternoon to last as long as possible.

'It's great,' I tell him. 'I'm already showing new customers the equipment and everything.'

'Cool, you'll be assistant manager in no time.'

I blush, secretly hoping it's true. 'You playing cricket?'

'Yeah, should be awesome. I'm still trying to work out the rules.'

'It's easy. My brother plays. He can give you some tips if you want.' Though except for Luke's words yesterday, I've never known him to actually want to help someone.

'That'd be awesome.'

My phone's vibrating non-stop like a bistro buzzer. I pull it out of my pocket and hit 'decline' when I see it's Mum. No one's going to cut into my Carter time. Especially her.

'Do you need to get that?' Carter asks, always so polite.

'Nah.' I shove my phone in my pocket. 'Um, Carter, I've been meaning to say, uh, sorry for what happened at *Hairspray*. I didn't mean to ruin your big finale.'

He stares at me and blinks twice. 'Ruin? What do you mean?'

'The lights going out. That was me.'

'That was you?' He tilts his head back and laughs. 'We thought a fuse had been tripped.'

Really? 'Well, okay, but sorry anyway.'

'Hey, don't sweat it. People thought it was a dramatic ending. They were even cheering for us.'

Cheering? I was sure they were chanting my name.

'No worries,' he adds.

My afternoon stroll with Carter is giving me such a natural high I can nearly feel a surge of endorphins, nourishing me on every level. I'm spending time with the hottest human being on the planet, I'm burning calories and I'm getting a healthy dose of nature. The trifecta.

'Man, is it always so dry this time of year?' Carter points

out the brown camellia buds that have fallen before they've had a chance to bloom.

'Not really,' I tell him. 'Just the planet protesting.'

At the start of last summer, The Mount came alive in a sea of emerald, like someone wrapped the hills in green velvet. Except for a few half-hearted drizzles, it's hardly rained since. Now, the ground is dusty and dry, cracked open in some places, desperate for a trickle of water. Nature is surrendering.

We walk nearly a block without saying anything.

I give up trying to figure out why the conversation has ground to a halt and focus on getting it back on track, which is hard to do when my phone keeps buzzing.

I run through new affirmations in my head, like an elite athlete before a meet.

I'm focusing on the present, one step at a time.

I have what it takes to win.

I am strong, capable and confident.

Why doesn't he just spit it out? What on earth is he waiting for?

'Hard to believe the year's nearly over,' I offer instead. 'I mean, can you believe the formal's only a few weeks away?'

'I know, can't believe I'm gonna miss it.'

I stop in my tracks and scan Carter's face, praying he's joking. When my phone buzzes again, I seriously think of ripping it out of my pocket and throwing it into the road.

'Are you okay?' Carter asks, his face serious.

I feel like I'm going to faint. 'Yeah, just a stitch,' I lie, grabbing my side when I really want to hold my heart. I think it just broke.

He ushers me to the bench outside the chemist. My phone's still buzzing.

I'm not sure what to say but aim for a cross between interested and carefree. 'So why are you going to miss the formal?'

He looks confused. 'Didn't I tell you?'

'Tell me what?'

'We're heading back to San Diego for the holidays. Dad has some big work thing there, so we're cutting out a few days early.'

I hear his words, but it's like he's speaking a different language. I can't even see his face – just my beautiful gown, its trail of rosettes along the back, withering like dead violets before my eyes. I can't breathe, there's no air.

'Maybe you should get that,' he says when my phone buzzes again. 'Could be important.'

And this isn't important?

There are seven missed calls and three texts from Mum. The latest: *Come home now!*

What's her problem?

My head feels like it's about to split open. It's a steady beat that slowly builds behind my temples while the rest of my body is numb, anaesthetised. A massive cloud passes in front of the sun, casting a long shadow across Carter's face.

I jump up. 'Sorry, I have to go. There's a problem at home.' My mind's racing.

Is Dad okay? Did he tell Mum about his affair?

An awful thought consumes me.

Did Falco get hit by a car?

I don't know what's happening anymore.

Carter's not asking me to the formal. He's not even going.

'I'll walk you home,' Carter insists.

I want this whole conversation to be over. I need it to be over.

'Thanks but I really need to call Mum,' I tell him, waving my phone.

Then I turn and run faster than I've ever run before.

When I get home Mum's waiting for me in the kitchen, drinking a cup of tea.

I drop my bag on the table. 'Thanks for ruining my afternoon with Carter!' I need to blame someone. 'We never even made it into town,' I add, 'with all your phone stalking.'

Her eyes are red, her face serious. 'Sit down, Harley.'

'What?' I bark, dragging out the chair with a loud screech.

'I wanted your father to be here, but he's not back until tomorrow and this can't wait.' She fiddles with her phone then holds it up for me to see. It's my selfie to Nan. 'Can you explain this please?' she asks. Her hand is shaking but her voice is calm, like she's asking for help with the TV.

I lean closer for a better look. My dress is too tight but at least I nearly got the damn thing on. 'How did you get this photo?'

'That's not important.' She shoves the phone centimetres in front of my nose. 'But this is!'

I don't know why she's in such a mood when she should be congratulating me on all my hard work.

'You're far too thin!'

I blow up the image and still don't know what she's talking about. *Too thin? Not in this lifetime.*

'Okay, so I've lost a bit of weight ...'

'A bit? Look at your arms in this photo!' She waves the phone in front of me again. 'Then look ...' She studies the photos under the glass tabletop, quickly settling on one.

'Here.'

It's a photo of me after school ended last year. I'm wearing a sky-blue tank top that would look half decent if my arms weren't so enormous.

'Can you see the difference?' she asks.

I'm not sure what she's looking at, or looking for. All I see is a fat girl in a blue top.

She sighs loudly, studying my selfie again. 'Look at your ribs, they're practically poking through.'

I pretend to study the photo then pass back her phone. 'That's because I bought the wrong dress size,' I insist, which is technically true.

'Harley, I'm not an idiot so please stop treating me like one.'

I can feel the heat of her glare.

'I know you switched sizes. If you can't see it in this photo, then take off your jacket right now and I'll show you.'

My mind is racing. My head hurts and it feels like my blood has stopped moving. There's no way I'm taking off my jacket.

That's not even the issue. Nan is. Somehow Mum has found the texts. She's going to think I've gone off the deep end. But Nan's here, I know it.

'I thought Nan might want to see my formal dress,' I try to explain, 'so I sent her a selfie.'

A look flashes across Mum's face that's too fast for me to process.

She places her hand on mine. 'Honey, you do realise Nan is gone, don't you?'

I try to calm my breath before speaking. 'Mum, I know this is going to sound a bit out there,' I start off, biting the dead skin off my lip. 'I know Nan's *body* isn't here, but in some weird way that I can't really explain, her spirit's here, helping me.'

Mum's tears fall silently.

'It's okay, Mum, I know it's hard for you too,' I tell her, patting her shoulder in a rare show of support. 'When Nan started texting me a while back, I didn't know what to think either.'

I show her my phone, scrolling through the thread with all the messages, but she turns away, blowing her nose long and hard.

'And just yesterday at her house I found a sign that said "Nan's Garden". Did you put it there?'

'No.'

'Neither did I. See?'

Mum pulls out another phone from her handbag, this one smaller and older. I'd recognise Nan's cover anywhere: clear with mini watermelon slices. She fiddles with it for a few moments then calls up the same thread.

'Harley, Nan's not texting you.' She shows me the screen. 'I am.'

If there's a giant rug in life, someone's just pulled it out from under me. Top is bottom, left is right. My eyes don't work properly and I'm pretty sure my heart has stopped.

'What? How did you ... why?'

She tries to take my hand, but I snatch it away.

'Honey, I saw you were hurting. We all were,' she starts to explain, but her words don't even make sense. 'Nan was a big presence in all of our lives.'

I can't believe what I'm hearing. There's a lump the size of a golf ball in my throat. I open my mouth to speak but nothing comes out. There are too many thoughts in my head.

'So, you thought you'd pretend to be her,' I finally manage to say, 'and that'd help me how?'

'I'm so sorry,' she tries to convince me, 'I never wanted to hurt you.'

Sorry? What is wrong with her? Does she think a few useless words are suddenly going to make everything better?

'I know what it's like to not want to let go,' Mum says, trying to fill the space with meaningless excuses, as though what she's been doing is normal. 'She was my mother and I loved her.'

She reaches for a tissue. 'Love her,' she corrects, dabbing her eyes.

I don't say anything because there's nothing to say. And because I want her to hurt like I do.

She takes a deep breath before speaking. 'Do you know I've been to your grandmother's house every few weeks or so, going through her belongings, trying to work out what to keep and what to get rid of?'

So *Mum* is the one moving things around.

'And I know you've been spending time there,' she tells me.

'Yeah, so?'

Her exhale is so deep it comes out as a groan. 'I spend most of the afternoon just sitting there, crying. Over simple things like a newspaper clipping, or an old photo or her favourite recipe. I see her in everything. I can't even bring myself to step into her garden. I want to but I'm not ready yet.' She's staring into her teacup like she's lost something in it. 'I went to the phone shop to cancel her account months ago,' she continues. 'And the poor manager, he tried to busy himself, waiting for me to stop crying. It's hard to explain but I felt like I was somehow cancelling my mother.'

She peers over the mug when she sips again but I just stare. I'm numb.

'So, I kept Nan's phone,' she continues, 'figuring I'd tuck it away in a drawer just till, I don't know, I was ready to deal with her not being here anymore.' She brushes her fingers against the teacup handle as though she's playing the harp. 'Then your message came through. *Are you there?* or something like that. That's when I realised you were struggling as much as I was. And then another message, *Send me a sign.* I can't even remember what was going through my head, but when I replied I think in some odd way I was trying to stay connected to my mother ... and maybe to you too.'

I replay each of Nan's messages in my mind, remembering how they gave me so much comfort, always saying the right thing, coming at the right time. But those were Mum's words, not Nan's.

For the first time I see Mum, really *see* her. She's a woman who had hopes and dreams, who put her husband's career before her own, a woman whose marriage has broken down. A woman who has lost her mother. Suddenly, everything I thought I knew about her no longer seems real.

'Honey, I'm worried about you. I see how much you're hurting over Nan, but it's taking over your life. It's like you're pulling away from everyone and everything.' She grabs my hand before I have a chance to yank it away.

'I want you to see someone.'

I manage to squirm free. 'Who?'

'A psychologist. Someone who specialises in eating disorders.'

Suddenly all the sympathy I feel for her vanishes. 'You're the one pretending to be my dead grandmother!' I shout, jumping up from the table. 'If anyone needs help, it's you!'

Mum flinches. Her eyes are huge with shock. 'I'm not sick, Harley. I'm grieving and you are too.'

She drops her face in her hands, her shoulders shuddering, and I know what's coming.

As I near the front door, I hear Mum's tears explode.

CHAPTER 30

Pulling Up Weeds

Falling down is not a failure.
Failure comes when you stay where you have fallen.
(Socrates)

When I get to Nan's house I can finally breathe. This day already seems like a week. I need silence, space. I manifest a life where Mum's not at me all the time. I pull out my phone, knowing all the buzzing is her, as if overkill will motivate me to reply. Buried in the *Mum*s is a message from Talia, who still hasn't learned the meaning of *Give up.*

For a moment, I feel sorry for Talia. Then I think back to the beginning of the year. How she came back from Italy with this I'm-better-than-you vibe. How she practically told me I was fat. How she's so obsessed with being popular that she took topless pics that probably half the guys in town have seen. How she's a stuck-up, two-faced liar.

I hit delete.

Just pulling up weeds, as Nan would say.

When the notification comes up, my first thought is to ignore it – something tells me it can't be good – but I click on the group page anyway. Judging by the photos, there must have been a sale at the Ugly Shop: shiny, trashy, metallic seems to be in, and sequins. Lots of them. Until the very end, when the most beautiful dress loads onto the screen.

My dress.

The comments keep coming.

Stunner.

Wow! Amaaaazing. Queen of the ball.

Simple but elegant.

Paris replies to each one with a <3.

My head starts to throb, a dull pain right behind my eyes. Just when my wish list was about to come true, everything is falling apart. Carter's not going to the formal. Mum's pretending to be Nan. Paris just bought my dress.

Just when I think my life couldn't be worse, I close my eyes and the backlog rears its ugly head. The ruined bake-off. Falling out with Talia. The pledge against Griff. The musical fail. Eden's party.

I didn't manifest this shit.

I make my way to the bathroom where I hardly recognise myself in the mirror: bloodshot eyes, broken capillaries on my cheeks and nose, chapped lips. There are countless pill bottles and blister packs in the medicine cabinet but no Panadol. I grab the tablets that look like the ones Nan always took for her migraines. The directions say, *Take one at bedtime.* I pop two. That ought to get rid of this headache.

I step out into garden, thinking some light exercise will help my head. Within three steps I'm frozen to the spot. My brain switches to pause while my thoughts try to catch up. My pulse is deafening and I can't breathe.

Nan's garden is dead. Totally dead.

The bushes are dry and woody. The azalea buds have shrivelled after a brief moment of glory. The camellia buds have dropped to the ground, surrounding the trees with a cream and mauve skirt. Even the supposedly hardy Japanese maple is sagging towards the ground as if weeping.

How could this have happened?

I check the irrigation lines and they're still intact.

All that time, wasted.

When I check the in-ground sprinklers they're bone dry. Then I remember something so obvious that I can't believe it never entered my head before. Nan's garden is irrigated by rainwater, collected off her roof. I haven't checked the rain tank. Ever. But I don't need to. I know it's empty.

I'm such an idiot.

I just want the pain to go away. I pop two more of Nan's tablets.

<hr>

My eyelids flutter like they have a mind of their own as the darkness slowly gives way to colour. Everything is patchy, distorted, as though I'm peering through lace. When I squint, I can just make out the shape of the birdbath and the trunk of a tree.

My head huuuuuuurts! I'm not sure if I think it or say it. My voice sounds detached – a low, long groan. I'm dreaming. A glass is being held to my lips but it slices straight through, blood shooting everywhere, a cut inside me that's still unstitched. I hear a voice, it's getting louder, more urgent.

'Come on, Harley! HARLEY!' A bright light flickers in my eyes. A second later it dims and I recognise the figure.

'Griff?' I hear the quiver in my voice. My hand isn't working properly, but I manage to bring the glass to my lips, checking my arms and face but there's no blood.

Am I dreaming?

I lock onto his watery, dark brown eyes, flecked with gold like a melted Crunchie.

'At your service.' He slumps against the stone wall with a massive sigh. 'You scared the crap out of me, Harls.'

I can't keep my eyes open. 'Sooooorrrrryyyy.'

'The front door was open but I couldn't find you anywhere. Then I looked out the window and saw you lying on the patio. What the hell happened?'

'I don't know, all I remember is feeling dizzy. I must've passed out.' My face feels funny, like my jaw's out of whack. 'What are you doing here, anyway?' I ask, opening my eyes when my brain finally kicks in.

'Looking for you.'

'Why?'

'Because I texted you all day and you didn't answer. Then when I went to your house, your mum said you ran off after a big fight.'

I try to smile. 'You'd make a good detective.'

The corners of Griff's mouth turn up ever so slightly. His smile isn't perfect, like Carter's. It's natural. Real. The little gap between his front teeth has closed up. Did he get braces this year and I didn't even notice?

'Griff?'

'Yeah?'

'But how'd you know I was *here*?' I try to sit up, changing my mind when the yard starts spinning.

'I figured you'd come here to hang out with your nan. You know, like when I go to The Mount to spend time with my mum.'

A sharp pain shoots from one side of my head to the other, but this time no amount of rubbing offers relief.

'Headache?' he asks.

I nod. 'Hard to believe after all those tablets.'

'What tablets?'

I shrug. 'The ones I found in Nan's medicine cabinet.'

He opens his mouth to speak but doesn't say anything.

'Oh, here they are,' I tell him, finding the bottle in my pocket. I don't remember putting it there.

He studies the label, letting out a deep sigh. 'These are painkillers, really strong ones.' His face is dead serious. 'Shit, Harls, you can't go around self-medicating.'

I laugh even though I don't mean to. 'Okay, doctor.'

He looks at me for ages and I wonder when he's going to speak.

He finally says, 'Remember when I disappeared over school holidays earlier this year?'

I can barely remember this afternoon let alone over six months ago, but vague memories resurface. 'Yeah, kind of.'

'Well, I was at Glendale.'

My brain snaps to attention. 'The psych hospital?'

'Yep,' he mutters, drumming his fingers on his knees.

I'm not sure if he's thinking of what to say next or waiting for me to speak. 'But why?'

His head is down like he's having a conversation with the floor. 'When Mum died I wasn't coping well so the doctor put me on meds.'

'Like those?' I ask, nodding to Nan's bottle.

He studies the bottle again. 'Mine were different. They were for depression.'

My thoughts are too jumbled to find their way out. Finally, I manage to ask, 'Did the meds help?'

He shrugs. 'I was feeling like a piece of me broke off, and they helped with that. The edges didn't feel so raw.'

So many thoughts are lurking in my head. Griff's mum

dying. Nan dying. Griff struggling. Me struggling. Hot tears roll down my face, burning my skin.

'But I don't get it. Why were you at Glendale *this* year?'

He blinks a few times and I wonder if it's some sort of code. My stomach is cramping but I'm not sure why.

'I went off the meds at the end of last year,' he starts to explain, 'and I was feeling much better. Then school started back and, before I knew it, I was back in a dark place again. And it scared me.'

He stares into space for what seems like an eternity but his eyes soon find mine. 'It was my decision to go. Dad's been great, supporting me every step of the way.'

I let his words wash over me. How could I not know this was happening? 'And you're better now?'

'Better than before,' he says, 'but not as good as I'd like to be.'

I try to get up but can't. 'I'm glad you told me.' He pulls me to my feet, his movements slow, mirroring mine. 'I know that couldn't have been easy.'

My headache kicks into overdrive and the dizziness strikes again. Griff holds out his arm to steady me. 'You okay, Harls? You don't look so good.'

I survey the garden, hoping it was just a dream. But the wall of brown around me says otherwise.

Everything's gone. All the blooms have died off. There are no buds left, no potential life. No colour. The climbers have stopped climbing, their shrivelled leaves bordering the trellis. The air is thick with dirt.

The *Nan's Garden* sign is poking out of the dry bed.

My tears come again, this time, so quickly and freely they startle me. And Griff.

'What's wrong?' he asks, throwing his arm around my

shoulder. His grip feels strong and certain.

'I can't do anything right,' I tell him, trying to catch my breath between sobs. 'I worked so hard, trying to make Nan proud. You remember how much she loved the garden?'

Griff nods.

'Now everything's dead. I'm going to smash that sign,' I tell him. 'Because this isn't Nan's garden anymore. She'd be too ashamed to call it hers.'

I stand up but don't get very far. The pavers sway left to right like I'm riding a wave.

'You need to take it easy,' Griff says, guiding me to the chair near the maple tree. 'Your nan would be super proud of you even if the garden needs a bit of ...' he takes a moment to survey the scrappy surrounds, 'attention.'

'The good thing about plants is they're resilient,' he adds with sudden energy in his voice.

He grabs the clippers and works his way around the bed, snipping the native grass to a stump, then the dried blooms from a few shrubs.

'You just need to trim here and get rid of the dead growth,' he explains, kneeling beside Nan's winter daphnes. 'A snip here and there, sometimes a bit deeper.'

The smooth cut of the stalk is bright green. New life waiting to blossom.

He crumples the leafy mix, scattering it around the roots. 'The dead bits make good mulch.'

Griff knows a lot about things. Less about people.

'But there's no water in the tank,' I remind him.

'That's okay. We just need to switch from the tank to the mains. The sensor's probably busted.'

When Griff says it, it sounds easy.

'And please leave my sign alone,' he insists.

'Your sign?'

'Yeah, I saw it in a garden shop and thought you'd like it. Looks homemade, right?'

A cool breeze kicks in but I feel warm inside. For the first time in a long time, I let my worries go. I close my eyes, knowing sleep is only moments away.

———

When I open my eyes, it's already dark. Griff's sitting on the grass, opposite me, rocking back and forth slightly. 'Do you know you talk in your sleep?'

'Huh? Really?'

He nods.

'What'd I say?'

'Carter.' He abandons rocking for foot tapping. 'Four times.'

'Oh.' I can feel Griff's eyes drift back to me. My mind is blank then I remember the formal. And Carter's words: *Too bad I'm gonna miss it.* 'I just thought we were going to the formal together, but that's not going to happen.'

'Why's that?'

'Because he won't be here,' I tell him, feeling the tears come again.

The brief silence lapses into a long, awkward moment.

Griff finally speaks. 'Well, I know I'm not Carter and I can't dance for shit ...' he starts off, fiddling with the cord of his hoodie, 'but I'll go with you to the formal. I mean, if you want to.'

'You will?' My heart skips a few beats. Probably the pills. 'You're not going with Addy?'

I can't read his lopsided grin.

'Why would I be going with Addy?'

'I thought you were friends. *Good friends.*'

He seems confused. 'She's nice, I guess, but ...'

'Didn't she plus-one you for Eden's party?'

His face tells me I'm not making any sense.

'Nup,' he offers just so I'm sure. 'It's just that I heard you raced out right before the show was over.'

I'd do anything to forget that night.

'So I went over to your house. But before I got there, I spotted you across the road, swinging a wine bottle.'

My cheeks feel hot.

'And I thought that couldn't be good,' he continues. 'So I followed you and snuck into Eden's party.' He hesitates. 'To make sure you were okay.'

The party. Griff and me, under the tree. Together.

Even in the dim light I can see Griff's blushing. I wonder if he's thinking about our kiss too.

I throw my arms around his neck, squeezing him tight. I feel his hand on my back; short, quick pats, like he's tapping a code, then slow, tentative strokes soon relaxing into an easy rhythm.

'Hey, early warning,' I tell him. 'You have to have at least *one* dance with me.' I can feel his whole body tense. 'It *is* a dance that we're going to,' I remind him, pulling back to look him in the eye, 'the point being that people *dance.*'

He leans against the stone wall with a loud sigh. 'Wish I'd paid attention in that social dance class last year.' He looks at me and smiles. 'But sure, why not?'

'Promise?'

He holds out his little finger, lacing it with mine for a pinkie promise, like we used to in kindergarten. I reach over for another hug, relaxing into the rhythm of his heartbeat.

He smells like hot chips and eucalypt and I smile, thinking those two scents hardly go together, then I realise they do. Because that's Griff. And that makes me realise how much I've missed talking to him. Missed *him*. I want to tell him about Mum and Dad splitting up, Talia turning feral, Mum pretending to be Nan and all the other crap in my life – maybe he could make sense of it. I want to tell him how sorry I am about everything I've done to him, about how I miss the way we used to be together.

I will, soon. I promise myself I will.

CHAPTER 31

State of Flux

*Happiness does not consist in pastimes and
amusements but in virtuous activities.*
(Aristotle)

When I get to school, I feel like a spectator. Manifesting is overrated. I'm just going to watch the last week of the school year gently unfold, let the universe come to me for a change.

The buzz of the formal is in the air. Thirty-four hours and counting. I try to muster enthusiasm but I can't. I'm relieved Griff is going. So why do I feel disappointed?

On the upside, I finally get to wear the dress I've practically tortured myself to fit into. And I haven't had a night out since Eden's party. Part of me is too afraid; the other part has nowhere to go.

Every day it's the same old thing: Rev, breakfast (boiled egg), school and lunch (two nuts and an apple), another Rev, gym, Nan's house to check the garden. Then back home for dinner (a small piece of chicken, broccoli if I want a treat), schoolwork, sleep. *Yawn.*

From my locker I watch cliques that formed long ago, groups that Mum said were around even in her day: freaks and geeks, learning-support kids, kids who don't speak English at home, greenies and goths. That's because school's a germ pool, where the genetically superior have a special immunity. They grow stronger while the weaklings orbit them like insects with broken wings, latching on to each other in random clusters. Anything to avoid being alone.

My mind drifts back to the opening scenes on the first day of the school year: Talia and I collapsing into each other with laughter, waiting for our bus, excited about the year ahead – a year when anything seemed possible. This year turned out to be a scavenger hunt, a maze of obstacles and challenges with the promise of a treasure. But there's no map. Or compass. I'm meant to be starring in my best year yet but it's like I'm an NPC, stuck in a crap video game. And no one pays attention to non-playable characters.

The temperature is cold and crisp, like winter came back for one last hurrah. But I seem to be the only one feeling the cold. Everyone's running around in short sleeves.

The sound of girls chattering carries like the annoying wind chimes Mum hung on our deck last summer. I feel a headache coming on. Eden bursts out of the group like a meteor, her brightness boring a hole in her satellite of admirers.

'Harley, aren't you boiling in that?' She nods to my jumper, darting off before I can even reply.

Stu's doing a handstand walk along the retaining wall. Ty's causing chaos, unable to control his longboard. Paris is using her locker mirror to perfect her eyeliner flick. Addy and Sydney are giggling over their keep cups near the canteen. I track everyone's movements but don't feel a thing – except my head throbbing.

With three minutes to the bell, I sprint around the corner

to Carter's locker, desperate to say goodbye, even though I'm thinking, *Thanks so much for ruining the formal for me.* The launch of New Harley is on hold till further notice.

None of my hard work means anything without Carter at my side.

I turn the corner to find Carter fiddling with his padlock, looking fine, as always, in his navy pleated pants and striped shirt. I lock in his magnificent face and body, morphing them ten years forward, like the drawings police use to track long-lost children. The future version's even better than the original.

'Bon voyage!' I call out as I near his locker. It takes so much energy to sound happy and light that I'm exhausted by the time I get there.

He flings his locker open and rests his arm on the door. 'Sorry?'

'Your trip!' Within seconds, my heart goes from racing to pounding in my ears. 'Aren't you cutting out at lunchtime?'

He stares at me for a few seconds without saying anything.

Something's not adding up.

'Oh sorry, thought I told you. Change of plans.'

I lean against the locker alongside his, waiting for the punchline.

'Trip's off,' he announces with a shrug.

My past, present and future come together in this moment. I can't find any words.

'You okay?' he asks, squeezing my shoulder.

My head is tingling but I manage to nod.

'I, uh, just realised I never handed in my subject selections.' As if I could be bothered thinking about next year. I'm lying so much lately that I'm not ever sure what I'm saying. 'So …

you're *not* going overseas?'

'Nah, Dad's work thing got cancelled so Mom said we'll go in April instead.'

'So, you *are* going to the formal?'

He grabs a bag of chips, taking his time to close his locker door. 'Yeah, I guess so.' He turns to me but there's something different about him – a sparkle in his eye, perhaps a hint of nerves. This is it, I can feel it.

His perfect lips break into a smile. 'Hey, we should go together ... I mean, if you're not already going with someone.'

I blink. 'No, I'm not,' I say, trying to act casual while inside I'm doing cartwheels, a backflip then a double round-off. 'Going with anyone, that is. So sure, I'd love to go.'

The second Carter walks off, I pull out my phone and message Griff:

ur off the hook for formal!

Carter not going o'seas. thx anyway! H xx

Then I message Talia for the first time in months.

Mission accomplished.

Dr Kanter is her usual bubbly self, like she can't wait to get stuck into all things philosophical.

'Okay, everyone, we've covered a lot of ground this term. We've talked about theories of knowledge and existence and notions of the good life. So, as the school year comes to an end, I thought it only fitting to focus on something more up your alley,' she tells us with a smile. 'Happiness.'

'Finally, something I can relate to,' Stu says, and everyone laughs.

'Of course, we can't do that without visiting our good

friend, Aristotle.' Dr Kanter chuckles, holding up her hands to stifle our groans. 'You'll be pleased to know Aristotle considered the pursuit of happiness to be the ultimate purpose of life.'

'That's my philosophy,' Eden calls out.

'But Aristotle didn't define happiness in terms of status or wealth,' Dr Kanter continues.

'So, it's a state of mind, like, I'm happy when my footy team wins?' Stu asks. He actually seems interested.

'Which is never,' Ty adds, punching his arm.

'Happiness, or *eudaimonia,* as the Greeks called it, is living your life well,' she explains. 'Aristotle defined it as *an activity of the soul in accordance with virtue.*'

'And that means?' asks Paris.

'It means living a life of balance rather than one of excess,' Dr Kanter replies. 'To put it in everyday language, happiness is having your act together and living up to your full potential.'

Paris breaks into a smile. 'Aristotle sounds a lot like my mother.'

'And the list of virtues is quite exhaustive,' Dr Kanter continues, 'things like friendship, honesty, temperance, self-respect, courage, patience, modesty ...'

'No wonder Talia's never happy,' Addy snipes, eliciting a chorus of *oohs.*

'Who's Talia?' Paris calls out and everyone laughs.

A small part of me wants to speak up, to defend Talia when she's not here to do the job herself. But what's there to say?

I'm not sure what happiness looks like, or what my full potential is, but I know Carter's a key part of it.

The bell rings, underlining the thought.

When I get home, Mum can tell straight away that this is the best day of my life. We've hardly spoken the past month. I'm still pissed off at her for pretending to be Nan, but I'm calling a truce ... till after the formal, at least.

'Harley, my goodness, I haven't seen such a spring in your step for months. Good day at school?'

I pluck an apple from the fruit bowl. *Great* day,' I tell her, sinking my teeth in.

She wraps her teabag around a spoon, squeezing the last drops into her cup. 'What happened? Did you get an A on your Philosophy assessment?'

'Better!'

'Wow, an A+?'

'No, Carter asked me to the formal!' I do a little Irish jig around the kitchen bench then run up to give her a hug.

'Really?' She's not nearly as excited as she should be. 'I thought he was heading overseas,' she says, bringing her cup to the table.

'He was,' I start to explain, following her, 'but they pushed back their trip.'

'I thought you were going with Griff.'

My sigh is louder than intended. I'm sure I already explained this to her at least twice. 'That was only a backup plan,' I explain. 'He didn't really want to go.'

She sips her tea, taking time to speak. 'Are you sure? What did he say?'

I shrug, taking another bite of my apple. 'Nothing yet. I just messaged him on my way home.'

Her eyes open wide. 'The formal's in two days and you ditched him in a message?'

'For God's sake, Mum, it's not like it was a *date*.'

When I close my eyes, I can feel the sensation of Griff's lips on mine, lost in a moment where anything seemed possible. But the face is Carter's. 'No offence, Mum, but you're the last person who should be giving me *relationship* advice, seeing as how you and Dad hate each other.'

Mum's body jerks. 'We don't hate each other, Harley,' she insists. 'What makes you think that?'

'Well, you live here and Dad lives somewhere else,' I say, like it's a no-brainer. 'And when he was here, you were always fighting.'

She tries to wave me away.

'I heard you fighting, Mum. So did Luke.'

'Harley, life gets complicated when you're older. Relationships get complicated. People your age are falling in and out of love every other day, but that head-over-heels feeling doesn't last forever.'

'Thanks so much, Mum. The boy I've been madly in love with all year has finally asked me out and you're already ruining the moment. Why can't you ever be happy for me?'

Mum's shoulders slump. 'I *am* happy for you, but, honey, love isn't about hooking up with the hot guy.'

I can't stifle my groan.

'I'm serious,' she insists. There's concern etched into her features. 'Love is being best friends. Love is having a history, a story. Love is making each other laugh.'

'Even when there's nothing to laugh about?'

'*Especially* when there's nothing to laugh about.'

I think for a moment, not sure how much I want to know, and how much she wants to say, but I ask anyway. 'Are you ever going to forgive Dad?'

Mum's eyebrows knit together. 'Forgive him? For what?'

'For having an affair.' Of course Dad denied it, but I know it's true.

Now Mum's eyebrows are unnaturally high. I can't believe she doesn't know.

'I have no idea where you got that from,' she says, 'but it's not true.' She takes a deep breath before continuing. 'Sometimes people just drift apart and need the time and space to figure out what they mean to each other, to remember why they fell in love in the first place.'

I'm getting this sick feeling that I've been blaming Dad all year for something he didn't do.

'There's something else I want to tell you,' Mum adds, 'something you need to know.'

She holds my gaze, but instead of looking away, I feel strangely connected, like we're on the same side.

'Yes?' my voice cracks.

'You need to know that it's easy to lose your sense of self in a relationship, to put everyone's needs before your own,' she tries to explain. 'And you need to know that when you feel lost and don't know who you are anymore then it's time to roll up your sleeves and get to work to find yourself again.'

'Is that what you did?'

'That's what I'm doing now.'

She grabs my hand and squeezes it tight. I squeeze hers even tighter.

CHAPTER 32

Freefalling

Blessed are the hearts that can bend;
they shall never be broken.
(Albert Camus)

Finally, the moment I've been waiting for all year is here.

Mount Pleasant High is unrecognisable. The entire building has been transformed, thanks to colourful projections that illuminate the brick façade, which is throbbing to the beat of an electronic-loving DJ.

Talia the text-stalker is pissed that she's been banned from the formal but rather than deal with it, she's trying to make me miserable too. Her latest message, timed for maximum impact on the ride over here: *Carter doesn't like you.* I so want to say, *Hello? Who's alongside me right now?* I try to relax with Carter in the back of his dad's fancy car, like I'm meant to on the best night of my life. But I can't do it, I can't let her words go unanswered, so I call up the video from Eden's party on my phone instead. I don't even remember taking it – maybe it was an accident and that's why the whole thirty-six seconds are of Eden's boots, but the audio's there ... Eden hissing, *I don't give two shits what that little slut thinks*, telling me Talia's the one who sent her nudes to everyone and let Ty take the fall. I hit send.

Carter and I walk up the steps together and my stomach flips anticipating Eden's reaction. I wish Talia wasn't suspended just so I could see the look on her face.

I can already imagine the girls' fake tans, fluorescent nails and skanky dresses. I do my best to push these thoughts away. Carter, the ideal boyfriend, is at my side and that's all that matters.

Tonight is the night my wish list comes true.

The moment we enter the hall we're transported to a magical winter wonderland, thanks to the planning committee quickly getting around my theme.

There's so much to take in. Every surface glistens in white, with touches of silver for added sparkle. Large stone pots filled with white hibiscus are placed strategically, creating intimate nooks without compromising the dance space.

At the back of the hall, clusters of tabletop candles in alternating sizes emit a warm glow, forming a romantic skyline.

'Cool,' Carter says, taking it all in.

Dr Kanter glides through the crowd, a standout in a floral-patterned cocktail dress that fits in with the season.

'I dance, therefore I am,' Ty calls out and she laughs.

I undo my wrap and fold it over my arm, eager to show off my dress. I love the feel of the organza. It's sheer and flowing and shorter than I'm used to, but still offers enough structure to flatter my shape while hiding my flaws. Mum nearly fainted when I walked into the family room tonight, wearing her old dress. I found it at the very back of Nan's wardrobe. Who would have thought I'd ever fit into it?

There's an unspoken rule. Girls should judge themselves by the reaction of other girls, and if the open-mouthed stares and roomful of eyes on me are any indication, I must look shit hot. I smile, meeting their gazes, chin up like I'm working the red carpet.

Carter spots Stu in the crowd and makes his way over to him. He walks away, taking all my confidence with him.

The voice is low and rough, like gravel. *Couldn't wait to ditch you, could he? Probably on the hunt for some skinny chick instead.*

I push the voice back down, determined to ignore it, but when I look around the hall, everyone's talking, dancing, laughing. Except me. Sydney and Paris walk over, looking shocked, probably because I'm here with Carter. Being alone is better than listening to their mindless chatter, but it's too late.

'Are you okay?' Sydney asks, her hand on my arm, offering her best I-care-about-you look.

'Uh, *yeah*,' I tell her, nodding in Carter's direction.

She just stands there, her eyes narrowing slightly like she doesn't believe me. Paris nods, though no one's saying anything.

It's time to state the obvious. 'Look, I know a lot of girls will be gutted that Carter's here with me,' I start off, wondering if they'll pick up the hint. 'I see everyone staring …'

'Harls,' Sydney cuts in, her eyes drilling right through me, 'everyone's staring because they're worried about you.'

'Yeah, you look sick,' Paris says. 'Really sick.'

For a second, I feel their words start to crush me, but I've come too far to let that happen. They are *not* going to ruin my night.

When the opening chords to 'Runaway' announce themselves, I push past a gawking Paris and Sydney, squealing, 'I love this song!'

I quicken my steps, my body tingling with anticipation from head to toe, desperate to find Carter.

Addy is slinking around the DJ who's busy mixing the tracks and seems unimpressed by her try-hard moves.

Then, the voice I've been waiting for. 'Want to dance?'

Carter takes my hand and leads me to the dance floor before I can even say *Yes*! He places his left hand on my hip like it belongs there and pulls me close, our bodies the perfect fit. I rest my head against his chest, admiring my gorgeous corsage – dark purple irises with sprigs of lavender and baby's breath. His heart's beating as fast as mine.

We glide around the dance floor and I'm so lost in the moment, in Carter, in the whole idea of him, that I don't even worry when I step on his foot a few times.

'Just follow my lead,' he whispers.

I try to clear my head, to banish all the doubt, the fear, the sadness this year. That's the price I had to pay to be here tonight. With Carter.

We ease into a rhythm, somehow making our way around the crowded dance floor without bumping into anyone. It takes a few moments to disentangle when the song comes to an end, like he doesn't want to let go either.

'Caaaaarter!'

The voice cuts through me like glass and I try to ignore it. But it gets louder and closer. That's when I realise it's coming from the dance floor. Carter's eyes lock on the far side of the hall.

A slim brunette is running towards me. She's beautiful, an angel in a slinky, strapless Mediterranean-blue dress. Her luscious long hair, the colour of whisky, sweeps around her shoulders with each bounding step. By the time I open my mouth to speak, Carter has already stepped between us. She leaps into his arms, kissing him passionately, their mouths hungry and urgent.

I can't breathe. The music's thumping so hard even my bones are vibrating, sending a loud reverb through my ears and jaw. My feet won't move and I'm forced to watch Carter and the girl embrace for an eternity. Her long, lean legs wrap around his waist as they circle the dance floor. The music is cranked, the beat gripping me hard. Strobes flash in sync with the song, ribbons of light tying them together. When they finally come up for air, Carter catches my eye and smiles, taking the girl's hand as they approach.

'Harley,' he says, his gaze quickly shifting to her. 'This is my girlfriend, Daisy.'

My head is on the verge of exploding. I didn't manifest this. But Tiktok did. *Daisy.*

'Nice to meet you, Harper,' Daisy leans in to say.

'It's Harley,' I croak, numb with shock.

'Sorry, it's hard to hear anything in here,' she shouts in a strong American accent, both hands over her ears. 'I just flew in so I'm a bit zoned.'

'A surprise visit,' Carter says, clearly shocked.

I can't speak. The room is spinning as the music fades out. So much for breaking up.

'Babe, you know I wouldn't miss your prom for anything,' Daisy giggles, throwing her arms around his neck. He leans in for a kiss, their bodies pressed so close that I can't tell where he ends and she begins.

I close my eyes, praying that this is a bad dream, but when I open them, the nightmare's still unfolding. Carter and Daisy are fused together, swaying to the song that he and I should be dancing to. The room buzzes with hushed whispers. More couples step onto the dance floor, leaving me at the fringe, an outcast. I watch connections form all around me. Some new, others rekindled.

Carter and Daisy.

The Year of Harley is over before it even started.

I spy rows of drinks on the table, amazed the school sprang for glass, and scull one, hoping it's spiked. The emptiness grows deeper and deeper. My skin's cold, but I'm burning up. The room starts to spin again. A raw, menacing shriek, like an animal at the point of capture, erupts. Mine.

'Harley, oh my God, you're bleeding!' Eden cries, appearing from nowhere. She takes my hand, gently easing the jagged shard from my grip, while Sydney picks up the broken glass at my feet. 'What were you thinking?'

I scream again, a primal rage so potent that it silences the hall in one breath. No one takes a step. Even the air doesn't move. I race to the toilet and stick my hand under the tap, watching the water turn red as blood seeps from the gash. When I look in the mirror, I see a grim-faced Dr Kanter standing behind me, first-aid kit in hand.

'Harley, are you all right?'

My eyes flood with tears. 'Yeah, I'm okay,' I whimper, even though I'm light years from okay. I don't recognise my voice. It sounds small, distant.

She inspects my hand, carefully blotting the wound before disinfecting and bandaging it. 'I don't think you'll need stitches, but keep this on for ... Girls, not now!' she shouts when Eden and Sydney burst through the doorway. 'Give us a few minutes.'

I rest my other hand on the edges of the sink to stop the room from spiralling out of control. In the mirror my hair has a life of its own, my eyes are smudged and my skin's flushed, red patches breaking through my contouring.

'Harley, I've watched you all year,' Dr Kanter starts off, talking to me in the mirror like a hairdresser. My head fills with scenes from that creepy movie where the teacher's obsessed with her student, but that doesn't seem like her thing. 'Something's changed in you. You might not see it but I do.'

With a trembling hand, I try to touch up the foundation above my cheekbones, but it flakes. My 'waterproof' mascara is anything but, judging from my panda eyes. Blotches of broken blood vessels are dotted across my face and neck. The concealer stick is even worse. It seems to have accentuated my flaws rather than hiding them. The peachy tint isn't even close to my complexion.

'I couldn't put my finger on it with those shapeless uniforms,' Dr Kanter continues.

I bite the dead skin off my lips and reapply my lipstick, but the colour's too bright. I may as well be wearing clown make-up.

Dr Kanter places her hands on my shoulders. 'But now, seeing you tonight in this dress, I know.'

'Know what?' I ask, finally meeting her gaze.

'That you're wasting away.' She tightens her grip, forcing me to confront my reflection. 'Open your eyes, Harley.'

I don't know what her problem is. Sure, I've lost some weight but she's making it sound like I'm skin and bones.

'You're dangerously thin, Harley,' she says, her gaze shifting from my face to the bruises on the back of my arms. 'Your body's deteriorating, struggling to repair itself. You're lacking nutrition.'

I snap my evening bag shut. 'Well, my dad's a scientist and knows health stuff. If I was sick, don't you think he would've said something?'

Dad's words flood back. *You're so ... thin.* And Mum's. And Griff's. And Luke's. But I don't have time to think about any of that right now.

'Harley, my sister almost died from starving herself,' Dr Kanter says. 'We didn't realise how sick she was until it was nearly too late.'

I'm sorry about Dr Kanter's sister and all but I'm already feeling like shit and I don't see why she's trying to bring me down even more.

'Is this a life of balance, Harley?' she asks, her eyes urgent. 'Is this expressing your full potential?'

My heart is racing in my chest and the entire year flashes before me. Every conversation with Carter, every laugh, every gesture. The girl in the mirror mocks me.

How could you be so stupid?

How could you think Carter liked you?

How could you think anyone would like you?

I want to run up to Carter and ask him why he led me on. But perception gives way to reality. He never kissed me or tried to hold my hand. He never promised me anything. He never said he was into me. It's only in this moment that I can see.

I have to get out of here.

'Who *are* you, Harley? That's the question you need to answer!'

The silence is so strong that it nearly has a beat. 'I'm just a girl trying to have fun at her formal,' I insist, focusing on what's important. 'That's who I am.'

I fly out the door and straight into a gigantic white plume poking out of Eden's dress. I thought it'd be a classy number, but it looks like she's wearing a stray chicken. Her shocking pink hair makes her look like My Little Pony.

'God, you're already stumbling and it's not even eight o'clock,' she scoffs, brushing past me. 'Let's not have a repeat of my party.'

A burst of colour flashes in the corner of my right eye. It's shiny and topaz. Talia.

'You bitch,' she screams, lunging at Eden, tackling her to the ground. 'I wasted all year in your shadow, listening to your bullshit.'

Guess she got the video. I can't work out what's more bizarre – the fact that she's showing her face here tonight or that she got dressed up for her wrestling match.

'Get off me, you psycho,' Eden squeals, her hand breaking free to land a few slaps to Talia's head. 'You wasted your own time wanting to be like me!'

Mrs Stevens flies across the room, trying to yank Talia off Eden.

'Leave me alone,' Talia screeches, eluding her grasp.

The battle of the bitches is over but a crowd's building, hoping for an encore. Talia's hair is as wild as her eyes, vaguely resembling a bird's nest, only fitting as she picks Eden's stray feathers from her topaz sequins. Eden is still on the floor, her hair untouched, as though she dipped her head in shellac. She rises with the help of Sydney and, then others, quickly walled off by an army of supporters.

Within seconds Talia's in my face but I brush past, pushing through the crowd, tears stinging my eyes. I'm exposed, an elephant in a cage. Fingers are pointing at me, hushed whispers cutting me down. I stumble, but quickly find my feet, refusing offers of help. I rip the corsage off my wrist. Then I do what any animal does under threat.

I run.

I chase the sunset, covering four blocks in no time, my legs pumping, adrenaline coursing through my veins. There's no one left who understands, no one who can help me. I'm in a race – a race to my future – and I need to shed everything I know, everything I believe is true, to find myself.

The last sliver of light disappears on the horizon, putting the star-freckled sky to sleep under a blanket of grey. But not before the brightest star winks, telling me anything's possible if I don't give up, if I just keep running. The shops whir past, then the primary school and church as the bitumen blurs beneath my stride, propelling me far from the pain, from the humiliation. From everything. Blood's pounding in my ears and I can't catch my breath. Daisy has taken Carter and all the oxygen in the world.

I take off my heels, not even caring if my feet get cut up because nothing can hurt more than my heart right now. The voice is low-pitched, raspy. No matter how fast I run, it's still there, reminding me that I'll never be smart enough, funny enough, pretty enough, thin enough.

When I turn the bend, a house comes into view. It doesn't take me long to realise I'm not running away from something.

I'm running towards someone.

CHAPTER 33

The Clearing

Know thyself.
(Socrates)

I pound on the front door until my knuckles are red raw, but no one answers. Then I remember where the spare key's hidden and let myself in.

'Anyone home?' I call out when I walk through the door. 'Mr Laettner? Griff?' I run from room to room, half expecting to see Griff's father asleep on his favourite recliner but he's not here.

My legs feel as heavy as lead. I grip the handrail, using the landing to catch my breath before scaling the last set of stairs. There's a dim green light from the solar system on Griff's ceiling. The glow-in-the-dark stickers orbit his overhead light, my birthday gift to him so long ago I'm amazed I remember. I wonder if he never got around to taking them down or if he still loves "sleeping under the stars". When I turn on the light, the sparse décor of his room looks straight out of a display home, reminding me how much he needs order in his life.

As I'm about to flick off the light, I spy something on his desk. It's a big book, the type Mum has on our coffee table.

On the front cover there's a baby photo of us, side by side in our bouncers. Underneath, there's a title in elegant script: *The Story of Harley and Griff.*

I open the cover and flick through the pages, each image taking me back to a happier time. Griff and me in our mothers' baby slings on The Mount, at the petting zoo, in the preschool reading corner, playing our recorders, climbing the giant spider web at the park. There's a 'Sport & Rec' section featuring our visits to the zoo, camping trips, pool high-dive adventures, and sandcastle villages at the coast. There's even the first photo that Griff ever took of me. I'm seated at his kitchen table, chocolate icing from his number eight cake smeared all over my face and shirt, my favourite 'Fur-ever' tee with all the puppies. As I turn the pages, the memories draw me into a story that began nearly sixteen years ago.

Last year's Drama trip dominates the double-page spread at the centre of the book. In our theatre seats, just before lights up. Sharing ice cream after the show. Getting lost downtown. Blending in with a streetscape mural. The sunset harbour cruise – me at the front of the boat, arms outstretched, doing my best *Titanic* impression. I look happy. Healthy.

When I turn the page, my stomach twists. The sepia tone is eerie, the photo taking up nearly the whole page. My eyes are puffy and glazed with tears, one of them nearly closed. It looks like it was taken at Nan's funeral, though I don't remember Griff having his camera there. I swallow my emotions, feeling the weight hit my gut. Opposite is a black and white photo, the last time I saw him at The Mount. I don't recognise the girl in the photos. Her eyes are cold and glassy, shutting out light, the images lifeless. She's unrecognisable, a shadow of herself.

Of me.

Pasted to the next page is Griff's poem for English, 'Before You'.

One the last page there is a message. Strange to find it at the back of the book, and not the beginning, but Griff has always done his own thing. His handwriting is neat, as always. I swallow hard but the lump at the base of my throat won't budge.

Dear Harley,

Don't be afraid to fall.

I'll catch you.

Griff x

I leave the book exactly where I found it. How could I not see what's been in front of me all along? Griff's the one who's always been there for me. He's the one who's stayed true to himself. And what did I do? I ditched him. Repeatedly.

Who's Harley?

She's the 'insensitive bitch'.

How could I be so cruel?

I spy the pill bottle on Griff's bedside table and my thoughts instantly turn to Glendale, how I was so absorbed in my own issues that I didn't even know he had depression. Is he better now or the same? I don't know how depression works. I haven't even tried to find out.

That's when an awful realisation hits me. Since that day at Nan's house I've never bothered to follow up, to ask him how he's feeling. I have to tell him sorry – sorry I haven't been there for him. Sorry that this whole year happened. I pull out my phone, amazed I haven't checked it all night. Just before my phone dies, I see his message.

Have fun 2nite. Won't bother u anymore.

The unthinkable hits me. I shake the pill bottle. Empty. I remember his message on the last page of the book. Is he saying ... goodbye?

He wouldn't. Would he?

Dark thoughts are fighting for space in my head. I'll never be able to say sorry. I'll never be able to show him how I truly feel. I'll never be able to make it up to him.

I snatch his torch, flying down the stairs and out the door. I know where he is.

<div align="center">~~~~~~~~~~~~~~~</div>

'Griff? *Griff?*' I sprint into the clearing, the bright beam slashing through the inky blackness. 'Where are you?'

Ribbons of light silhouette our favourite tree.

'Griff? Griff!' I shout again, trying to catch my breath. My heart splits in two. I was sure he'd be here.

Sounds overhead are amplified by my stillness. Tapping, creaking, whispering. Is the tree trying to tell me something?

When I sweep the beam across the trunk, a zap of white light nearly blinds me.

Something's there. On the branch.

Griff's camera strap.

Darkness tightens around me, every murky thought multiplying. When my eyes finally adjust, I spy his jacket, wedged into the base of the tree. I open my mouth to scream, but there's no sound.

The world is spinning but no matter how I claw and clutch, I can't find my way. When I open my mouth this time, the sound is big enough to create a black hole that would suck in the entire universe.

I finally see myself.

My *essence*.

And I see everything I've lost in trying to find it.

There's a rustling noise above, whisperings of leaves carried off by the wind. My feet give way but the tree breaks my fall. Vibrations hum through the trunk.

If I didn't know better, I'd swear the tree was saying my name.

It is.

'Hold on, Harley, I'm coming!' Griff says, as though he's rescuing me. Which he is. I just never realised it until now.

I want to yell at him for scaring me, for making me think he was gone, but I'm too relieved to be angry. The emotions escape in loud, blubbery sobs.

'Grab my hand,' he says, emerging from the dark canopy.

I nod. When our fingers touch, he wraps his hand around mine, lifting me effortlessly to the first branch. I reach up behind him for the next one, hoisting myself higher, climbing instinctively, like when we were kids. I try to be careful, not wanting to wreck Mum's dress, but I know she'd understand if I did.

We make our way to the largest branch that overhangs the clearing like a treetop verandah. I squirm cautiously, trying to squeeze into the opposite limb, creating a nook alongside Griff where I finally rest.

My thoughts are racing. If only I had an off switch for all the chatter in my head this year. Nan dying, Carter monopolising my thoughts, Dad moving out, all that madness with Griff, Talia going off the rails, Eden's party. But none of that seems to matter right now.

'Why aren't you at the formal?' Griff asks.

'Because I'd rather be here.' I aim the torch at his face, trying to read his expression, but he takes it from me. The clearing comes to life in a soft yellow glow.

'What happened? he asks, turning the beam to my hand. Are you hurt?'

'I'll explain later,' I tell him.

His inspects my bandage, stroking it gently. 'You okay?'

I position the torch so I can see his face. 'Yeah, I think so,' I tell him, even though I'm not really sure.

'Are *you* okay?' The words come out so easily that I can't believe it's taken me so long to ask.

'I am.'

Griff's eyes look lighter than usual, the colour of honey. I rest my head on his shoulder and for the first time in a long while, I feel like I can finally breathe.

Wispy clouds hang in the night sky and I trace them like I'm finger-painting. 'Look at all the stars,' I tell him. 'Just like your bedroom.'

'You were in my room?'

'I was looking for you,' I explain.

Suddenly it hits me. The stars. Daisies. *Signs.*

He sighs, straddling the branch to face me but doesn't say anything.

'I love the photo book,' I tell him, and he blushes. Then I notice there's something in his hand. It looks like ... no, it can't be.

'Is that what I think it is?'

He smiles. 'Yeah. You'll probably think this is crazy but sometimes I carry it around with me. You know, as a reminder. He shows me his words:

Take risks.

Make memories.

Help someone.

Griff took a lot of risks this year. Confiding in me about

his depression. Telling me I was too thin. Staying true to himself rather than trying to be just like everyone else.

'I'm still working on the second one,' he says.

I nod. There aren't many good memories from this year but that can change, starting now.

'Promise me something, Harls,' he says, suddenly serious.

'Sure, what?'

'Promise me you'll get help.'

I let his words sink in. If he'd said that any other time this year, I would have told him he was crazy. That there was nothing wrong with me. But in this moment, I can finally see – not what I want to see, but what is.

'I will,' I reply. And I mean it.

The wind picks up, bringing a chorus of sounds and an earthy smell.

'What was that?'

Griff turns to me. 'What was what?'

'A rustling sound,' I try to explain, although now the only thing I hear is the first splatter of rain.

'Probably birds.'

A light flashes in the distant trees.

'There! Do you see that?' I squeeze his arm tight.

The light splits into two. The smaller one's moving quicker, dancing near the ground. It's getting bigger. Closer.

I'd recognise Falco's bark anywhere. He bounds across the clearing, the light on his collar skipping with every step.

Seconds later, Luke emerges from the scrub.

'Come quick. It's Talia.'

CHAPTER 34

The Lies We Tell Ourselves

That which does not destroy me makes me stronger.
(Friedrich Nietzsche)

When I walk into the hospital room after midnight, I nearly don't recognise Talia. She looks pale, weak. Fluids are being pumped into her, and she's wearing one of those oxygen things up her nose. I count four screens, two of them beeping steadily, flashing green and orange. I hope that's normal.

'It's not so ... bad,' she says, waving away all the high-tech gear as though it serves no purpose. Her voice sounds different. Timid.

'A punctured lung. Cracked ribs? Two broken teeth?'

'No big deal,' she assures me with a faint smile.

'It *is* a big deal, Talia,' I insist.

She turns her head, like she doesn't want to accept it.

I squeeze her hand.

'I can't believe you didn't hear me,' she says. 'I ran down the road after you, shouting your name. Then that car turned the corner.' She grimaces. 'The paramedics said I was lucky.'

Talia's cheeks are streamed with tears. Like a yawn that's

contagious, her emotions give permission to my own. My tears fall freely as I think of all we've been through this year. The things we've said. And done.

'Ya know how girls are always bitching about each other?' I ask Talia, thinking back on the whole year.

Her whole body shudders. 'Yeah.'

I unfold the blanket on the foot of the bed and drape it over her.

'Well, I was thinking, what if we're all going through the same stuff? What if we're all so focused on what everyone thinks that we're missing what's inside?'

Talia turns to me, smiling weakly. 'Well, that'd blow a giant hole in my bitch theory.'

Typical Talia. Always the entertainer.

'I'm serious, Tal. I'm tired of all the lies. The lies we tell each other. The lies we tell ourselves.'

The machine's beeping faster and I wonder if that's normal.

'I really fucked up. Big time,' Talia exclaims. 'Wanting to be popular, the pics. Everything.'

I pat her hand, the one without all the tubes.

'Ya know, when I got caught up in all the bullshit with Ty and Eden,' she continues, her voice starting to crack, 'I couldn't find my way out, so ... I don't know.' She looks away to utter the words. 'Guess I tried to drag you in.'

We don't say anything for a while, settling into a soundtrack of machine beeps. But the silence isn't awkward. It's real. More real than anything we've said until now.

My phone buzzes nonstop. I pull it off the charger, thinking thank goodness for Snap Maps or I'd still be on The Mount. And thank God for Luke, because Mum can barely work out Facebook. It's 2019 but Mum's stuck in the past.

'Everyone's asking about you, Tal,' I tell her, scrolling through the messages.

'You mean I'm finally popular?' She tries to laugh but winces, clutching her ribs. I think her lungs hurt.

'Carter wants to know how you are,' I tell her.

'He should be asking how *you* are.'

'He is, listen to this.' I read Talia his message. '*Hope ur doing ok, Harls. Soz if I misled u. NOT my intention.*'

I say the words as I reply. '*Not ur fault. Had other stuff going on.*'

'Other stuff,' Talia echoes. '*That's* an understatement.'

A frazzled nurse appears out of nowhere, drawing back the curtain around Talia's bed, not so subtly telling me to get lost. I move to the chair in the corner to finish my conversation with Carter. I feel like I need to broach the girlfriend thing. Daisy probably thinks I'm a psycho.

ME: *btw, Daisy seems nice*

CARTER: *she is. you'd like her. wanna catch a movie before she heads back?*

ME: *I can't tell if you're joking*

CARTER: *she wants to get to know my Aussie friends.*☺

ME: *me, you, her … slightly awks*

CARTER: *maybe Stu can come ….*

ME: *how 'bout Griff?*

CARTER: *sure thing. so we're all good?*

ME: *Bob's ur uncle*

With her lips slightly parted and a faint smile on her face, Talia drifts off to sleep. I watch the gentle rise and fall of her chest, unable to leave. Outside, the night has faded but the moonlight lingers. It's always there, even when no one notices, every day a new version of itself.

Tomorrow is the first day of summer. I think of Griff's

favourite tree, how the new growth will soon ripen, thanks to long, warm days. Then the thick skin of the figs will soften, and occasionally bruise, before the sweet, mature fruit is ready to harvest.

Book of Revelation

The journey of a thousand miles begins with a single step.
(Lao Tzu)

The warmth of the January sun nearly coaxes me back to sleep. I'm still in my pyjamas, cocooned in our hammock, but I don't care. As Dr Halaby says, 'With stillness comes strength.' She's a psychiatrist who specialises in eating disorders. Even though I've only been seeing her for the past two months, I'm already feeling stronger.

My whole family went to the first session the week after the formal. Hard to believe that was nearly two months ago. Mum and Dad were in a bad state, blaming themselves for 'misplaced priorities' and 'taking our eye off the ball'. Luke stepped up, apologising again for all his fat comments and for getting in my head.

None of this is their fault. It's no one's fault. Talking to Dr Halaby and my GP and nutritionist is helping me realise that.

People often hold on to grief because they're not ready to let go of their loved ones, Dr Halaby told us. That's when Mum broke down, saying she was so ashamed of all those texts, how she's been holding on to Nan's house, to Nan. I told her not to worry, we'd get through it together.

In an odd way our family has never seemed stronger. It took a crisis for us to realise what we mean to each other. It's nice having Dad back home. Mum will probably always drive me a bit crazy but I'm seeing her with new eyes. I wouldn't have believed I'd ever say this, but she's actually good to talk to. As she reminded me the other day, she was a teenage girl once. She's given me a lot of support, but also space. So has Dad. And Luke.

I nibble my Vegemite toast. It's salty, soothing. My stomach's saying, *Have another bite,* but my head's still saying, *No.*

Dr Halaby said the focus shouldn't be on food, or Nan, but on how I'm feeling. She encouraged me to write every day, so I'm using my journal again. My *second* journal. I filled up the other one quickly.

I swing on the hammock, my hands ruffling through tufts of green below, thanks to recent rains. Nothing ever keeps the grass away for long, not a bushfire or the scorching sun. I wonder if life is like that – hardy, but soft enough to cushion a fall, hurdles always poking through, like weeds in a footpath, the new growth never far behind.

Later that evening, I curl up on the lounge-room couch, Falco draped across my feet. Nothing's happened and everything's happened in a summer – a year – that's zipped by at lightening pace. It's hard to believe school starts tomorrow.

When I glimpse a photo of Nan on the mantel, I suddenly realise it's been a year since she died. A year of learning to live life without her, to work out what to do when the grief comes out of nowhere, swallowing my heart like a freak wave, dumping me breathless on the shore. But this time, instead of tears, I feel a warm embrace, as though Nan's wrapping me up in one of her big hugs.

I pick up the pen, ready to jot down today's journal entry. There are so many issues that I'm still trying to unpack, so many thoughts that I need to work through. Dr Halaby told me I shouldn't worry about what to say, to just write what I feel … a paragraph, a sentence — anything. I turn to a blank page, write today's date and then a single word:

Heal.

'Tackling your memoirs already?' Griff's here again, this time with a large box of chocolates in hand. I wonder whether he actually knocked for once or simply walked in. Dad's convinced he somehow has a key.

Griff and I have seen each other all summer but still haven't talked about the formal. Or the pledge, the kiss – everything that's happened this year.

'Probably should have given this a bit more thought,' he says with an awkward smile, handing over the box.

'Don't worry.' I laugh. 'Chocolate is a good goal to work towards.'

Dr Halaby said healing is going to take time. It's complicated. It's about being comfortable in my skin, not pushing my body beyond its limits. It's about giving myself permission to eat. And it's about being mindful: doing a lot of self-talk, asking questions, challenging opinions, training my heart and my head to work together. Like a philosopher! Dr Kanter would be proud.

I sink into the sofa, tucking my bare feet under the cushion, the one Nan made when she was teaching me how to embroider. Griff sits alongside me.

'I'm still trying to make sense of everything,' I start off, not sure where I'm heading. 'I think I was trying to find myself in everyone else, in what they had that I didn't.' I keep talking, I need to get things out. 'All the other girls were thinner, prettier … better. At least that's what the mirror told me.'

It's only now that I realise the mirror lies.

'Then Carter turned up and started paying attention to me,' I continue, 'and I felt special, like some rare gem … until I held up my heart and found out it was made of glass, and I realised all this time I was cutting it, distorting it, making it something it wasn't and could never be.'

The late sun streams through the window, bathing the sky in a watercolour of deep maroons and burnt orange, the prelude to a slow summer sunset.

'Gems are tricky,' Griff says, reaching for my hand. His touch is warm, reassuring. 'They can look ordinary. But hold them up to the light and they sparkle.'

Just when I think he's about to let go, our fingers intertwine. And it feels like the most natural thing in the world.

The next morning, the girl in the mirror smiles back at me.

The uniform has changed this year – goodbye shapeless dress, hello comfy shorts and shirt – for everyone. My quality of life doubled when I read that announcement on the school website. I'm dressed in no time and quickly gather my gear – a new backpack to start 2020 afresh, some new notebooks and the healthy snacks I packed after breakfast.

My phone vibrates and I read Talia's message: *8.05 bus? x*

After sending a quick *k*, I let Griff know and remind him to bring his wish list. On my way out the door, I grab a sheet of paper and pen. This time, the words come easy:

Harley's Year II Wish List
Be myself.

ACKNOWLEDGMENTS

The seeds of this story were planted in high school. That sense of being untethered – of not knowing who I was and, at the time, not liking some aspects of my appearance – burrowed into my consciousness, resurfacing from time to time in my adult years. I'm not alone. Millions of people are preoccupied with perceived flaws in their appearance that cloud how they see themselves and engage with the world. Yet few are talking about it.

That's why I wrote this book.

Whether reading or writing, literature is a powerful mirror that allows us to see ourselves on the page, explore complex issues in a safe space, and identify healthier ways to deal with internal struggles. But we humans are walking contradictions. We crave understanding, acceptance and genuine connection yet tend to shy away from sensitive topics, especially when the hard stuff involves young people. We're all about minimising, rather than embracing, risk. Nowhere is this more apparent than in the publishing industry, a highly risk-averse landscape that proved challenging to navigate for this story.

The Lies We Tell Ourselves is not just a culmination of a ten-year journey from idea to publication. The book reflects the collective encouragement, wisdom, and support of countless others who have walked alongside me: manuscript assessors, editors, publishers, proofreaders, writing group buddies, beta readers and friends. While it's impossible to rattle off all their names individually, I am indebted to everyone for the vital role they played. I'm also grateful for industry recognition of this work, with earlier drafts named winner of the Children's Book Council of Australia (CBCA) NSW Aspiring Writers Mentorship Program, the Charlotte Waring Barton Award, Varuna's Publisher Introduction Program (shortlisted), and the NSW Writers Centre (now Writing NSW) Varuna Fellowship (runner up), to name just a few honours.

A special thank you to my agent, Debbie Golvan, Golvan Arts Management, who fought tirelessly, but unsuccessfully, to get this manuscript over the line. Enormous gratitude to Samantha Tidy, Alison Hill, Yvette Walker, Georgina Ballantine and James Hartley, whose keen insights helped to nurture and shape the early story, and to Aleesah Darlison, Cameron Macintosh and Irma Gold, whose editing magic sharpened, streamlined and refined the narrative later in its life cycle. Thanks to graphic designer Nicola Matthews, whose creative eye enriches this story and the reader's experience. To my family, especially Kieran and Liam, who read more drafts than one would think humanly possible, thank you from the bottom of my heart – your thoughtful comments, honesty, support and encouragement kept me going every step of the way. And infinite thanks to my dearest friend, Miri – my cheerleader, confidante, sounding board, listener, motivator, and humour barometer – whose unwavering belief in me and this story means more than she could ever imagine.

Although my name is on the front cover, this story now belongs to its readers – those who see themselves, or someone they know, on its pages and who will open their minds and hearts to occupying space with empathy, positivity, self-respect and forgiveness. Here's to the healing power of stories and the courage to share them.

ABOUT THE AUTHOR

Maura grew up in the Bronx and spent her high school years in New Jersey before travelling and eventually settling in Australia. She's been writing all her life, usually what other people have paid her to write about. A decade ago, she stepped back from the family business to reconnect with her creative self. When she put pen to paper, *The Lies We Tell Ourselves* was born.

Today, Maura is an author, playwright, filmmaker, art therapist and mental health advocate. She loves big ideas, particularly exploring where identity, self and belonging collide and the role of memory in who we were, who we are, and who we're becoming. She holds a PhD in philosophy, specialising in ethics, and was a former medical news reporter, ethicist and editor of *Australian Medicine*.

Maura is the Founder of The Book Bench Project, a Canberra region initiative that celebrates community and a shared love of reading. She enjoys author visits to schools, reviewing children's books for CBCA's online magazine, *Reading Time*, and serving as a Role Model and Sponsor for Books in Homes Australia. When she's not busy writing, and even when she is, Maura enjoys spending time with her family at their avocado farm in Jamberoo, a peaceful sanctuary between the mountains and the sea, shared with a host of native wildlife.

To find out more about Maura and her work, visit
maurapierlot.com

www.ingramcontent.com/pod-product-compliance
Lightning Source LLC
Chambersburg PA
CBHW020259120726
47904CB00001B/260